JOHN CREASEY'S
CRIME COLLECTION 1983

JOHN CREASEY'S CRIME COLLECTION 1983

An Anthology by members of the
Crime Writers' Association

edited by

HERBERT HARRIS

ST MARTIN'S PRESS
NEW YORK

Library of congress Catalog Card Number 82–647147

ISBN 0-312-44297-1

First published in Great Britain by
Victor Gollancz Ltd
First U.S. Edition
10 9 8 7 6 5 4 3 2 1

CONTENTS

ACKNOWLEDGEMENTS

Five original stories are included in this edition, those by Cyril Donson, Antonia Fraser, Peter Godfrey, Herbert Harris and Jeffry Scott.

We are grateful to *Ellery Queen's Mystery Magazine* for "The Virgin and the Bull" by Peter Lovesey, "Something Evil in the House" by Celia Fremlin, "Terror Ride" by Berkely Mather, and "Fair and Square" by Margaret Yorke; to Macmillan's *Winter's Crimes* series for "Juno's Swans" by Celia Dale; to *Mr Calder and Mr Behrens* (Harper & Row) for "The Mercenaries" by Michael Gilbert; to *The Times* (London) for "The Day It Rained in Singapaw" by Madelaine Duke; to *Blackwood's Magazine* for "The Adventure of the Suffering Ruler" by H. R. F. Keating; to *Francis Quarles Investigates* (Panther Books) for "The Santa Claus Club" by Julian Symons; to *Hjemmet* (Norway) for "Tarantella" by Ella Griffiths.

INTRODUCTION

This edition of *John Creasey's Crime Collection* coincides with the thirtieth birthday of the Crime Writers' Association, which Creasey brought into being on (appropriately enough) Guy Fawkes Day, 1953.

Since then it has achieved an international membership of four hundred, including the world's leading crime writers, and the Association is naturally a rich source of short stories in the heterogeneous fields of detection, mystery, suspense, horror and adventure, so often carelessly lumped together under the heading of "thrillers".

In the thirty years of the C.W.A., there have been twenty-two anthologies of members' short stories, totalling 353 stories altogether, a handsome legacy for posterity's students of this eternally fascinating fictional art-form.

Nowadays, with so few outlets for short-story writers, we are always delighted when somebody initiates new opportunities, and we are grateful to the partnership of Veuve Clicquot and *The Times* for jointly promoting a short-story contest for C.W.A. members, the first winner of which ("The Day It Rained In Singapaw") appears in this volume.

Last year's Crime Collection was described by one authoritative judge as "the best yet", and I believe this year we have done at least as well and perhaps even better, but this is for our readers to decide.

HERBERT HARRIS

THE VIRGIN AND THE BULL

Peter Lovesey

SHE WAS THE daughter of the vicar and he was the publican's son. She had been sent into the vicarage garden to pick greengages for the jam her mother always made in the last week of August. Alision was seventeen, with fine flaxen hair, the envy of every girl in the village. She dressed plainly and she had no use for make-up, yet there was not a man in Middle Slaughter whose thoughts had not been disturbed by her.

Shyly she pretended not to notice the bare-chested farm worker repairing the stone wall in the field adjoining the garden. Tom Hunt had not impressed her in the least when they had been at school together. Large, rough and rebellious, he had ruled the playground by sheer tyranny. She had been pleased to forget him when she had transferred to boarding school. The bullying in a school for girls was of a different order from his brutish behaviour. He had become as unreal as the ogres in the story books she had left behind on her bedroom shelf.

His work on the wall brought him to a point where the greengage tree overhung the field. Alison moved around the trunk so that she would not be forced to catch his eye.

He was not to be ignored. A large, ripe greengage landed neatly in the basket she was using. She heard him say, "Funny how the best ones are always out of reach."

She made no response.

"I mean the plums, of course. Remember me, Alison?" He sat astride the wall where she could not fail to see his grinning features and bare, brown torso. He had the physique of a man now, a strong, broad man, but she recognized his smile.

She said, "Tom Hunt. You used to chase the girls with nettles and sting their legs."

He laughed. "I've given it up now."

It was strange to trace the obnoxious features of six years ago in this undeniably good-looking face.

At the church fête the following Sunday he helped her sell programmes at the gate. He seemed popular with the villagers, even girls and boys he had once persecuted shamefully.

That evening there was a barn dance in aid of parish funds. As soon as Alison appeared with her father, Tom Hunt crossed the floor and asked her to join him in a St Bernard's Waltz.

"That's the way I do things," he told her as they linked arms. "Straight to it, like a bull at a gate. I don't stand on ceremony."

"And you'd better not stand on my feet," she said, as their shoes touched. "Haven't you danced a St Bernard's before?"

"Not very often. Have you? You seem to know the steps."

"Yes."

"Where did you learn—at school?"

She gave a nod. She did not like being reminded that she was still a schoolgirl.

"I thought so," Tom said with a trace of condescension. "Girls' schools do a lot of that, don't they? Singing and dancing and skipping."

"They do other things too," Alison pointed out.

"Cookery?"

"Farming. My school has a Jersey herd and twelve acres put out to wheat and barley. The girls do all the work. It's not just skipping and dancing. So it follows," she said with a level look at Tom, "that bulls don't impress me overmuch."

Against all the indications, the friendship between them took root. They were seen together hand-in-hand walking the lanes and footpaths around the village each evening after work until it got dark. Then Tom would escort her to the vicarage porch and kiss her briefly before making his way, whistling, to the Harrow. There, over his beer, he would shrug aside the good-natured banter of the regulars, the enquiries after the vicar's health and whether Tom proposed to join the choir. Any young man who courted a village girl was a target for the locals' wit. The wooing of the vicar's daughter was better than a game of darts.

The baiting of Tom was rendered more entertaining by the knowledge that not many months before, it would have roused him to violence. Perhaps it was the onset of maturity, or perhaps it was the fact that his father was landlord of the Harrow that kept

Tom in check. He managed to accept the chaffing in good sport, which of course was demanded by the time-honoured ritual. He even summoned an occasional smile.

On some evenings Rufus Peel added his comments to the rest. Rufus was the only one of the regulars capable of rankling Tom. He was of Tom's generation. He had been the star pupil in the village school, the boy who had played Joseph in the nativity play to Alison's Mary, when Tom had not even aspired to the part of third shepherd. At secondary school, Rufus had collected every honour possible. The head had chosen him for school captain. He had become the first Middle Slaughter boy ever to win a place at agricultural college. Now he was regarded with awe. He treated the older men like contemporaries, and they accepted it. His middle-aged manner and short, portly stature undoubtedly helped, as did the rounds he bought in the Harrow. His grant was topped up with a sponsorship from the fertilizer industry.

When Rufus joined in the wisecracks at Tom's expense, there was a cutting edge to his comments calculated to test the victim's passivity to the limit. "Tom's no fool," he told the others. "He's after a cheap wedding. There'll be no church fees, you see. It's all on the Lord if you're smart enough to marry a vicar's daughter."

Tom tried to ignore the remarks. He knew what lay behind them. Rufus had wanted Alison for years. He had pestered her for friendship ever since they were in junior school. He had passed notes to her and tried to arrange meetings. He had thought at first that she would be flattered by his interest. Each success in his life—the biology prize, the commission in the CCF, the school captaincy—had cued another bid for Alison's approval.

Alison had lately described to Tom how difficult her life had become through Rufus's persistence. She had treated him politely, but coolly. In reality she disliked everything about him.

Rufus had refused to give up. One Saturday in May, Alison had been playing tennis at school, when she had noticed a persistent giggling from the benches by the sidelines. Along one side of the courts was a beech hedge, intended to isolate the daughters of the clergy from the pernicious world at large. The smaller girls had spotted a young man peering through a gap in the hedge: Rufus. He had cycled sixty miles to let Alison know that he had won a place in agricultural college. Burning with embarrassment and with the second-formers tittering in chorus, Alison had approached the gap, lowered her head and listened to Rufus's jubilant announcement. She had stared at the ridiculous, smug face framed by the beech leaves and she had told Rufus that she was glad he would be going to agricultural college, and she hoped it was as far away as possible. They had not spoken since.

The summer passed. In September, Rufus went off to college in a dark blue suit and a striped scarf, and Alison started her last year at boarding school. Tom stayed in Middle Slaughter and helped burn the stubble on Hopkin's Farm. In the next few weeks, he wrote a few letters to Alison, but he had difficulty in expressing himself in words.

When she came home for Christmas he met the train. They went for long walks on the frost-white footpaths. They always parted at the vicarage porch with a short embrace and a token kiss. Alison was very proper. Tom had more than once invited her home, but she had resolutely declined. The reason was that his home was the Harrow and her father would be shocked if she set foot in a public house. She told Tom, "I'll be eighteen next holiday, and then my father says I can make my own decisions. Let's wait till then."

So the next vacation, on the Friday after Easter, the day arrived when Tom treated Alison to her first drink in the Harrow. She secretly dreaded the amusement it would give the regulars, but as it turned out, her appearance caused no comment at all, for there was a bigger diversion. There were strangers in the Harrow.

They were a couple from London on their way, as the man explained with a wink, to spend the weekend at a cottage in Wales. He was a freelance journalist, a fluent, amusing talker who was soon entertaining the entire clientele with stories of famous people whose secrets he had somehow uncovered. He had one of those prodigious moustaches once known as "RAF", though he belonged to a later generation. He smoked cigars and claimed to have rubbed shoulders with everyone of note in London. A cynic quietly remarked that if his suit was anything to go by, he was telling the truth.

If either of them had money, it was she. Her sable jacket was the real thing and so were the diamond and ruby rings. She had blonde hair worn long, with silver highlights. She wore a musky perfume that penetrated the cigar fumes. She might have been thirty-nine:

forty was unthinkable. The thoughts that were abroad in the Harrow that night were tinged with envy of her weekend companion.

He emptied his glass. "Not a bad beer. Not bad at all."

"Have another?" offered Rufus, back from college with some of his grant unspent.

"That's very decent of you. The lady's is a Pimms'."

"I don't think I'd better, Charlie," said the woman.

"Of course you will. I'll drive the rest of the way. I'm steady as a rock if I stay on beer." Charlie turned to Rufus. "You take the order, old chum, and I'll collect the empties."

Rufus had clearly not intended to buy drinks for everyone, but that was what happened. The regulars chanted their orders with the familiarity of monks at prayer.

While the order was being set up, the man called Charlie said confidentially to Rufus, "You know who she is, of course?"

"Who do you mean?"

"My travelling companion—who else?"

Rufus shook his head. "Should I know her?"

Charlie nodded. "You've seen her picture plenty of times. Come on, you recognize her."

Rufus gave the woman another look. "I'm sorry. I'm damned sure I don't."

Charlie looked as if he had taken offence. "She's famous, man."

"I'm a student at college," said Rufus in his defence. "I don't watch the telly."

"You read the papers, don't you?"

"She's not a politician?"

"Does she look like one? Which paper do you read?"

"The *Chronicle*."

"I thought so. You really ought to know her."

"Well, there's something familiar, I admit," lied Rufus.

Charlie addressed the room in general. "Anyone got a copy of the *Chronicle*?"

On the window-seat to the right of the door, Tom and Alison were drinking white wine, grateful for the attention the strangers were getting. Nobody had passed a comment yet about Alison's presence.

Tom's father, the landlord, retrieved a copy of the *Chronicle* from under the counter and handed it to Charlie, who passed it to Rufus. The mystery of the woman's identity was now the focus of every person present.

"Turn to the centre pages, lad," instructed Charlie. "Now turn over again. What do you find?"

"*Letters to the Editor*," Rufus read aloud. "*Your Stars Today*. Well, I'll be damned!" He stared at the page and across the room at the woman. Her large brown eyes returned his gaze without self-consciousness. She was used to being pointed out as a celebrity. "Deborah Kristal!" said Rufus. "The fortune-teller."

"Don't call her that, for Heaven's sake," said Charlie between his teeth. "She's not some gypsy at the Derby with a crystal ball. She's an astrologer, and she takes it very seriously. It's highly technical. They use computers these days." He picked up a tray of drinks and carried it across the room. "Anyone had a birthday lately?"

The question produced a sudden silence in the room.

In the window-seat, Alison whispered urgently to Tom, "Take me home now." They got up to leave.

Charlie turned back to Rufus. "Never mind. What's your birth month, old boy?"

Desperate to escape the spotlight, Rufus had an inspiration. "It's Alison's birthday today. Her eighteenth!"

"Marvellous!" said Charlie. "Come over here, my dear, and Miss Kristal will tell you what the future holds."

"No, thank you," said Alison quickly.

"She's the vicar's daughter," someone explained. "She's shy, poor child. She's had a very sheltered life."

"Do it for both of 'em, then," Tom's father suggested. "My Tom isn't bashful."

"What a splendid idea," said Rufus at once. "Cast their horoscopes and tell them if they have any future together."

"I would need more information," said Miss Kristal. "I do not have my charts with me. I can only make a few broad observations."

"Tom was born on 28th August," said his father.

"In that case he is not afraid of a good day's work," said Miss Kristal. "He is healthy and strong, loyal and courageous. He does nothing by halves. He knows what he wants out of life and he will move mountains to get it. His manner may be a shade overbearing at times, but he hides nothing from the world. He is an honest, open-hearted man."

"Tom, I'd like to leave," said Alison for the second time, but Tom lingered by the door, too interested to move.

"The young lady has positive qualities, too," went on Miss Kristal. "She has the highest standards and she expects others to conform to them."

"That's true," said Tom. "It's absolutely true!"

"She has exceptional powers of concentration," said Miss Kristal. "She is not easily deceived. But when she gives her word, she means it."

"What about the future?" asked Tom's father. "Would you advise them to get hitched?"

"Dad!" said Tom in embarrassment.

There was a pause.

"I would rather not say," said Miss Kristal. "Charlie, it's getting late. We still have a long way to drive."

Rufus had been listening intently. The answer had not satisfied him. "But you must have *some* idea whether he is suited to her."

"In general," said Miss Kristal, choosing her words with care, "I would not recommend a partnership between a Virgoan and a Taurean."

"A what?" said Tom's father.

"A Virgoan and a Taurean. Virgo and Taurus are the virgin and the bull."

"The virgin and the bull! I like that!" said Charlie.

"It's laughable," said Rufus with a sneer.

"What do you mean?" demanded Tom in a spasm of anger. "What's there to laugh about?"

"It's so ridiculous," Rufus answered insensitively. "The virgin and the bull. It's a joke. It's got to be a joke!"

Rufus had scarcely spoken before Tom was across the floor and gripping him by the shirt-front. "What are you getting at, you louse?"

"Tom!" ordered his father. "Take your hands off him! I want no violence here."

"He's going to take back every word," said Tom, tightening his grip. "He insulted Alison. She's not like that. She's decent."

Rufus hissed at Tom, "Is that what you think, or what she told you?"

Behind Tom, Alison gave a whimper of distress and ran from the pub.

Tom brought back his fist to strike Rufus, but his arm was seized from behind and forced against his back in a savage half-nelson. "There'll be no brawling in this house," his father's voice snarled in his ear. "Not from my own son, or anybody. You're going out to cool off." Tom was strongly built, yet in that grip he could do nothing to prevent his father marching him to the door and thrusting him outside. It was debatable whether the father or the son suffered the greater humiliation.

The subdued atmosphere in the Harrow lasted only a short time. At Charlie's prompting, Miss Kristal obligingly cast more horoscopes. Rufus, who had two quick double brandies and left early, was one of the few who professed to be uninterested in knowing the future. As events turned out, this proved a fatal error, because he never reached home that night.

It was morning before his disappearance was reported by his parents. The overnight absence from home of a young man in his late teens is not usually treated by the police as a matter of grave concern. Yet in this case it was difficult to understand what might have happened. It was established that Rufus had left the Harrow soon after 9.45 p.m. He would have taken some twenty minutes to walk the mile and a quarter along the Harford Road. It was a minor road that eventually linked with the A436, and it would have led him past a couple of cottages and Hopkin's Farm. A search of the road, ditches and adjoining fields yielded no clue.

The enquiries were concentrated on the incident in the Harrow. Everyone present was questioned except Miss Kristal and her companion Charlie, who had left in their Alfa-Romeo about 10 p.m. As they had driven along the Harford Road, it was possible that they would have passed Rufus, but no one knew where to trace them in Wales, not even Miss Kristal's newspaper office. It seemed that Miss Kristal had anticipated a longish absence, because before leaving Fleet Street she had filed *Your Stars Today* for the next four weeks.

Tom and his father were questioned closely. Tom stated that after his father had ejected him, he ran after Alison and escorted her home. The vicarage was in the opposite direction from Rufus's route. Alison corroborated what Tom had said.

A theory was advanced in the village that the journalist, Charlie, well over the limit by the time he had left the Harrow with Miss Kristal and taken the wheel of the Alfa-Romeo, had run Rufus down and killed him, then taken fright and bundled the body into the boot of the car and disposed of it in some remote lake in Wales. But at the end of the month Charlie and Miss Kristal were traced by the police, and the car was examined by forensic experts. There was no evidence to support the theory. The couple claimed that they had no recollection of having seen Rufus or anyone else on the Harford Road after they had left the Harrow.

So Rufus Peel was listed as a missing person, one of the thousands on the police computer. For two years there were no developments in the case. Tom and Alison were married in the village church and the reception was held at the Harrow. Then, within a fortnight of the wedding, the remains of Rufus were discovered at the bottom of a septic tank on Hopkin's Farm.

The autopsy revealed that he had died violently. Both legs and one arm were shattered, the rib-cage had been crushed, the spinal column severed and the skull splintered. The Home Office pathologist stated his opinion that the multiple injuries had been caused by a heavy motor vehicle, probably a tractor. It was likely that the victim had been run over not once, but repeatedly, as if deliberately.

The police picked up Tom and took him to Gloucester for questioning. After several hours he made a confession. He admitted having caused Rufus's death. He stated that on the night his father had ejected him from the Harrow he had not, as previously claimed, taken Alison home. He had made his way to the farm, sat in the seat of a tractor at the farm entrance and waited for Rufus to come along the road. His fury at what had happened in the Harrow, the slanderous insinuation Rufus had made about Alison in the public bar the first time she had ever set foot in the place, had turned him crazy for vengeance. He had driven the tractor straight at Rufus and felled him. He had driven over him and then reversed the tractor and crushed the body again. He had dragged it into the yard and disposed of it in the tank.

At the assizes, Tom pleaded guilty to murder. In sentencing him, the judge allowed that there had been strong provocation, but ruled that the interval between the provocation and the crime did not allow sufficient grounds for a verdict of manslaughter. Tom was given a life sentence.

In Middle Slaughter there was strong sympathy for Tom. When he was released on parole after serving eleven years, he was given back his job on Hopkin's Farm. He lived there in a tied cottage with Alison, who had waited loyally for him to serve his sentence. The villagers still spoke of them as the virgin and the bull.

One lunchtime shortly after Tom's release, Deborah Kristal chanced to meet Charlie in a Fleet Street wine bar. The conversation got round to Middle Slaughter. "I thought I might go down there again," said Charlie. "Care to join me, sweetie? Another cosy weekend in Wales?"

"Using my car, I suppose? No thank you, Charlie. Nothing personal, just the price of petrol. What do you want to go to Middle Slaughter for?"

"Tom Hunt's out. I thought of offering the poor devil something for his story. It's worth another airing in the Sundays. It made a big enough impact when it happened."

"I shouldn't if I were you," said Miss Kristal.

"I'll be all right, my love. He had no grudge against me. I won't antagonize the fellow."

"It's a waste of time going," said Miss Kristal emphatically. "He won't tell you a thing."

But Charlie would not be dissuaded. He drove down to Middle Slaughter alone the following weekend.

"Sometimes I think you really are clairvoyant," he told Deborah Kristal the next time they met. "Ruddy fellow clammed up completely. Wouldn't say a word. And nor would anyone else in the village. His father still runs the pub, and he's no help. Nor are his customers. I spent a fortune at the bar trying to coax something out of 'em."

"I did warn you."

"How did you know I was wasting my time?"

"Because they don't want the story opened up again. It was full of holes when he made the confession."

Charlie's eyes narrowed. "What do you mean?"

"Tom didn't kill Rufus Peel. A man as strong and as angry as he was didn't need to lie in wait with a tractor. He could have strangled Rufus with his bare hands."

"But he confessed, for Heaven's sake!"

Miss Kristal shook her head. "For *Alison's* sake, darling. She was the killer of Rufus Peel. Everyone in that village knows it, but no one will say a thing. And nor will you, if you've any romance in you at all."

Charlie, wide-eyed, said, "Are you seriously telling me that an eighteen-year-old girl murdered a man by driving a tractor at him? A vicar's daughter? She wouldn't know the front of a tractor from the back."

"Wrong. I went to see the school she attended. A boarding school for daughters of the clergy. They believe in self-sufficiency. Every girl is taught to plough on the school farm."

"You checked on this? You're a dark horse, darling. Why on earth would she have wanted to kill Rufus?"

"Really, Charlie, if you can't see that, you'll never understand the way a woman thinks. Alison was enraged by what Rufus insinuated in the Harrow. He slandered her reputation in front of her prospective husband and father-in-law and most of the village. Instead of going home, she went to the farm and took out a tractor and took her revenge when Rufus came along the road. My guess is that Tom turned up later and helped her hide the body. When it was found, he made the false confession to save her."

"What a story!" said Charlie wistfully. "His heroic sacrifice for her act of violence. Is it really possible?"

"It was in the stars," said Miss Kristal with logic in her voice. "You see, he was the virgin and she was the bull."

HAVE A NICE DEATH

Antonia Fraser

EVERYONE WAS BEING extraordinarily courteous to Sammy Luke in New York.

Take Sammy's arrival at Kennedy Airport, for example: Sammy had been quite struck by the warmth of the welcome. Sammy thought: how relieved Zara would be! Zara (his wife) was inclined to worry about Sammy—he had to admit, with some cause; in the past, that is. In the past Sammy had been nervous, delicate, highly strung, whatever you liked to call it—Sammy suspected that some of Zara's women friends had a harsher name for it; the fact was that things tended to go wrong where Sammy was concerned, unless Zara was there to iron them out. But that was in England. Sammy was quite sure he was not going to be nervous in America; perhaps, cured by the New World, he would never be nervous again.

Take the immigration officials—hadn't Sammy been warned about them?

"They're nothing but gorillas"—Zara's friend, wealthy Tess, who travelled frequently to the States, had pronounced the word in a dark voice. For an instant Sammy, still in his nervous English state, visualized immigration checkpoints manned by terrorists armed with machine guns. But the official seated in a booth, who summoned Sammy in, was slightly built, perhaps even slighter than Sammy himself, though the protection of the booth made it difficult to tell. And he was smiling as he cried:

"C,mon, c'mon, bring the family!" A notice outside the booth stated that only one person—or one family—was permitted inside at a time.

"I'm afraid my wife's not travelling with me," stated Sammy apologetically.

"I sure wish my wife wasn't with me either," answered the official, with ever increasing bonhomie.

Sammy wondered confusedly—it had been a long flight after all—whether he should explain his own very different feelings about his wife, his passionate regret that Zara had not been able to accompany him. But his new friend was already examining his passport, flipping through a large black directory, talking again:

"A writer . . . Would I know any of your books?"

This was an opportunity for Sammy to explain intelligently the purpose of his visit. Sammy Luke was the author of six novels. Five of them had sold well, if not astoundingly well, in England and not at all in the United States. The sixth, *Women Weeping*, due perhaps to its macabrely fashionable subject matter, had hit some kind of publishing jackpot in both countries. Only a few weeks after publication in the States its sales were phenomenal and rising; an option on the film rights (maybe Jane Fonda and Meryl Streep as the masochists?) had already been bought. As a result of all this, Sammy's new American publishers believed hotly that only one further thing was necessary to ensure the vast, the *total* success of *Women Weeping* in the States, and that was to make of its author a television celebrity. Earnestly defending his own position on the subject of violence and female masochism on a series of television interviews and talk shows, Sammy Luke was expected to shoot *Women Weeping* high, high into the bestseller lists and keep it there. All this was the firm conviction of Sammy's editor at Porlock Publishers, Clodagh Jansen.

"You'll be great on the talk shows, Sammy," Clodagh had cawed down the line from the States. "So little and cute and then—" Clodagh made a loud noise with her lips as if someone was gobbling someone else up. Presumably it was not Sammy who was to be gobbled. Clodagh was a committed feminist, as she had carefully explained to Sammy on her visit to England, when she had bought *Women Weeping*, against much competition, for a huge sum. But she believed in the social role of bestsellers like *Women Weeping* to finance radical feminist works. Sammy had tried to explain that his book was in no way anti-feminist, no way at all, witness the fact that Zara herself, his Egeria, had not complained . . .

"Save it for the talk shows, Sammy," was all that Clodagh had replied.

While Sammy was still wondering how to put all this concisely, but to his best advantage, at Kennedy Airport, the man in the booth asked: "And the purpose of your visit, Mr Luke?"

Sammy was suddenly aware that he had drunk a great deal on the long flight—courtesy of Porlock's First Class ticket—and slept too heavily as well. His head began to sing. But whatever answer he gave, it was apparently satisfactory. The man stamped the white sheet inside his passport and handed it back. Then:

"Enjoy your visit to the United States of America, Mr Luke. Have a nice day now."

"Oh I will, I know I will," promised Sammy. "It seems a lovely day here already."

Sammy's experiences at the famous Barraclough Hotel (accommodation arranged by Clodagh) were if anything even more heart-warming. Everyone, but everyone at the Barraclough wanted Sammy to enjoy himself during his visit.

"Have a nice day now, Mr Luke": most conversations ended like that, whether they were with the hotel telephonists, the agreeable men who operated the lifts or the gentlemanly *concierge*. Even the New York taxi drivers, from whose guarded expressions Sammy would not otherwise have suspected such warm hearts, wanted Sammy to have a nice day.

"Oh I will, I will," Sammy began by answering. After a bit he added: "I just adore New York," said with a grin and the very suspicion of an American twang.

"This is the friendliest city in the world," he told Zara down the long-distance telephone, shouting, so that his words were accompanied by little vibratory echoes.

"Tess says they don't really mean it." Zara's voice in contrast was thin, diminished into a tiny wail by the line. "They're not sincere, you know."

"Tess was wrong about the gorillas at Immigration. She could be wrong about that too. Tess doesn't *own* the whole country, you know. She just inherited a small slice of it."

"Darling, you do sound funny," countered Zara; her familiar anxiety on the subject of Sammy made her sound stronger. "Are you all right? I mean, are you all right over there all by yourself—?"

"I'm mainly on television during the day," Sammy cut in with a laugh. "Alone except for the chat show host and forty million people." Sammy was deciding whether to add, truthfully, that actually not all the shows were networked; some of his audiences being as low as a million, or, say, a million and a half, when he realized that Zara was saying in a voice of distinct reproach:

"And you haven't asked after Mummy yet." It was the sudden illness of Zara's mother, another person emotionally dependent upon her, which had prevented Zara's trip to New York with Sammy, at the last moment.

It was only after Sammy had rung off—having asked tenderly after Zara's mother and apologized for his crude crack about Tess before doing so—that he realized Zara was quite right. He *had* sounded rather funny: even to himself. That is, he would never have dared to make such a remark about Tess in London. Dared? Sammy pulled himself up.

To Zara, his strong and lovely Zara, he could of course say anything. She was his wife. As a couple, they were exceptionally close as all their circle agreed; being childless (a decision begun through poverty in the early days and somehow never rescinded) only increased their intimacy. Because their marriage had not been founded on a flash-in-the-pan sexual attraction but something deeper, more companionate—sex had never played a great part in it, even at the beginning—the bond had only grown stronger with the years. Sammy doubted whether there was a more genuinely united pair in London.

All this was true; and comforting to recollect. It was just that in recent years Tess had become an omnipresent force in their lives: Tess on clothes, Tess on interior decoration, especially Tess on curtains, that was the real pits—a new expression which Sammy had picked up from Clodagh; and somehow Tess's famous money always seemed to reinforce her opinions in a way which was rather curious, considering Zara's own radical contempt for unearned wealth.

"Well, I've got money now. Lots and lots of it. Earned money," thought Sammy, squaring his thin shoulders in the new pale blue jacket which Zara, yes Zara, had made him buy. He looked in one of the huge gilded mirrors which decorated his suite at the Barraclough, pushing aside the large floral arrangement, a gift from the hotel manager (or was it Clodagh?) to do so. Sammy Luke, the conqueror of New York, or at least American television; then he had to laugh at his own absurdity.

He went on to the little balcony which led off the suite's sitting-room and looked down at the ribbon of streets which stretched below; the roofs of lesser buildings; the blur of green where Central Park nestled, at his disposal, in the centre of it all. The plain truth was that he was just very, very happy. The reason was not purely the success of his book, nor even his instant highly commercial fame, as predicted by Clodagh, on television, nor yet the attentions of the Press, parts of which had after all been quite violently critical of his book, again as predicted by Clodagh. The reason was that Sammy Luke felt loved in New York in a vast, wonderful, impersonal way: Nothing was demanded of him by this love; it was like an electric fire which simulated red-hot coals even when it was switched off. New York glowed but it could not scorch. In his heart Sammy knew that he had never been so happy before.

It was at this point that the telephone rang again. Sammy left the balcony. Sammy was expecting one of three calls. The first, and most likely, was Clodagh's daily checking call: "Hi, Sammy, it's Clodagh Pegoda . . . listen, that show was great, the one they taped. Our publicity girl actually told me it didn't go too well at the time, she was frightened they were mauling you . . . but the way it came out . . . Zouch!" More interesting sounds from Clodagh's mobile and rather sensual lips. "That's my Sam. You really had them licked. I guess the little girl was just protective. Sue-May, was it? Joanie. Yes, Joanie. She's crazy about you. I'll have to talk to her; what's a nice girl like that doing being crazy about a man, and a married man at that. . . ."

Clodagh's physical preference for her own sex was a robust joke between them; it was odd how being in New York made that, too, innocuous. In England Sammy had been secretly rather shocked by the frankness of Clodagh's allusions: more alarmingly she had once goosed him, apparently fooling, but with the accompanying words "You're a bit like a girl yourself, Sammy," which were not totally reassuring. Even that was preferable to the embarrassing occasion when Clodagh had playfully declared a physical attraction to Zara, wondered—outside the money that was now coming in—how Zara put up with Sammy. In New York, however, Sammy entered enthusiastically into the fun.

He was also pleased to hear, however lightly meant, that Joanie, the publicity girl in charge of his day-to-day arrangements, was crazy about him; for Joanie, unlike handsome, piratical, frightening Clodagh, was small and tender.

The second possibility for the call was Joanie herself. In which case she would be down in the lobby of the Barraclough, ready to escort him to an afternoon taping at a television studio across town. Later Joanie would drop Sammy back at the Barraclough, paying carefully and slightly earnestly for the taxi as though Sammy's nerves might be ruffled if the ceremony was not carried out correctly. One of these days, Sammy thought with a smile, he might even ask Joanie up to his suite at the Barraclough . . . after all what were suites for? (Sammy had never had a suite in a hotel before, his English publisher having an old-fashioned taste for providing his authors with plain bedrooms while on promotional tours.)

The third possibility was that Zara was calling him back: their conversation, for all Sammy's apologies, had not really ended on a satisfactory note; alone in London, Zara was doubtless feeling anxious about Sammy as a result. He detected a little complacency in himself about Zara: after all, there was for once nothing for her to feel anxious about (except perhaps Joanie, he added to himself with a smile).

Sammy's complacency was shattered by the voice on the telephone:

"I saw you on television last night," began the voice—female, whispering. "You bastard, Sammy Luke, I'm coming up to your room and I'm going to cut off your little—" A detailed anatomical description followed of what the voice was going to do to Sammy Luke. The low, violent obscenities, so horrible, so surprising, coming out of the innocent white hotel telephone, continued for a while unstopped, assaulting his ears like the rustle of some appalling cowrie shell; until Sammy thought to clutch the instrument to his chest, and thus stifle the voice in the surface of his new blue jacket.

After a moment, thinking he might have put an end to the terrible whispering, Sammy raised the instrument again. He was in time to hear the voice say:

"Have a nice death, Mr Luke."

Then there was silence.

Sammy felt quite sick. A moment later he was running across the ornate sitting-room of the splendid Barraclough suite, retching; the bathroom seemed miles away at the far end of the spacious bedroom; he only just reached it in time.

Sammy was lying, panting, on the nearest twin bed to the door—the one which had been meant for Zara—when the telephone rang again. He picked it up and held it at a distance, then recognized the merry, interested voice of the hotel telephonist.

"Oh, Mr Luke," she was saying. "While your line was busy just now, Joanie Lazlo called from Porlock Publishers, and she'll call right back. But she says to tell you that the taping for this afternoon has been cancelled, Max Syegrand is still tied up on the Coast and can't make it. Too bad about that, Mr Luke. It's a good show. Anyway, she'll come by this evening with some more books to sign. . . . Have a nice day now, Mr Luke." And the merry telephonist rang off. But this time Sammy shuddered when he heard the familiar cheerful farewell.

It seemed a long time before Joanie rang to say that she was downstairs in the hotel lobby, and should she bring the copies of *Women Weeping* up to the suite? When she arrived at the sitting-room door, carrying a Mexican tote bag weighed down by books, Joanie's pretty little pink face was glowing and she gave Sammy her usual softly enthusiastic welcome. All the same Sammy could hardly believe that he had contemplated seducing her—or indeed anyone—in his gilded suite amid the floral arrangements. That all seemed a very long while ago.

For in the hours before Joanie's arrival, Sammy received two more calls. The whispering voice grew bolder still in its descriptions of Sammy's fate; but it did not grow stronger. For some reason, Sammy listened through the first call to the end. At last the phrase came: although he was half expecting it, his heart still thumped when he heard the words:

"Have a nice death now, Mr Luke."

With the second call, he slammed down the telephone immediately and then called back the operator:

"No more," he said loudly and rather breathlessly. "No more, I don't want any more."

"Pardon me, Mr Luke?"

"I meant, I don't want any more calls, not like that, not now."

"Alrighty." The operator—it was another voice, not the merry woman who habitually watched television, but just as friendly. "I'll hold your calls for now, Mr Luke. I'll be happy to do it. Goodbye now. Have a nice evening."

Should Sammy perhaps have questioned this new operator about his recent caller? No doubt she would declare herself happy to discuss the matter. But he dreaded a further cheerful, impersonal New York encounter in his shaken state. Besides, the very first call had been put through by the merry television-watcher. Zara. He needed to talk to Zara. She would know what to do; or rather she would know what *he* should do.

"What's going on?" she exclaimed. "I tried to ring you three times and that bloody woman on the hotel switchboard wouldn't put me through. Are you all right? I rang you back because you sounded so peculiar. Sort of high, you were laughing at things, things which weren't really funny; it's not like you, is it; in New York people are supposed to get this energy, but I never thought . . ."

"I'm not all right, not all right at all," Sammy interrupted her; he was aware of a high, rather tremulous note in his voice. "I was all right then, more than all right, but now I'm not, not at all." Zara couldn't at first grasp what Sammy was telling her, and in the end he had to abandon all explanations of his previous state of exhilaration. For one thing, Zara couldn't seem to grasp what he was saying, and for another Sammy was guiltily aware that absence from Zara's side had played more than a little part in this temporary madness. So Sammy settled for agreeing that he had been acting rather oddly since he had arrived in New York, and then appealed to Zara to advise him how next to proceed.

Once Sammy had made this admission, Zara sounded more like her normal brisk but caring self. She told Sammy to ring up Clodagh at Porlock.

"Frankly, Sammy, I can't think why you didn't ring her straightaway." Zara pointed out that if Sammy could not, Clodagh certainly could and would deal with the hotel switchboard, so that calls were filtered, the lawful distinguished from the unlawful.

"Clodagh might even know the woman," observed Sammy weakly at one point. "She has some very odd friends."

Zara laughed. "Not *that* odd, I hope." Altogether she was in a better temper. Sammy remembered to ask after Zara's mother before he rang off; and on hearing that Tess had flown to America on business, he went so far as to say that he would love to have a drink with her.

When Joanie arrived in the suite, Sammy told her about the threatening calls and was vaguely gratified by her distress.

"I think that's just dreadful, Sammy," she murmured, her light hazel eyes swimming with some tender emotion. "Clodagh's not in the office right now, but let me talk with the hotel manager right away. . . ." Yet it was odd how Joanie no longer seemed in the slightest bit attractive to Sammy. There was even something cloying about her friendliness; perhaps there was a shallowness there, a surface brightness concealing nothing; perhaps Tess was right and New Yorkers were after all insincere. All in all, Sammy was pleased to see Joanie depart with the signed books.

He did not offer her a second drink, although she had brought him an advance copy of the *New York Times* Book Section for Sunday, showing that *Women Weeping* had jumped four places in the bestseller list.

"Have a nice evening, Sammy," said Joanie softly as she closed the door of the suite. "I've left a message with Clodagh's answering service and I'll call you tomorrow."

But Sammy did not have a very nice evening. Foolishly he decided to have dinner in his suite; the reason was that he had some idiotic lurking fear that the woman with the whispering voice would be lying in wait for him outside the Barraclough.

"Have a nice day," said the waiter, automatically, who delivered the meal on a heated trolley covered in a white damask cloth, after Sammy had signed the chit. Sammy hated him.

"The day is over. It is evening." Sammy spoke in a voice which was pointed, almost vicious; he had just deposited a tip on the white chit. By this time the waiter, stowing the dollars rapidly and expertly in his pocket, was already on his way to the door; he turned and flashed a quick smile.

"Yeah. Sure. Thank you, Mr Luke. Have a nice day." The waiter's hand was on the door handle.

"It is evening here!" exclaimed Sammy. He found he was shaking. "Do you understand? Do you agree that it is *evening*?" The man, mildly startled, but not at all discomposed, said again: "Yeah. Sure. Evening. Goodbye now." And he went.

Sammy poured himself a whisky from the suite's mini-bar. He no longer felt hungry. The vast white expanse of his dinner trolley depressed him, because it reminded him of his encounter with the waiter; at the same time he lacked the courage to push the trolley boldly out of the suite into the corridor. Having avoided leaving the Barraclough he now found that even more foolishly he did not care to open the door of his own suite.

Clodagh being out of the office, it was doubtless Joanie's fault that the hotel operators still ignored their instructions. Another whispering call was let through, about ten o'clock at night, as Sammy was watching a movie starring the young Elizabeth Taylor, much cut up by commercials, on television. (If he stayed awake till midnight, he could see himself on one of the talk shows he had recorded.) The operator was now supposed to announce the name of each caller, for Sammy's inspection; but this call came straight through.

There was a nasty new urgency in what the voice was promising: "Have a nice death now. I'll be coming by quite soon, Sammy Luke."

In spite of the whisky—he drained yet another of the tiny bottles—Sammy was still shaking when he called down to the operator and protested: "I'm still getting these calls. You've got to do something. You're supposed to be keeping them away from me."

The operator, not a voice he recognized, sounded rather puzzled, but full of goodwill; spurious goodwill, Sammy now felt. Even if she was sincere, she was certainly stupid. She did not seem to recall having put through anyone to Sammy within the last ten minutes. Sammy did not dare instruct her to hold all calls in case Zara rang up again (or Clodagh, for that matter; where was Clodagh, now that he needed protection from this kind of feminist nut?) He felt too desperate to cut himself off altogether from contact with the outside world. What would Zara advise?

The answer was really quite simple, once it had occurred to him. Sammy rang down to the front desk and complained to the house manager who was on night duty. The house manager, like the operator, was rather puzzled, but extremely polite.

"Threats, Mr Luke? I assure you you'll be very secure at the Barraclough. We have guards naturally, and we are accustomed . . . but if you'd like me to come up to discuss the matter, why I'd be happy to. . . ."

When the house manager arrived, he was quite charming. He referred not only to Sammy's appearance on television but to his actual book. He told Sammy he'd loved the book; what was more he'd given another copy to his eighty-three-year-old mother (who'd seen Sammy on the *Today* show) and she'd loved it too. Sammy was too weary to wonder more than passingly what an eighty-three-year-old mother would make of *Women Weeping*. He was further depressed by the house manager's elaborate courtesy; it wasn't absolutely clear whether he believed Sammy's story, or merely thought he was suffering from the delightful strain of being a celebrity. Maybe the guests at the Barraclough behaved like that all the time, describing imaginary death threats? That possibility also Sammy was too exhausted to explore.

At midnight he turned the television on again and watched himself, on the chat show in the blue jacket, laughing and wriggling with his own humour, denying for the tenth time that he had any curious sadistic tastes himself, that *Women Weeping* was founded on any incident in his private life.

When the telephone rang sharply into the silence of the suite shortly after the end of the show, Sammy knew that it would be his persecutor; nevertheless the sight of his erstwhile New York self, so debonair, so confident, had given him back some strength. Sammy was no longer shaking as he picked up the receiver.

It was Clodagh on the other end of the line, who had just returned to New York from somewhere out of town and picked up Joanie's message from her answering service. Clodagh listened carefully to what Sammy had to say and answered him with something less than her usual loud-hailing zest.

"I'm not too happy about this one!" she said after what—for Clodagh—was quite a lengthy silence. "Ever since Andy Warhol, we can never be quite sure what these jokers will do. Maybe a press release tomorrow? Sort of protect you with publicity *and* sell a few more copies. Maybe not. I'll think about that one, I'll call Joanie in the morning." To Sammy's relief, Clodagh was in charge.

There was another pause. When Clodagh spoke again, her tone was kindly, almost maternal; she reminded him, surprisingly, of Zara.

"Listen, little Sammy, stay right there and I'll be over. We don't want to lose an author, do we?"

Sammy went on to the little balcony which led off the sitting-room and gazed down at the street lights far far below; he did not gaze too long, partly because Sammy suffered from vertigo (although that had become much better in New York) and partly because he wondered whether an enemy was waiting for him down below. Sammy no longer thought all the lights were twinkling with goodwill. Looking downwards he imagined Clodagh, a strong Zara-substitute, striding towards him, to save him.

When Clodagh did arrive, rather suddenly at the door of the suite—maybe she did not want to alarm him by telephoning up from the lobby of the hotel?—she did look very strong, as well as handsome, in her black designer jeans and black silk shirt; through her shirt he could see the shape of her flat, muscular chest, with the nipples clearly defined, like the chest of a young Greek athlete.

"Little Sammy," said Clodagh quite tenderly. "Who would want to frighten you?"

The balcony windows were still open. Clodagh made Sammy pour himself yet another whisky and one for her too (there was a trace of the old Clodagh in the acerbity with which she gave these orders). Masterfully she also imposed two mysterious bomb-like pills upon Sammy which she promised, together with the whisky, would give him sweet dreams "and no nasty calls to frighten you."

Because Clodagh was showing a tendency to stand very close to him, one of her long arms affectionately and irremovably round his shoulders, Sammy was not all that unhappy when Clodagh ordered him to take both their drinks on to the balcony, away from the slightly worrying intimacy of the suite.

Sammy stood at the edge of the parapet, holding both glasses, and looked downwards. He felt better. Some of his previous benevolence towards New York came flooding back as the whisky and pills began to take effect. Sammy no longer imagined that his enemy was down there in the street outside the Barraclough, waiting for him.

In a way of course, Sammy was quite right. For Sammy's enemy was not down there in the street below, but standing silently right there behind him, on the balcony, black gloves on her big, capable, strong hands where they extended from the cuffs of her chic black silk shirt.

"Have a nice death now, Sammy Luke." Even the familiar phrase hardly had time to strike a chill into his heart as Sammy found himself falling, falling into the deep trough of the New York street twenty-three stories below. The two whisky glasses flew from his hands and little icy glass fragments scattered far and wide, far far from Sammy's tiny slumped body where it hit the pavement;

the whisky vanished altogether, for no one recorded drops of whisky falling on their face in Madison Avenue.

Soft-hearted Joanie cried when the police showed her Sammy's typewritten suicide note with that signature so familiar from the signing of the books; the text itself, the last product of the battered, portable typewriter Sammy had brought with him to New York. But Joanie had to confirm Sammy's distressed state at her last visit to the suite; an impression more than confirmed by the amount of whisky Sammy had consumed before his death—a glass in each hand as he fell, said the police—to say nothing of the pills.

The waiter contributed to the picture too.

"I guess the guy seemed quite upset when I brought him his dinner." He added as an afterthought: "He was pretty lonesome too. Wanted to talk. You know the sort. Tried to stop me going away. Wanted to have a conversation. I shoulda stopped, but I was busy." The waiter was genuinely regretful.

The hotel manager was regretful too, which considering the fact that Sammy's death had been duly reported in the Press as occurring from a Barraclough balcony, was decent of him.

One of the operators—Sammy's merry friend—went further and was dreadfully distressed: "Jesus, I don't believe it. For Christ's sake, I just saw him on television!" The other operator made a calmer statement simply saying that Sammy had seemed very indecisive about whether he wished to receive calls or not in the course of the evening.

Zara Luke, in England, told the story of Sammy's last day and his pathetic tales of persecution, not otherwise substantiated. She also revealed—not totally to the surprise of her friends—that Sammy had a secret history of mental breakdown and was particularly scared of travelling by himself.

"I shall always blame myself for letting him go," ended Zara, brokenly.

Clodagh Jansen of Porlock Publishers made a dignified statement about the tragedy.

It was Clodagh, too, who met the author's widow at the airport when Zara flew out a week later to make all the dreadful arrangements consequent upon poor Sammy's death.

At the airport Clodagh and Zara embraced discreetly, tearfully. It was only in private later at Clodagh's apartment—for Zara to stay at the Barraclough would certainly have been totally inappropriate—that more intimate caresses of a richer quality began. Began, but did not end: neither had any reason to hurry things.

"After all, we've all the time in the world," murmured Sammy's widow to Sammy's publisher.

"And all the money too," Clodagh whispered back; she must remember to tell Zara that *Women Weeping* would reach the Number One spot in the bestseller list on Sunday.

THE SANTA CLAUS CLUB

Julian Symons

I

IT IS NOT often, in real life, that letters are written recording implacable hatred nursed over the years, or that private detectives are invited by peers to select dining clubs, or that murders occur at such dining clubs, or that they are solved on the spot by a process of deduction. The case of the Santa Claus Club provided an example of all these rarities.

The case began one day a week before Christmas, when Francis Quarles went to see Lord Acrise. He was a rich man, Lord Acrise, and an important one, the chairman of this big building concern and director of that and the other insurance company, and consultant to the Government on half a dozen matters. He had been a harsh, intolerant man in his prime, and was still hard enough in his early seventies, Quarles guessed, as he looked at the beaky nose, jutting chin and stony blue eyes under thick brows. They sat in the study of Acrise's house just off the Brompton Road.

"Just tell me what you think of these."

These were three letters, badly typed on a machine with a worn ribbon. They were all signed with the name James Gliddon. The first two contained vague references to some wrong done to Gliddon by Acrise in the past. They were written in language that was wild, but unmistakably threatening. "You have been a whited sepulchre for too long, but now your time has come . . . You don't know what I'm going to do, now I've come back, but you won't be able to help wondering and worrying . . . The mills of God grind slowly, but they're going to grind you into little bits for what you've done to me."

The third letter was more specific. "So the thief is going to play Santa Claus. That will be your last evening alive. *I shall be there*, Joe Acrise, and I shall watch with pleasure as you squirm in agony."

Quarles looked at the envelopes. They were plain and cheap. The address was typed, and the word "Personal" was on top of the envelope. "Who is James Gliddon?"

The stony eyes glared at him. "I'm told you're to be trusted. Gliddon was a school friend of mine. We grew up together in the slums of Nottingham. We started a building company together. It did well for a time, then went bust. There was a lot of money missing. Gliddon kept the books. He got five years for fraud."

"Have you heard from him since then? I see all these letters are recent."

"He's written half a dozen letters, I suppose, over the years. The last one came—oh, seven years ago, I should think. From the Argentine." Acrise stopped, then said abruptly, "Snewin tried to find him for me, but he'd disappeared."

"Snewin?"

"My secretary. Been with me twelve years."

He pressed a bell. An obsequious, fattish man, whose appearance somehow put Quarles in mind of an enormous mouse, scurried in.

"Snewin? Did we keep any of those old letters from Gliddon?"

"No, sir. You told me to destroy them."

"The last ones came from the Argentine, right?"

"From Buenos Aires to be exact, sir."

Acrise nodded, and Snewin scurried out. Quarles said, "Who else knows this story about Gliddon?"

"Just my wife." Acrise bared yellow teeth in a grin. "Unless somebody's been digging into my past."

"And what does this mean, about you playing Santa Claus?"

"I'm this year's chairman of the Santa Claus Club. We hold our raffle and dinner next Monday."

Then Quarles remembered. The Santa Claus Club had been formed by ten rich men. Each year they met, every one of them dressed up as Santa Claus, and held a raffle. The members took it in turn to provide the prize that was raffled—it might be a case of Napoleon brandy, a modest cottage with some exclusive salmon fishing rights attached to it, a Constable painting. Each Santa Claus bought one ticket for the raffle, at a cost of one thousand guineas. The total of ten thousand guineas was given to a Christmas charity. After the raffle the assembled Santa Clauses, each accompanied by one guest, ate a traditional Christmas dinner. The whole thing was a combination of various English characteristics: enjoyment of dressing up, a wish to help charities, and the desire also that the help given should not go unrecorded. The dinners of the Santa Claus Club got a good deal of publicity, and there were those who said that it would have been perfectly easy for the members to give their money to charities in a less conspicuous manner.

"I want you to find Gliddon," Lord Acrise said. "Don't mistake me, Mr Quarles. I don't want to take action against him, I want to help him. I wasn't to blame—don't think I admit that—but it was hard that Jimmy Gliddon should go to jail. I'm a hard man, have been all my life, but I don't think my worst enemies would call me mean. Those who've helped me know that when I die they'll find they're not forgotten. Jimmy Gliddon must be an old man now. I'd like to set him up for the rest of his life."

"To find him by next Monday is a tall order," Quarles said. "But I'll try."

He was at the door when Acrise said casually, "By the way, I'd like you to be my guest at the Club dinner on Monday night."

Did that mean, Quarles wondered, that he was to act as official poison-taster if he did not find James Gliddon?

II

There were two ways of trying to find Gliddon—by investigation of his career after leaving prison, and through the typewritten letters. Quarles took the job of tracing the past, leaving the letters to his secretary, Molly Player.

From Scotland Yard Quarles found out that Gliddon had spent nearly four years in prison, from 1913 to late 1916. He had joined a Nottinghamshire Regiment when he came out, and the records of this Regiment showed that he had been demobilized in August, 1919, with the rank of Sergeant. In 1923 he had been given a sentence of three years for an attempt to smuggle diamonds. Thereafter, all trace of him in Britain vanished.

Quarles made some expensive telephone calls to Buenos Aires, where letters had come from seven years earlier. He learned that Gliddon had lived in the city from a time just after the war until 1955. He ran an import-export business, and was thought to have been living in other South American Republics during the war. His business was said to have been a cloak for smuggling, both of drugs and of suspected Nazis, whom he got out of Europe into the

Argentine. In 1955 a newspaper had accused Gliddon of arranging the entry into the Argentine of a Nazi war criminal named Hermann Breit. Gliddon threatened to sue the paper, and then disappeared. A couple of weeks later a battered body was washed up just outside the city.

"It was identified as Gliddon," the liquid voice said over the telephone. "But you know, Señor Quarles, in such matters the police are sometimes happy to close their files."

"There was still some doubt?"

"Yes. Not very much, perhaps, but—in these cases there is often a doubt."

Molly Player found out nothing useful about the paper and envelopes. They were of the sort that could be bought in a thousand stores and shops in London and elsewhere. She had more luck with the typewriter. Its key characteristics identified the machine as a Malward portable of a type which the company had ceased producing ten years ago. The type face had proved unsatisfactory, and only some three hundred machines of this sort had been made. The Malward Company was able to provide her with a list of the purchasers of these machines, and Molly started to check and trace them, but had to give it up as a bad job.

"If we had three weeks I might get somewhere. In three days it's impossible," she said to Quarles.

Lord Acrise made no comment on Quarles's recital of failure. "See you on Monday evening, seven-thirty, black tie," he said, and barked with laughter. "Your host will be Santa Claus."

"I'd like to be there earlier."

"Good idea. Any time you like. You know where it is—Robert the Devil Restaurant."

III

The Robert the Devil Restaurant is situated inconspicuously in Mayfair. It is not a restaurant in the ordinary sense of the word, for there is no public dining-room, but simply several private rooms, which can accommodate any number of guests from two to thirty. Perhaps the food is not quite the best in London, but it is certainly the most expensive.

It was here that Quarles arrived at half past six, a big suave man, rather too conspicuously elegant perhaps in a midnight blue dinner jacket. He talked to Albert, the *maître d'hôtel*, whom he had known for some years, took unobtrusive looks at the waiters, went into and admired the kitchens. Albert observed his activities with tolerant amusement. "You are here on some sort of business, Mr Quarles?"

"I am a guest, Albert. I am also a kind of bodyguard. Tell me, how many of your waiters have joined you in the past twelve months?"

"Perhaps half a dozen. They come, they go."

"Is there anybody at all on your staff—waiters, kitchen staff, anybody—who has joined you in the past year, and who is over sixty years old?"

Albert thought, then shook his head decisively. "No. There is not such a one."

The first of the guests came just after a quarter past seven. This was the brain surgeon Sir James Erdington, with a guest whom Quarles recognized as the Arctic explorer, Norman Endell. After that they came at intervals of a minute or two—a junior minister in the Government, one of the three most important men in the motor industry, a General promoted to the peerage to celebrate his retirement, a theatrical producer named Roddy Davis, who had successfully combined commerce and culture. As they arrived, the hosts went into a special robing room to put on their Santa Claus clothes, while the guests drank sherry. At seven-twenty-five Snewin scurried in, gasped, "Excuse me, place names, got to put them out," and went into the dining-room. Through the open door Quarles glimpsed a large oval table, gleaming with silver, bright with roses.

After Snewin came Lord Acrise, jutting-nosed and fearsome-eyed. "Sorry to have kept you waiting," he barked, and asked conspiratorially, "Well?"

"No sign."

"False alarm. Lot of nonsense. Got to dress up now."

He went into the robing room with his box—each of the hosts had a similar box, labelled "Santa Claus"—and came out again bewigged, bearded and robed. "Better get the business over, and then we can enjoy ourselves. You can tell 'em to come in," he said to Albert.

This referred to the photographers, who had been clustering outside, and now came into the room specially provided for holding the raffle. In the centre of the room was a table and on this table stood this year's prize, two exquisite T'ang horses. On the other side of the table were ten chairs arranged in a semi-circle, and on these sat the Santa Clauses. The guests stood inconspicuously at the side.

The raffle was conducted with the utmost seriousness. Each Santa Claus had a numbered slip. These slips were put into a tombola, and Acrise put in his hand and drew out one of them. Flash bulbs exploded.

"The number drawn is eight," Acrise announced, and Roddy Davis waved the counterfoil in his hand. "Isn't that *wonderful?* It's my ticket." He went over to the horses, picked up one. More flashes. "I'm bound to say that they couldn't have gone to *anybody* who'd have appreciated them more."

Quarles, standing near to the General, whose face was as red as his robe, heard him mutter something uncomplimentary. Charity, he reflected, was not universal, even in a gathering of Santas. More flashes, the photographers disappeared, and Quarles's views about the nature of charity were reinforced when, as they were about to go into the dining-room, Erdington said: "Forgotten something, haven't you, Acrise?"

With what seemed dangerous quietness Acrise answered, "Have I? I don't think so."

"It's customary for the Club and guests to sing 'Noel' before we go in to dinner."

"You didn't come to last year's dinner. It was agreed then that we should give it up. Carols after dinner, much better."

"I must say I thought that was *just* for last year, because we were late," Roddy Davis fluted. "I'm sure that's what was agreed. I think myself it's rather pleasant to sing 'Noel' before we go in and start eating too much."

"Suggest we put it to the vote," Erdington said sharply. Half a dozen of the Santas now stood looking at each other with subdued hostility. It was a situation that would have been totally ludicrous, if it had not been also embarrassing for the guests. Then suddenly the Arctic explorer, Endell, began to sing "Noel, Noel" in a rich bass. There was the faintest flicker of hesitation, and then guests and Santas joined in. The situation was saved.

At dinner Quarles found himself with Acrise on one side of him and Roddy Davis on the other. Endell sat at Acrise's other side, and beyond him was Erdington. Turtle soup was followed by grilled sole, and then three great turkeys were brought in. The helpings of turkey were enormous. With the soup they drank a light, dry sherry, with the sole Chassagne Montrachet, with the turkey an Alexe Corton, heavy and powerful.

"And who are *you*?" Roddy Davis peered at Quarles's card and said, with what seemed manifest untruth, "Of course I know your name."

"I am a criminologist." This sounded better, he thought, than private detective.

"I remember your monograph on criminal calligraphy. Quite fascinating."

So Davis did know who he was—it would be easy, Quarles thought, to underrate the intelligence of the round-faced man who beamed innocently to him.

"These beards really do get in the way rather," Davis said. "But there, one must suffer for tradition. Have you known Acrise long?"

"Not very. I'm greatly privileged to be here." Quarles had been watching, as closely as he could, the pouring of the wine, the serving of the food. He had seen nothing suspicious. Now, to get away from Davis's questions, he turned to his host.

"Damned awkward business before dinner," Acrise said. "Might have been, at least. Can't let well alone, Erdington." He picked up his turkey leg, attacked it with Elizabethan gusto, wiped mouth and fingers with his napkin. "Like this wine?"

"It's excellent."

"Chose it myself. They've got some good Burgundies here." Acrise's speech was slightly slurred, and it seemed to Quarles that he was rapidly getting drunk.

"Do you have any speeches?"

"What's that?"

"Are any speeches made after dinner?"

"No speeches. Just sing carols. But I've got a little surprise for 'em."

"What sort of surprise?"

"Very much in the spirit of Christmas, and a good joke too. But if I told you it wouldn't be a surprise now, would it?"

Acrise had almost said "shurprise." Quarles looked at him and then returned to the turkey.

There was a general cry of pleasure as Albert himself brought in the great plum pudding, topped with holly and blazing with brandy.

"That's the most wonderful pudding I've ever seen in my life," Endell said. "Are we really going to eat it?"

"Of course we're going to eat it," Acrise said irritably. He stood up, swaying a little, and picked up the knife beside the pudding.

"I don't like to be critical, but our Chairman is really *not* cutting the pudding very well," Roddy Davis whispered to Quarles. And indeed, it was more of a stab than a cut that Acrise made at the pudding. Albert took over, and cut it quickly and efficiently. Bowls of brandy butter were circulated.

Quarles leaned towards Acrise. "Are you all right?"

"Of course I'm all right." The slurring was very noticeable now. Acrise ate no pudding, but he drank some more wine, and dabbed at his lips. When the pudding was finished he got slowly to his feet again, and toasted the Queen. Cigars were lighted. Acrise was not smoking. He whispered something to the waiter, who nodded and left the room. Acrise got up again, leaning heavily on the table.

"A little surprise," he said. "In the spirit of Christmas."

Quarles had thought that he was beyond being surprised by the activities of the Santa Claus Club, but still he was astonished by sight of the three figures who entered the room. They were led by Snewin, somehow more mouselike than ever, wearing a long white smock and a red nightcap with a tassel. He was followed by an older man dressed in a kind of grey sackcloth, with a face so white that it might have been covered in plaster of paris. This man carried chains which he shook. At the rear came a young middle aged lady, who sparkled so brightly that she seemed to be completely hung with tinsel.

"I am Scrooge," said Snewin.

"I am Marley," wailed grey sackcloth, clanking his chains.

"And I," said the young middle-aged lady, with abominable sprightliness, "am the ghost of Christmas past."

There was a murmur round the table, and slowly the murmur grew to a ripple of laughter.

"We have come," said Snewin in a thin mouse voice, "to perform for you our own interpretation of *A Christmas Carol*—oh, sir, what's the matter?"

Lord Acrise stood up in his robes, tore off his wig, pulled at his beard, tried to say something. Then he clutched at the side of his chair and fell sideways, so that he leaned heavily against Endell and slipped slowly to the floor.

IV

There ensued a minute of confused, important activity. Endell made some sort of exclamation and rose from his chair, slightly obstructing Quarles. Erdington was first beside the body, holding the wrist in his hand, listening for the heart. Then they were all crowding round, the red-robed Santas, the guests, the actors in their ludicrous clothes. Snewin, at Quarles's left shoulder, was babbling something, and at his right were Roddy Davis and Endell.

"Stand back," Erdington snapped. He stayed on his knees for another few moments, looking curiously at Acrise's puffed, distorted face, bluish around the mouth. Then he stood up. "He's dead."

There was a murmur of surprise and horror, and now they all drew back, as men do instinctively from the presence of death.

"Heart attack?" somebody said. Erdington made a non-committal noise. Quarles moved to his side.

"I'm a private detective, Sir James. Lord Acrise feared an attempt on his life, and asked me to come along here."

"You seem to have done well so far," Erdington said dryly.

"May I look at the body?"

"If you wish."

As soon as Quarles bent down he caught the smell of bitter almonds. When he straightened up Erdington raised his eyebrows.

"He's been poisoned."

"Bravo."

"There's a smell like prussic acid, but the way he died precludes cyanide I think. He seemed to become very drunk during dinner, and his speech was blurred. Does that suggest anything to you?"

"I'm a brain surgeon, not a physician." Erdington stared at the floor, then said "Nitro-benzene?"

"That's what I thought. We shall have to notify the police." Quarles went to the door, spoke to a disturbed Albert. Then he returned to the room and clapped his hands.

"Gentlemen. My name is Francis Quarles, and I am a private detective. Lord Acrise asked me to come here tonight because he had received a threat that this would be his last evening alive. The threat said: 'I shall be there, and I shall watch with pleasure as you squirm in agony.' Lord Acrise has been poisoned. It seems certain that the man who made the threat is in this room."

"Gliddon," a voice said. Snewin had divested himself of the white smock and red nightcap, and now appeared as his customary respectable self.

"Yes. This letter, and others he had received, were signed with the name of James Gliddon, a man who bore a grudge against Lord Acrise which went back nearly half a century. Gliddon became a professional smuggler and crook. He would now be in his late sixties."

"But dammit man, this Gliddon's not here." That was the General, who took off his wig and beard. "Lot of tomfoolery."

In a shamefaced way the other members of the Santa Claus Club removed their facial trappings. Marley took off his chains and the young middle aged lady discarded her cloak of tinsel.

"Isn't he here? But Lord Acrise is dead."

Snewin coughed. "Excuse me, sir, but would it be possible for my colleagues from our local dramatic society to retire? Of course, I can stay myself if you wish. It was Lord Acrise's idea that we should perform our skit on *A Christmas Carol* as a seasonable novelty, but—"

"Everybody must stay in this room until the police arrive. The problem, as you will all realize, is how the poison was administered. All of us ate the same food, drank the same wine. I sat next to Lord Acrise, and I watched as closely as possible to make sure of this. I watched the wine being poured, the turkey being carved and brought to the table, the pudding being cut and passed round. After dinner some of you smoked cigars or cigarettes, but not Acrise."

"Just a moment." It was Roddy Davis who spoke. "This sounds fantastic, but wasn't it Sherlock Holmes who said that when you'd eliminated all other possibilities, even a fantastic one must be right? Supposing that some poison in powder form had been put on to Acrise's food—through the pepper pots, say—"

Erdington was shaking his head, but Quarles unscrewed both salt and pepper pots and tasted their contents. "Salt and pepper. And in any case other people might have used these pots. Hallo, what's this?"

Acrise's napkin lay crumpled on his chair, and Quarles had picked it up and was staring at it.

"It's Acrise's napkin," Endell said. "What's remarkable about that?"

"It's a napkin, but not the one Acrise used. He wiped his mouth half a dozen times on his napkin, and wiped his greasy fingers on it too, when he'd gnawed a turkey bone. He must certainly have left grease marks on it. But look at this napkin." He held it up, and they saw that it was spotless. Quarles said softly, "The murderer's mistake."

"I'm quite baffled," Roddy Davis said. "What does it mean?"

Quarles turned to Erdington. "Sir James and I agreed that the poison used was probably nitro-benzene. This is deadly as a liquid, but it is also poisonous as a vapour, isn't that so?"

Erdington nodded. "You'll remember the case of the unfortunate young man who used shoe polish containing nitro-benzene on damp shoes, put them on and wore them, and was killed by the fumes."

"Yes. Somebody made sure that Lord Acrise had a napkin that had been soaked in nitro-benzene but was dry enough to use. The same person substituted the proper napkin, the one belonging to the restaurant, after Acrise was dead."

"Nobody's left the room," said Roddy Davis.

"No."

"That means the napkin must still be here."

"It does."

"Then what are we waiting for? I vote that we submit to a search."

There was a small hubbub of protest and approval. "That won't be necessary," Quarles said. "Only one person here fulfils all the qualifications of the murderer."

"James Gliddon?"

"No. Gliddon is almost certainly dead, as I found out when I made inquiries about him. But the murderer is somebody who knew about Acrise's relationship with Gliddon, and tried to be clever by writing the letters to lead us along a wrong track. Then the murderer is somebody who had the opportunity of coming in here before dinner, and who knew exactly where Acrise would be sitting. There is only one person who fulfils all of these qualifications.

"He removed any possible suspicion from himself, as he thought, by being absent from the dinner table, but he arranged to come in afterwards to exchange the napkins. He probably put the poisoned napkin into the clothes he discarded. As for motive, long-standing hatred might be enough, but he is also somebody who knew that he would benefit handsomely when Acrise died—stop him, will you."

But the General, with a tackle reminiscent of the days when he had been the best wing three quarter in the country, had already brought to the floor Lord Acrise's mouselike secretary, Snewin.

THE DAY IT RAINED IN SINGAPAW

Madelaine Duke

N O JETLAG. N OT much energy either. I'd have gone back to sleep if the snoring hadn't become intolerable. Out of bed, out on the balcony. Black ceramic tiles almost cool under my feet. Snores rasping from the room below. Must have left his balcony door open. Like me, not keen on air conditioning. Forget it. Have fun in this five-star luxury, this holiday brochure come alive.

No mere glass and concrete cubes here. Each suite has a balcony, which juts out over the tropical gardens like the thick bottom lip of a smiling Buddha. And all the lips spill great cascades of bougainvillaea, purple and orange, white and coral, an onslaught of colours above the palm-trees that surround the pool.

There is nothing to indicate whether the solitary swimmer is male or female, except the cap, a cluster of rubber frangipani blooms. She is cutting length after length, barely disturbing the surface of the pool. From above she looks weightless.

She is still travelling while a Chinese attendant brings me a garden bed and table, and while the waiter serves my breakfast. She must have completed a couple of miles yet shows no sign of flagging.

At close quarters she looks tall, lean, sunburned. She's as agile as the water snake I'd seen at Malindi. I wonder what it feels like to move with such unselfconscious ease.

"Excuse me." She is sitting on the edge of the pool, peeling off her cap. "You've just arrived from England?"

"Last night."

She shakes down her hair. Faded blonde. She has shy grey eyes. Not in the habit of buttonholing strangers. "I hope you don't mind . . . This hazy sun's rather deceptive. One must protect oneself. You haven't put on cream?"

"Not yet. Thanks, I will."

"First time in Singapore even my leathery skin got quite burned."

"I wish I was as brown."

"Give it time . . . a few years. You're so fair . . . and young."

She might be any age between forty-five and sixty. I wouldn't mind getting old, looking like her. "Have you spent a lot of time in the tropics?"

"Just our annual holidays. My husband's the one who used to travel. For his firm. He was in engineering." She goes to a cluttered daybed and picks up a plastic bottle. "Not taking chances." She squirts a colourless liquid on her palm and begins to work over her limbs. The black one-piece swimsuit, the type I hated wearing at school, is right for her. "I've got to use real grease. My skin's so dry, it eats the stuff." She massages her ankles, then the soles of her feet. "If you're going to tramp around the city like us, make sure your feet are comfortable."

"Right."

"Are you with a group?"

"No. I prefer going to new places on my own. Not that I've travelled a lot."

She nods. "You see more when you don't have to worry about companions. I once went abroad on my own. To Italy." A remote smile. "It was the only time. The year after it was quite different, like another country. I went with the team."

"Swimming?"

"Yes."

"I thought you must be a professional."

"No, an amateur. In the Olympic team. Not good enough though. I didn't bring home a medal. With hindsight, I think I should have tried again."

"Why didn't you?"

"Why?" She wipes oil on her face. "Because I married Lloyd, I suppose. In those days wives were expected to give up doing their own thing."

"You're still a super swimmer."

"I could be . . . I think. If I lived by the sea, in a tropical climate. Somewhere like Penang. We've just had a week in Penang. The Malayans don't mind English people. There are bungalows for sale . . ."

*

A man comes stalking to the pool, a bony Briton with a sharp jaw and thin lips. He wears a silly red cotton hat, white shorts and black leather shoes. Not an outfit he'd wear at home. As he approaches, the swimmer slides back into the water.

He lifts a camera to his eyes and watches her through the viewer. "Margaret!"

She is making for the far end.

"Margaret, come here! Don't play games."

She turns under water and surfaces below him. "Yes Lloyd?"

"Where's my blue shirt?"

"Laundry."

"Could have washed it yourself, couldn't you? What am I supposed to wear?"

"The khaki set's clean. Are you going into town?"

"You know perfectly well where we're going. I'm not in Singapaw to waste time."

His drawl sounds phoney, not like my grandfather's. Gran, according to my mother, speaks with an Oxford accent, an English that's almost died away with the British Empire.

"Dawling," Lloyd, now aware of my presence, is adjusting his approach to Margaret. "If we don't go soon it'll get frightfully sticky."

"Mind if I don't come?"

"Mind . . . mind. Bugger it up as usual . . . Listen, we must call the airline. Confirm our flight home."

"Will you, Lloyd?"

"You do it."

"You know more about it."

"Any fool can confirm an okay booking . . . Hell, I'll see to it. Are you going to flop around all day?"

"I'd like to invite this young lady for lunch at the Lotus. Miss . . ."

"Morgan." Stupid of me. I don't want to get involved with elderly couples. "Celia."

Lloyd offers me his hand. "Pleased to meet you, Celia." His wife knows that I've recognized her husband's pedigree. People with a hereditary drawl don't say, *pleased to meet you*; they'd mutter something suitably unintelligible. "Our name's Baker," he tells me. "Lloyd and Margaret . . . Stinking hot, isn't it? How about a drink?" He snaps his fingers at a passing waiter. "Boy! Bring us your special . . . Sort of liquid fruit salad," he informs me, "pineapple, paw-paw, litchi, cherries, soaked in some local hooch and ice. All right for you, Celia?"

"Fine."

He pulls up a deckchair. "You on holiday?"

"Partly. I also have some work."

"What do you do?"

"I'm a journalist."

"Nice racket. I have a friend who's a journalist. Travels tax-free all over the place. So-called business expenses. Your first time in Singapaw?"

"Yes."

"Good old Sweatypaw. Changed out of all recognition. Should have seen it thirty years ago . . . all ramshackle native houses, shops open to the street . . . people cooking, tailoring, selling silks and spices; lots of rats. Good old-fashioned Far East. Not much of it left. City of high-rise blocks, cleanest I've seen. Acres of elegant shopping plazas; goods from all over the world. Worth coming here for photographic equipment alone . . . The population decently housed. Each group of high-rise apartments holds a quarter of a million. Would you believe it!"

"Oh yes." Margaret watches the waiter serve our drinks. "Poor things. I wonder how they like it, filed away in boxes."

"Twaddle." Lloyd examines the chit presented by the waiter and signs it. "They're proud of their city. Ask any taxi driver."

"Lloyd does," says Margaret, "ask taxi drivers." She squirts oil on her palm, contemplates it for a while, and massages her feet.

Never noticed anyone else grease the soles.

Lloyd gives me his run-down on Singapore; the economic miracle, statistics, politics. Mr Who-d'ya-Bang, whom he's met at a business banquet, is the genius behind it all. Not generally understood, except by men in the know. Such as Lloyd, of course. Amazing man, Who-d'ya-Bang.

"What about Lee-kuan-Yu?" asks Margaret. "That is the name of the head of state, isn't it?"

"Well, what about him?" demands Lloyd.

"I thought he was the creator of all the affluence."

"Rubbish. What do you know about it!" Lloyd turns to me.

"She's seen Lee-kuan-Yu on TV. She's fallen for him, therefore he must be the tops . . . How do you like the drink, Celia?"

"Nice."

Margaret has almost finished hers and is trying to spear the pineapple from the bottom of the glass. The plastic cocktail stick being too short for the purpose, she puts in her fingers.

Lloyd is angry. "What d'you think you're doing?"

"Fishing out my pineapple."

"Don't be disgusting. Leave it alone."

The fruit slides back into the glass, Margaret's fingers in pursuit.

"You heard me." Lloyd glares at her. "Must you advertise your slum upbringing?"

"It was happy," she murmurs into her glass.

"Oh sure. And you'd still feel at home in Gorbals gutters. But while you're with me I won't have you . . ."

"Lloyd," I cut in. No reason why I should suffer. "*My* pineapple's stuck, and I'm going to pull it out with my fingers."

He watches me, thin lips in a clamped smile. "Celia, *you* know how to do it . . . Well, Margaret? Coming?"

"I'd rather stay."

"Then call the airline. I never can find a phone in town."

"There's one in our room."

"But I'm going out."

"What? Without a shirt?"

"Hell! All right, I'll see to it. You'd only make a hash of it." He lifts his red hat, "Pleased to have met you, Celia. See you later."

Change into a cotton dress. Put my swim suit out to dry. Now the sky is overcast, an English grey. The heat is pressing me down like my flabby ex-boyfriend. On the balcony below sprawls Margaret's black one-piece suit. So it's Lloyd who snores.

Margaret is waiting for me in a trishaw. "Lloyd calls these little carriages tourist-traps. Nothing shameful about being a tourist, is there?"

The young cyclist pedals us down Orchard Street, winding in and out between cars and buses. At Lucky Plaza, the huge modern shopping complex, Margaret spots her husband, binoculars in hand, apparently lecturing a well-groomed Chinese.

"He wants field glasses," she tells me, "but he won't buy until he's visited every likely shop in town."

We finish up in a warren of narrow streets where multitudes of Chinese trade with Chinese, a place of gaudy colours, alien sounds and unfamiliar smells—a romantic traveller's Singapore.

The Lotus consists of a kitchen, with the cooks on display, and an adjacent garden restaurant. We are the only Europeans among immaculately laundered Chinese men with briefcases.

I let Margaret choose our food. She has fun wandering along the range of cookers, picking out pieces of duck, selecting exotic vegetables. We take our plates to a table under a plane tree.

"Be prepared to run." She squints at the dark sky. "You get no warning when it rains here. The heavens open. It also stops suddenly, like someone turning off a tap." She uses her chopsticks with skill. "Lloyd doesn't know what he's missing. He won't eat in what he calls native slums . . . What are your plans, Celia?"

"I'll see what there is."

"Temples, the snake farm, the harbour." She smiles. "Buy the obligatory silk and watch Chinese dancing. You didn't expect to land in a commercial centre that could be anywhere in the world, did you?"

"My grandfather says everything is built over something else. He was here in the war. You're not keen on Singapore?"

"I see enough of supermarkets at home. Not complaining. Lloyd has compromised. Emporiums for him, the swimming pool for me; and the week in Penang . . . the blessed warm sea. Lloyd's just retired. We could live in Penang. But Lloyd wouldn't even consider it. In Northampton there are no language problems, and he's got the bowling club. Next year he'll be president . . ." She opens her handbag and takes out a fragile disc, mother of pearl, gleaming pastel colours. "Have you ever seen a shell like this?"

"No. It's beautiful."

"Yes." Her fingers contract. I can hear the shell crack in her fist. "There are plenty in Penang."

Margaret hasn't been hard to get rid of. She's sensitive enough to know when her company is no longer welcome. I don't think she minded going back to the swimming pool on her own. She understands about a person wanting to be alone in a foreign country.

She was right; I am disappointed in the metropolis. My fault. Having seen pictures of modern Singapore I should have known what to expect. Seemingly the old images, the ones grandfather conjured up, had the effect of confusing me.

Still jet-weary. Wandering aimlessly through siesta-sluggish streets. Here and there a small tumbledown house or a homely temple. Nothing grand, just fragments of grandfather's Singapore, the place he'd loved before he became a war-prisoner of the Japanese. Even while he rotted in Changi jail—he says the parasites are still feeding on his guts—the proximity of the magic city sustained him. The nostalgia hasn't rubbed off on me. Not much. But I'll go wherever he's told me to go, even to Changi. A proxy sentimental journey.

Raffles Hotel, and I haven't even been looking for it. So this was gran's playground. Raffles. Haven of British officers in tropical kit, the Ritz of the East. Eating, drinking, dancing to the boom of Japanese guns. Ornate white building against the grey sky. An oriental commissionaire under tropical palms. How come Mr Who-d'ya-Bang hasn't yet swept this icing sugar relic into the trash-can of history?

Lofty Victorian foyer. Cool. An American group drinking English tea around a swimming pool small enough to be a gesture rather than an amenity. Well manicured garden, almost English. A serene stage set, bar one disruptive apparition who appears to have strayed into the wrong scene. Lloyd, in khaki drill, beside the pool, eyes behind hefty binoculars. Absorbed in his new toy, yet bored. I dare say he was a martyr to boredom a couple of World Wars ago, jabbing sticks into the soft bodies of slugs or snails. There he goes, passing my table without seeing me.

Rain. Not the kind Margaret described. Just a soft patter. At Raffles, modom, we insist on the traditional English rain. We confine the tropical floods to the rest of Singapore.

Will Margaret be in her pool? Or does rain stop play?

Taxi home, the nearest thing to home because someone is there who knows me. Margaret and Lloyd, face it, have served a positive function in providing a transition between the familiar and the foreign. Had they not acknowledged my existence I mightn't have been too sure of my identity. Did gran need a transition when he landed at the other end of the world? Raffles perhaps?

Margaret and Lloyd are leaving the day after tomorrow. It'll be good to see the last of Lloyd. I'd like to know how Margaret put up with him most of her life. Would I? Perhaps not. Some things one learns have a diminishing effect, curiosity killing the cat—slightly.

My hotel is steeped in siesta somnolence. Best sleep off what's left of the lassitude. The rain is splashing down on the tiles of my balcony, drops bouncing and breaking, leaping and shattering.

Key in my lock. A Chinese maid; my clothes, shrouded in plastic, over her arm. "Your dresses, miss. Pressed very nice." She drapes the parcel over a chair. "You sleep good?"

"Too good. What's the time?"

She consults her digital watch. "A little after five."

"Thank you."

She stares at my balcony door and closes it. "Rain, very bad." The poor Mr Baker. Mr Woo, he say, bad for business."

Lloyd? "Why's Mr Baker bad for business?"

"It is the rain make Mr Baker fall down." She raises her hand and lets it drop. "Break his head . . . inside open like a coconut."

"You mean, Mr Baker is dead?"

"Oh yes. Mr Woo say unlucky for the hotel. Please, say nothing to guests."

"How did it happen?"

"Mr Woo say, the rain stop a little and Mr Baker go out . . . so." She opens the balcony door but immediately closes it again. "He look . . ." she mimes binoculars, "and his feet go, so . . ." she slips back a leg. "The guests see nothing. I see, and Mrs Baker in the pool. They take him away quick, quick." She shivers, blue-black hair quivering on her cheeks. Suddenly a big smile. "Tonight you enjoy Chinese dances? In the Hibiscus Room. Very nice."

Margaret is in the denim skirt and jacket she'd worn at lunch. "Celia. You've heard?"

"Yes. I'm sorry."

"Kind of you to come. Please sit down." She pushes a second chair to the open balcony door. "Drink?"

I manage a meaningless mutter.

"It'll help." She goes to the wardrobe. "Scotch and mineral water?"

"Thanks."

She hands me a tumbler and sits, facing me. "He *would* wear his black shoes. Thin leather soles. So unsuitable in this climate."

"Is there anything I can do?"

"No. Please don't let this upset you. After all . . . yesterday you didn't know we existed. I've phoned his brother. He always knows what to do . . . There must be some machinery . . ."

"The rain's going to stop." I can't think of anything less inane.

"So it is. The sun's coming out . . . There was a storm in Penang. Afterwards the beach was covered in shells, all washed and polished. Everything was so new and clean. People were beach-combing . . . English, of course . . ."

The rain has stopped. Gossamer mists rising from the balcony floor. Suddenly the tiles are dry, matt black except for the sheen of oily marks—footprints all along the outer edge of the balcony. Size four prints.

Bungalows for sale in Penang. Better not dwell upon something mentioned in passing.

THE MERCENARIES

Michael Gilbert

IT WAS ELEVEN o'clock on a fine February morning when Mr Calder's car gave up the struggle and rolled to a halt on the outskirts of Winterbourne Vaisey.

Mr Calder knew enough about cars to realize that whatever had happened needed expert attention. He was glad that the breakdown had occurred on the outskirts of a sizeable village. It looked the sort of place which might boast a garage.

He found both a garage and a helpful mechanic who ran him back in his own car to the stranded vehicle. Mr Calder sat in the sun, smoked a cigarette, and waited for the verdict.

"It's the petrol pump."

"How long will it take to put right?"

"Depends. If I can fix it up, maybe two, three hours. If I can't, and you have to have a new pump, maybe two, three days."

Mr Calder said "Humph", and started rearranging his plans in the light of alternative contingencies.

"I'll give you a tow back to the garage. Know more about it when we've got the pump off."

Half an hour later Mr Calder, attended by his Persian wolfhound Rasselas, was strolling down the main street of the village. The prognosis had been favourable. It seemed he might be able to resume his journey that afternoon. Meanwhile he had a telephone call to make, putting off a lunch appointment with a certain Brigadier Totton; and he had at least three hours to kill.

The delay was annoying, but not serious. For the last few days he had been touring round the home counties, talking to retired Army officers and Colonial policemen. He was engaged in tracing the early careers of the Croft brothers, Martin and Selby, a pair of middle-aged thugs who had been deported, by sea, from Egypt and were on their way to England. What the Home Office wanted was evidence sufficient either to send them on somewhere else, or to put them straight into detention. All that he had discovered so far was that they were a tough and resourceful couple.

A woman from whom he sought directions said, after admiring Rasselas, "There's the Crown Inn, at the end of the High Street. A lot of motorists stop there. Or if you don't mind a bit of a walk, you could take the first lane to the right outside the village, that'll bring you down to the river. There's an old inn there. The Pike and Eels. Boating people and fishermen go there a lot in the summer, but it's quiet at this time of year."

Mr Calder, who preferred anglers to motorists at any season of the year, thanked the lady and set off down the lane.

It went on for a long way, but at last it emerged on the towpath. The Thames is a quiet river in its upper reaches. Here it was still fairly broad, and was split by an island, which rode like a ship at anchor. Most of the island seemed to be occupied by a sprawling and pretentious house, with a big glassed-in balcony looking downstream.

Some millionaire's folly, thought Mr Calder. Ugly, and out of place in these surroundings. Much more to his taste was the Pike and Eels, a two-storeyed clap-board building with a long garden which straggled along the river bank. At the far end of the garden a youth was planting something in a leisurely way. Potatoes? Surely too early for potatoes? Might be broad beans. Apart from him the place seemed to be dozing in the sun.

He approached a door which was labelled "Public Bar". The notice painted above it in faded letters announced that Samuel Garner was licensed to sell Beer, Wines and Spirits for Consumption on or off the Premises. The tell-tale fixed over the door fetched out a stout man in shirt-sleeves and braces from the back premises. Mr Garner himself, no doubt.

"What can we do for you, sir?"

"A pint of your best bitter," said Mr Calder, "and a bowl of water for Rasselas."

"Is that your dog?"

"That's Rasselas." The dog had looked up as Mr Calder spoke his name. "If he isn't allowed in here, I'll turn him out."

"That's all right, sir. I never mind dogs in here, so long as the other customers don't object. And seeing we haven't got any other customers in the bar right now, they can't very well object, can they?"

"Do you get many people here?"

"In the summer, when the boating parties are all up and down the river, we get quite crowded. In winter it's quiet."

Mr Calder had been aware, for some time, of two things. The first was that they were not, whatever Mr Garner might say, the only customers. The second was that Mr Garner was uneasy.

In the far corner of the bar, down a couple of steps, was a door labelled "Private Bar". It was a thick door, built to maintain privacy. But he had been picking up a low rumble of dialogue from behind it. One voice, the deeper of the two, seemed to be laying down the law. The second seemed to be protesting, though without much conviction, against having the law laid down. None of this would have interested Mr Calder unduly. If people wished to carry on arguments in private bars that was their affair. What intrigued him was the noticeable and growing agitation of the landlord.

He said, "They seem to be having a bit of a debate in there. What is it? Two anglers arguing about who caught the biggest fish last season?"

"A friendly argument of that sort I expect, sir."

"Not so friendly," said Mr Calder.

There had been a sudden flurry of movement. A crash of a table going over. A rush of footsteps. It sounded as if one of the debaters had made a dash for the door and had been headed off at the last moment.

Mr Calder was now listening unashamedly.

He heard the second voice saying, "You've got no right—" and then, in a tone of panic which came clearly through the closed door, "Don't do it, please," followed by the sound of a blow.

Mr Calder said, "It sounds to me as if the argument is getting out of hand. Do you think, perhaps, you ought to break it up?"

The landlord leaned forward, with both his arms on the bar, and said, "If I was you, sir, I should just finish up that drink, and push off."

Up to that point Mr Calder had had no intention of interfering. He had enough troubles of his own in the ordinary line of business not to wish to intervene in other people's quarrels. But the threat in the landlord's voice had annoyed him.

He said, "I think I'll have a look. Perhaps I shall have a calming influence on them. I'll tell them the story of the angler who caught Brighton Pier."

"I'm telling you, you can't go in there."

"Oh! Why not?"

"Major Porter won't like it. It's a private room, see. And he's reserved it."

"It's labelled 'Private Bar'. If your pub's open, all the bars in it are open to the public. That's the law."

"Law or no law—" began the landlord. But he got no further, because Mr Calder had already moved across and opened the door.

There were three men in the private bar.

A red-faced, white moustached military character, dressed in a tight-fitting grey suit, was standing in front of the fireplace, with his thumbs hooked in the arm-holes of a checked waistcoat. A young man wearing corduroy trousers and a pullover was sitting in a chair. He was sitting with his chin up and his head tilted back, the reason for this uncomfortable position being that the third man, standing behind the chair, had his hand enlaced in the youngster's hair, and was pulling his head back over the top rail.

"I don't know who the hell you are," said the red-faced man, "but get the bloody hell out of it, and shut the bloody door."

Mr Calder said, "Good morning."

"Didn't you hear me? I said get the bloody hell out of it. And I'm not going to say it again."

Mr Calder said, "I ought to warn you, Major. It is Major Porter, isn't it? The louder you shout, the more angry my dog gets. If he gets really angry, he'll probably eat a bit out of you."

"Naylor. Boot him out. And his dog with him."

Mr Calder transferred his attention to the man behind the chair. During these exchanges he had not moved.

Now he released the boy's hair, and came forward cautiously, manoeuvring to avoid the legs of a table which had been knocked over.

"Naylor?" said Mr Calder thoughtfully. "You were in D Division. Got booted out for taking bribes from street bookies. You're getting a bit old for this strong-arm stuff, aren't you?"

"Mr Calder, ennit?"

Having made this discovery, he seemed even less anxious to

come forward. He said, "I know this man, sir. He's a—well—he's sort of official, you see."

"I don't care if he's your Aunt Tabitha," said the major. "He's got no right in here. Remove him."

"The major's right," said Naylor, sidling up cautiously. "It's a private room. You'd better be off."

"How are you going to make me?" said Mr Calder genially. "You're much too fat to fight."

"If you're afraid to tackle him alone," said the major, "I'll give you a hand."

"That you won't," said Mr Calder. And to Rasselas, "Guard."

The great dog had moved like a shadow on springs, and was standing in front of the major, his lips lifted over long white teeth. Naylor made a tentative lunge at Mr Calder, who dodged, caught the arm as it came past and pulled. The combined effect of the lunge and the pull swung Naylor half round. Mr Calder chopped him, with economical force, at the point where his spine joined his skull. Naylor keeled over, hitting his head on the protruding table leg as he did so. The major's hand slid inside his open coat and came out with a gun in it. It was a quick, smooth move, but Rasselas moved even more quickly. His teeth sank into the major's hand. The gun dropped to the floor and Mr Calder put his foot on it.

The major had given a brief cry as the teeth went in. Now he stood very still.

Mr Calder picked up a linen runner from the sideboard, said "Loose" to Rasselas, who let go of the major's hand. Mr Calder wrapped the runner round it to stop the spurt of blood. Then pulled the silk scarf off Naylor's neck as he lay on the floor, and tied it firmly round the runner.

Whilst he was doing all this, Mr Calder was cursing himself, silently but steadily. He had committed an unpardonable offence. He had interfered in something which was not his business. Moreover he had made a mess. The nursery rule held good. If you make a mess, you clear it up.

He said, "That should hold until you get to hospital."

The major still said nothing. It was partly shock, Mr Calder thought, but there was a lot of hatred in it too.

He said to the landlord, who had at last ventured into the room, "Major Porter has had a severe shock. Take him into the bar and fix him up with a brandy. And when you've done that come back here."

Mr Garner looked at the man on the floor, looked at the man in the chair, looked at the major, who still said nothing, and finally looked at Mr Calder.

"Get on with it," said Mr Calder impatiently. "There's a lot to do."

He had picked up the gun from the floor, and was holding it, loosely wrapped in his handkerchief. The sight of the gun seemed to make up Mr Garner's mind for him. He said, "Come on, then, Major," and led him out into the public bar.

Mr Calder turned his attention to the young man, who seemed glued to the chair. He said, "I think you'd better clear off now. Have you got some transport?"

"Y-yes. My moped. It's in the y-yard."

"Then that's all right, isn't it."

"Don't you want to know about—I mean—about me, and what they were doing?"

"If it's important, I'll find out later. You'd better go out the back way. That door probably leads into the yard."

"Y-yes. That would be best."

The young man stopped at the door. He seemed to have something on his mind. Then he said "Thank you", and went out closing the door behind him.

Mr Garner came back. He said, "That's a nasty wound."

"He shouldn't wave a gun around." Mr Calder put it carefully in his own pocket. "My dog's funny that way. He doesn't like guns. They make him nervous."

Rasselas rumbled happily.

"It'll have to be seen to."

"Of course. A deep bite like that can be very dangerous. Has the major got a car?"

"He keeps his car here."

"Keeps it?"

"He couldn't keep it on the island, could he?"

That made sense. The major was exactly the sort of man to live in the sort of house he had seen on the island.

"Could you drive it?"

"I expect so."

"Then run him to the nearest hospital. The sooner they get an anti-tetanus injection into him the better. They'll probably want to keep him overnight. Have you got someone who could keep an eye on the place?"

"Ernie can do it."

He went to the door and shouted down the garden. Then he came back and said, "What about him?"

Naylor had turned over and groaned.

"He'll be all right," said Mr Calder. "Just banged his head as he went down. Might be concussion. Nothing worse."

Mr Garner said, "Look here. I don't know nothing about you. You come here. Stir up trouble. And now you're giving orders. This is *my* place."

"It's your place," said Mr Calder softly, "and it's your licence. And if anyone found out that you'd allowed Major Porter and his hired thug to use your private bar to bully that young man, and if they knew that the major was carrying a gun, and had drawn it, and threatened a member of the public with it, then I think you might say good-bye to that licence."

Mr Garner stood for a moment, in silence. Then he said, "All right. We'll do it your way."

As soon as Mr Garner and the major had departed, Mr Calder hoisted Naylor into a chair, fetched the brandy bottle from behind the bar and poured out a half tumbler full. By the time Naylor had finished it he seemed to be himself again. The only mark on him was a large, purpling bruise on the side of his forehead.

Mr Calder said, "Now, talk."

"I haven't got nothing to say."

"And I haven't got any time to waste," said Mr Calder. "If you don't talk, I'll get my dog to chew off your fingers. He's had a taste of blood already this morning. He won't need much telling."

"You leave me alone."

"Guard," said Mr Calder.

Rasselas jumped to his feet.

"All right, all right," said Naylor, hastily. "What do you want to know? Good dog. Sit down."

Rasselas advanced stiff legged.

"It's all right," said Mr Calder. "He won't actually start on you until I tell him to. The only thing is, once he does get going, I'm not sure that even I can stop him."

"Then don't let 'im get going. What do you want to know?"

"Just exactly what was going on here this morning."

When the landlord came back he found Mr Calder playing darts with Ernie. Mr Calder said, "Your other guest has gone. He won't come back. I've had two pints of beer, and Ernie found me some bread and cheese in the kitchen. Oh, and he's already won two pints off me at darts. If you'll tot it all up, I'll pay you and be off. And Ernie, if you wouldn't mind, I want a word in private with your boss."

Ernie grinned and departed to resume his gardening. He was a simple soul, but threw a good dart.

"What did you tell them at the hospital?"

"I told them what you said. That a man had come in with a dog, and the dog had thought the major was threatening him, and had bitten him."

"Did you mention my name?"

"I didn't mention it, because I didn't rightly know it. I heard that other man call you Corder, or something like that."

"Right," said Mr Calder. "Now listen to me. This episode is finished. It's over and done with. Practically, you might say it never happened. If the major wants to take it any further that's up to him. My guess is he won't."

Here Mr Calder underestimated Major Porter, but he was not to know this. Back in the village he found that his car was once again in working order. "Temporarily," said the mechanic. "You'll need a new pump soon, but it'll do for the moment." Mr Calder thanked him, paid him and drove into Sonning. There was one more loose end to tidy up.

He found the young man, whose name was James Bird, half asleep in a chair in front of the fire in his lodgings. He said, "I got your address from that ape, Naylor. I want a few details from you. I gather that Major Porter is quite a lad. Owns a chain of betting shops, and at least three gaming clubs."

"Four, actually. The largest, and the most profitable, is the one on that island."

"And you know all about that because you're his accountant."

"One of his accountants. He uses several."

"And you ran into a bit of trouble."

"I was a fool. When the major invited me to come over and have a go I was rather flattered. Normally the only people who get invited to the island are his special friends, and people with a lot of money. I thought I understood the odds. I'd worked out a system."

"Oh, dear."

"All right. You can't kick me any harder than I've been kicking myself. I did make a bit of money—to start with."

"Then you started losing. How much?"

"In the end, just over eight hundred pounds. Of course, I hadn't got it. I gave them an IOU."

"And this morning's effort was Major Porter doing a bit of debt-collecting?"

"It wasn't just the money. He knew that was safe enough. He's only got to mention the matter to my firm, and I'd have got the sack on the spot. Anyway I'd made him an offer. Two hundred pounds, every three months, with interest at fifteen per cent. I could have managed that. Just."

"And he wouldn't accept it."

"It wasn't the money he was after. He said he'd tear up the IOU and forget about the debt if I did what he wanted. I look after the accounts for some of his betting shops. I do the annual audit. Well—you can guess."

"He wanted you to fiddle the books for him," said Mr Calder brutally. "And you said you wouldn't, and he set Naylor on to you."

"He told me what Naylor was going to do. He said Naylor would knock out two or three of my teeth and fracture my jaw. I guess he'd have enjoyed watching it. He's that sort of man."

"And if I hadn't turned up, would you have said yes or no?"

Young Mr Bird's face was crimson. In the end he said, "I think I might have said yes."

"Nasty either way," said Mr Calder. "Just as well, perhaps, you didn't have to find out, wasn't it?"

Mr Fortescue pursed his lips and said, "I am astounded that Calder should have behaved in such a stupid way."

"Yes," said Mr Behrens.

When Mr Fortescue was astounded in that tone of voice there was little point in arguing with him.

"A recruit to the service would have known better than to embroil himself with something which was not his concern."

The events at the Pike and Eels had been reported to him, as a matter of course, by Mr Calder, though in a much abbreviated version; but Mr Fortescue had had no difficulty in reading between the lines.

"Up to that point he had been doing some useful work. He had accumulated quite a comprehensive dossier on Martin and Selby Croft. They appear to be a pair of unscrupulous mercenary adventurers with a taste for violence and a flair for keeping out of trouble. Brigadier Rooke, who had had them as recruits in their para-corps days, writes"—Mr Fortescue picked up one of the papers in front of him—"'they had the making of first-class fighting men, but more trouble than they were worth. The best I can say about them is that they were attached to each other. On one occasion I know of, Martin saved Selby's life at some risk of his own.' Hmph. Major Sholto, who knew them in Rhodesia, says, 'You'd need wheels on your shoes to catch up with that pair.' What a curious expression. I wonder what he meant?"

Mr Behrens, who knew that Mr Fortescue understood exactly what Major Sholto meant, replied patiently. "He means that you'd have to move very fast to get ahead of them."

"We're ahead of them at this moment. They are docking at Tilbury tomorrow. The Egyptian authorities deported them by the slowest available ship. Which was thoughtful of them."

"Do we know why they were deported?"

"It appears that they shot a taxi-driver."

"Fatally?"

"Fortunately for them, a flesh wound only. It involved them in the payment of compensation. They are not short of money."

"They sound quite a pair."

"They were on the losing side in Tanzania, but removed themselves to America in time to avoid any unpleasant consequences. They lasted there for eighteen months, and then were deported on suspicion of being associated with various criminal activities. After that they spent some time in the Caribbean, allegedly running a cocoa plantation. There was some trouble about a labour dispute, and the use of unnecessary violence, and they moved on to Tunisia, where they were associated with the oil industry, although in what capacity I am not clear. Finally they gravitated to Egypt."

"It's all a bit vague, isn't it," said Mr Behrens. "Suspicion of association with criminals. Some trouble or other."

"As I told you, they are experts at avoiding specific charges."

"What are our instructions?"

"To keep an eye on them. To persuade them to behave whilst they are here. And to deport them as soon as they give us the least excuse to do so."

"If they are British, how can we deport them?"

"At some time in their career they acquired Panamanian citizenship."

"It sounds thin to me, but I suppose we could try. What is the immediate plan?"

"I want you to go to Tilbury and talk to them."

"I see," said Mr Behrens.

"Normally it is the sort of assignment I should have entrusted to Calder, but in his present state of mind there's no saying what he might do. If they made some remark which annoyed him, he'd probably set that dog of his on to them."

"It sounds more like a job for the police."

"They have committed no offence in this country, as yet."

"Let's hope that their first one won't be an aggravated assault—on me."

"I'm sure you'll be able to make suitable arrangements."

"It's a funny thing, Mr Berrings," said Martin Croft, "how people get ideas about us. They seem to think we're always roaring drunk and dripping with blood, or something like that. What they don't realize is we're just a pair of sober citizens. Isn't that right, Selby?"

"That's right."

The three of them were sitting in a small back room in a dockside pub at Tilbury which Mr Behrens had hired for the occasion. He said, "You weren't entirely sober that night in Cairo."

"Ah, but we were provoked. Our moral sense was outraged."

"That's right."

"I mean, it's one thing for a taxi-driver to offer to sell you his sister. That's fair enough. But when he offers to sell you his mother! Anyone might let fly if they had a proposition like that made to them. You might yourself, Mr Berrings."

"The situation is unlikely to arise. In any event, it's your intentions for the future, not your past that I'm here to talk about."

Martin Croft looked at him thoughtfully. Fortyish, Mr Behrens thought. Chunky. His wits about him. His younger brother was a malevolent lump. Both self-confident, with the confidence which came from coping successfully with various violent situations.

"You know," said Martin, "when you invited us in here for a little talk I thought, hullo, he's a copper. Then I thought, no. Can't be. Too old. So perhaps he's a reporter. Wants to buy our life stories. But I shall have to disappoint him."

"Oh, why? You must have had very interesting lives."

"The fact is, we've been paid too much, one way and another, *not* to publish them. It's one of the things I've found out in life Mr—"

"Behrens."

"Mr Berrings. Sometimes you get paid more for not doing things than for doing them. For instance, when Selby and me was in America there was this Senator—Hochstatter his name was—we was paid five thousand dollars each for not killing him. Which was funny, since we'd no idea of doing anything of the sort."

"Was that why you were deported?"

Martin looked disconcerted for a moment. He said, "Oh, you knew about that did you?"

Selby said, abruptly, "Just who are you, mister?"

"You got something there, Selby. He isn't a copper, he isn't a reporter. So who is he?"

Mr Behrens said, "I've been sent down by certain people who have an interest in seeing you behave yourselves."

"No one's got the right to put a finger on us. We're clean. Who are these people behind you? What do they want?"

"My instructions come from the Home Office, who are officially concerned with you because you've been the subject of at least one deportation order."

Selby lumbered to his feet. He said, "I've had enough of this bloody monkey-talk."

Martin Croft said, "Lay off, Selby. I want to get to the bottom of this. Why should anyone suppose we're *not* going to behave? Perhaps you can tell me that?"

Mr Behrens took a deep breath. He said, "Your record speaks for itself. You've spent the last twenty years of your life peddling violence—in places where violence was appreciated. The message I'm trying to get through to you is this. There's no market for it here."

Martin Croft said, slowly, "I think you've got a nerve, coming down here, lecturing us, like we was a couple of naughty kids. What'd you do if I threw you through that window?"

"Is that a threat?"

"Take it any way you like. We've done more than that to people who've annoyed us. Remember that American reporter in Cuba, Selby? We took him by an ankle each and swung him against a tree. They were hours and hours picking his teeth out of the trunk."

Mr Behrens said, in his gentlest voice, "I quite understand. And now you are threatening me with the same sort of violence."

"I wonder," said Martin equally softly, "what happens if we say yes?" He seemed to be listening. "Got men outside? Come rushing in? Search me and Selby? They won't find a thing."

"It's true you're not carrying guns at this moment," said Mr Behrens. "But you both own them. Yours, Martin, is a P.38, number RN9688. Selby's is a Mauser. I can't tell you the number, because it's been filed off. The steward who carried them ashore for you has been arrested and charged. Whether he implicates you depends on how much he loves you—or how much you've paid him."

Silence descended again. The brothers seemed to sense, for the first time, something menacing in the spare, grizzled, scholarly man in front of them.

At last Martin said, "Let him say what he likes, you've still got nothing you can pin on us." Selby growled his agreement.

"A little matter of threatening me with violence, wasn't there?"

"Two to one. Who's going to believe you?"

"If it comes to the point," said Mr Behrens, "I expect they'll believe the tape recorder."

"Are you telling me you've got this place bugged?"

"Naturally. Why do you think I brought you in here?"

Martin got slowly to his feet. He looked at his brother. He said, "We've got work to do, Selby. We're going to take this bloody room to pieces and find that bloody recorder, and break it on this character's head."

"Waste of time," said Mr Behrens. "Everything's gone straight through on the wire to London. It's probably been typed out in triplicate by now."

"You did that very nicely," said Mr Fortescue. "I did wonder, for a moment, whether they would take a chance on it, and assault you. In a way that would have suited us very well."

"I was fairly sure they wouldn't," said Mr Behrens. "They're not young tearabouts. They're middle-aged professionals. Even if they'd thought I was bluffing, they wouldn't have taken a chance on it. Incidentally, that steward wouldn't give them away. It wasn't just money. He was afraid of them."

"Thoroughly undesirable customers," said Mr Fortescue. He sounded as though he was refusing them an overdraft at his bank.

"What do you plan to do next?"

"Calder has an idea about that."

"I did think," said Mr Calder, "that it'd be a good idea if we put them somewhere where they'd have plenty of opportunities to get involved in trouble. Suppose we let them have a tip-off that Major Porter was looking for new talent. He sacked a rather ineffective muscle man called Naylor last week, so he's got at least one vacancy on his staff."

Mr Fortescue thought about it. He said, "If it can be done discreetly, it might work well. We would, at least, know where they were. But I don't want any unnecessary violence."

Mr Calder promised, meekly, that there would be no unnecessary violence. He knew that the episode of the Pike and Eels was neither forgotten nor forgiven.

Managing matters with discretion took time. Time to get the information, at fourth hand, to the Crofts. Time for them to vet the major and the major to vet them. It was on a fine morning in early May that they turned up at the Island Club to be given their instructions by Leo Harris, the major's chief of staff.

"In the ordinary way," he said, "it isn't a hard job. Most of the work's at night, when the tables are going. Perhaps someone loses money and gets a little bit upset about it. Or perhaps they've had too much to drink. Then you have to cool them off."

"Bounce them," said Martin. "That shouldn't be too difficult. What's amusing you, Selby?"

"He said, cool them off. All we've got to do is drop 'em in the river, right?"

"Certainly not," said Mr Harris. "For the most part they are thoroughly respectable people. You put them in the motor launch, land them on the bank, and persuade them not to return."

"And that's all there is to it?"

"Not quite. There are the betting shops that have to be looked after. It's a cash trade, so no bad debts to be collected. But it does happen, sometimes, that one of the managers gets ideas. Puts the money in his pocket, not in the books. When the auditors spot anything like that, you and Selby pay the manager a visit—"

"And hold him upside down until the money runs out of his pockets."

"You've got the idea exactly."

It was nearly a fortnight before they saw the major, who'd been away on business. When he summoned them to his office, they noticed that his right hand was in a glove. He said to the Crofts, "Sit down. Harris has been giving me a good report on you. You seem to handle the work very competently."

"Well, you see, Major, it's the sort of job we've done in rougher places than this."

"I'm sure the routine work gives you no trouble at all. What I've got for you now is a special job."

Martin looked at him speculatively. He said, "Special job, special pay?"

"Naturally."

"If there's someone you want done, it'll come expensive. Selby and me are aiming to keep our noses clean just now."

"Not someone. Something. There's a dog I want to have destroyed. A dangerous and savage dog. It attacked me the other day."

"Is that why you're wearing that glove?"

"Yes." The major removed the glove and Martin looked curiously at the hand. The print of Rasselas' teeth showed clearly on the back. "He severed two tendons. I've got the use of the hand back now. But it was painful."

"I'll say. It sounds the wrong sort of animal to mix with."

"I wasn't suggesting you mix with it. I've been making some enquiries. The animal belongs to a Mr Calder. He lives in a cottage, two miles from the village of Lamperdown in Kent. I suggest—"

"That's all right Major," said Martin. "Leave all the details to

Selby. He's the marksman. Less you know about it the better."

At six o'clock in the morning, three days later, Mr Behrens' telephone rang in his bedroom at the Old Rectory, Lamperdown. Mr Behrens sat up in bed, couldn't find his glasses, swore, found his glasses, picked up the receiver and said, "Hullo."

"It's me," said Mr Calder.

"I guessed as much. What do you want now?"

"A little help," said Mr Calder. "There's a man holed up in an oak tree on the edge of the wood opposite my front door."

"How do you know?"

"Rasselas spotted him. He refused to let me open the front door, and he's been 'pointing' him for the last five minutes."

"But you haven't actually seen him?"

"No. When I used my binoculars, I did think I spotted a slight movement. What I guess he's done is knock a hole in the hollow part of the trunk, and fixed his rifle up inside. That'd give him a rest for the gun, and good cover."

"He sounds like an old hand," said Mr Behrens appreciatively.

"That's why you'll need to take him very carefully."

"*I'll* need."

"Well, I can't come out. They may have the back covered too."

"I haven't had breakfast yet."

"It won't take long," said Mr Calder. "You know the back path through the wood. All you've got to do is follow it, and you'll come out right behind this joker."

Selby had reconnoitred the place the evening before and had fixed up his hide before it was light. He was wearing a camouflage jacket. He was a careful and experienced sniper. The range he had estimated as two hundred yards. The telescopic sight was focussed on the front door of the cottage, about eighteen inches above the ground. He was happy to wait. Sooner or later the door would open.

He tensed. The door had swung half open—showing a black gap. Who would fill it first? Man or dog?

The voice behind him said, "Don't turn round too quickly."

Selby froze.

"Leave that rifle exactly where it is, and come out. What I've got here is a twenty-bore shot gun. It's got such a comfortable spread that I couldn't possibly miss you. Come out, and stand up."

"I know you," said Selby stupidly.

"We met at Tilbury, and had a short talk. I remember warning you against peddling your brand of violence in this country."

"Violence," said Selby. "Who's talking about violence? I came here to shoot a fox."

"In some parts of the country, that's regarded as worse than murder. Have you got a licence for that rifle?"

"What's it got to do with you?"

Keep him talking.

"Look," he said, "let's be reasonable about this, shall we?"

Get one step closer, then duck under the barrel and collar him round the legs. Would the old coot have the nerve to pull the trigger?

"I didn't mean any harm to you. Right? It's just a job I'm doing for a friend. As a matter of fact, it isn't a fox. It's a dog. A nasty dangerous animal."

"I shouldn't say anything to upset him," said Mr Behrens.

Selby heard a slight sound and swung round.

Rasselas was standing just behind him. His nose was a few inches from Selby's leg, and he was grinning.

"Listen," said Martin Croft. "You've *got* to get him out."

He was trying to speak reasonably, but there was an under-current in his voice which Major Porter found disturbing. He had employed rough people before, but never anyone of quite this calibre.

He said, "They can't pin anything on him except the licence business. It'll only be a fine. I'll see it's paid."

"You don't understand, do you? You're not trying to understand. The way we've always worked is not to get mixed up with the law. Once they convict you of *anything* you've got a record. They've got your prints. You're pegged."

"Selby ought to have thought of that before he let himself be caught."

"Let himself?" Martin's voice went up. "Let himself nothing. He was doing your dirty work. A private grudge job."

"I chose him because I thought he could do a simple job. Not make a mess of it."

"When you talk like that," said Martin slowly, "I don't like you."

The major was not a fool. He knew when he had gone too far.

He said, "There's no point in quarrelling. That won't get us anywhere. Tell me what you want me to do, and if it's reasonable, I'll do it."

"What you've got to do is buy Selby out."

"Buy him?"

"That's right. Slip what's necessary to the top policeman or judge, and kill the case."

"You can't do it. Not in this country."

"Let me tell you," said Martin, "I've bought my way out of trouble in every bloody country I've ever operated in. The only difference is, some cost more and some cost less. Don't tell me they're so snotty-nosed in this country they don't know folding money when they see it."

The major considered the matter. Then he said, "First things first. Your brother's been committed for trial by the magistrates. They refused him bail. But they don't have the last word. There's an appeal to a judge in chambers. We'll do that next Monday. Get the best lawyers—a QC if necessary. It'll take a bit of organizing. We'll have to put up two sureties. You can be one. I'll be the other."

"Now you're talking," said Martin.

"Fortescue doubts if we can hold him," said Mr Behrens.

Mr Calder said, "As soon as he gets bail, he and his brother will skip. They've probably got half a dozen different passports, and as many ways out."

"Which is exactly what we want."

"It's not what I want," said Mr Calder, coldly. "I want Major Porter."

"You're taking this very personally."

"You seem to forget that he arranged to have Rasselas murdered."

Later that day he had a word with Superintendent Hadow, with whom he was on friendly terms, having known him when he was attached to the Special Branch.

"Certainly I've heard stories about this club," said Hadow. "Crooked play, and people being roughed up when they wouldn't pay up. The trouble is, nobody's ever been prepared to stand up in court and say so."

"But you'd like to shut the place up?"

"Certainly. Give me an excuse to take away its gaming licence, or even its drink licence, and it'd be dead."

"A bad case of disorderly conduct? Fighting? Use of firearms? Would that do it?"

"If it was reported to us."

"Suppose you actually heard it. You've got two police launches which make regular patrols. Next Monday, suppose one of them put me quietly on shore at the end of the island? Let's say at half past eight. Then they both cruise downstream, turn round and come back timing their arrival for exactly nine o'clock."

"And you think," said the Superintendent, "that if they did that, they might, at nine o'clock, just by coincidence, hear enough evidence of disorderly conduct to justify them investigating?"

"I'm a great believer in coincidences," said Mr Calder.

At half past four on Monday afternoon Martin Croft came out of the High Court, into the Strand. He was accompanied by his solicitor and Mr Mortleman, QC. He said, "Well, what do we do next?"

"Better come back to my Chambers and talk about it," said Mr Mortleman.

The Chambers were in Queen Elizabeth Buildings and overlooked the Embankment.

"I've never known an application for bail more strenuously resisted," said Mr Mortleman. "The charge is trespass when armed with a rifle for which no licence had been obtained. In simpler terms, you might call it poaching. A first offence, too. We offer them two sound sureties, who are prepared to deposit the money in court if necessary. If it had been you alone, Mr Croft, if you'll excuse me saying so, they might have hesitated. You're no longer, I believe, a national of this country, and have no fixed residence here. But Major Porter is quite different. He's a substantial citizen, with a house, and a business."

"Then why did the beak say no?"

"He didn't say no. He agreed to adjourn the matter for a week so that the police could complete their enquiries. He didn't like doing it. And I'm quite certain that when we do come up next week he'll grant the application."

"That means Selby's got to stay inside."

"But only for a week."

"As long as that's all it is," said Martin.

When he came out of the building two men were waiting for him. They introduced themselves as detective sergeants and invited Martin, very politely, to accompany them back to Scotland Yard.

"What's it all about?" said Martin.

"Superintendent Knox would like to have a word with you."

"And who the hell is Superintendent Knox?"

"He's in charge of the police proceedings against your brother."

Martin thought about it. It occurred to him that possibly a deal was going to be offered.

Superintendent Knox came straight to the point. He said, "In court this afternoon your Counsel informed the Judge that the owner of the Island Club, Major Porter, was prepared to stand bail for your brother."

"That's right."

"We thought you ought to know that he's changed his mind."

"He's done *what*?" said Martin, his face going first red and then white.

"The message from the local station simply says that he's withdrawn his offer of bail. We thought you ought to know this, so that you can go down at once and sort it out."

"I'll sort it out," said Martin thickly. He looked at his watch. If he could find a taxi, he could just make the seven-fifty from Paddington.

On a fine summer evening business started early at the Island Club. When Martin got there just before nine o'clock dusk had fallen. The lights were shining from the glassed-in balcony which looked downstream, and there was already a sizeable crowd round the gaming tables.

Martin came storming into the club. Leo Harris took one look at his face, and said, "What's up, Martin? How did it go up in court?"

"Never mind about the bloody court," said Martin. "I want a word with the major."

"I'm not sure—"

"And I want it *now*."

Harris could see that it was not a moment for argument. He said curtly, "You'll find him in his office," and went back into the gaming room.

Mr Calder, who had been standing unobtrusively by the door,

saw his chance. The moment that Harris's back was turned, he slipped into the passageway and followed Martin. As he did so, he looked down at the watch on his wrist. It showed two minutes to nine. The timing could not have been more exact.

As he reached the door of the office he heard the first explosion of anger from Martin and the major's voice, also raised in answer.

He opened the door a few inches. The two men in the room were too engrossed to take any notice.

"If the police hadn't blown the gaff, I'd never have known, would I? Or not until next week. Then what was supposed to happen?"

"You're talking nonsense."

"Who am I supposed to believe? Them or you? You double-crossing bastard."

"Personally," said Mr Calder, "I should believe the police. They're much more reliable."

Both men swung round. Mr Calder had shut the door carefully behind him and was standing there, holding a gun in his gloved right hand.

The major said, "Who the hell are you? That's my gun. Put it down and get out."

He seemed more angry than frightened.

Mr Calder said, "We've met before. If I'd brought my dog along, I imagine you'd recognize him. He became quite—er—attached to you."

The major said, "Take the gun from him, Croft. He's not got the guts to use it."

"No?" said Mr Calder. His head was cocked, and he seemed to be listening. "I shouldn't bank on it." He raised the gun and took careful aim.

The first shot went through the glass of the window overlooking the river. The next shot hit Martin Croft in the upper part of his right arm. The third shot went into the ceiling.

The next moment the whole place seemed to be full of policemen.

"Ah," said Martin. "I've been waiting for you to put in an appearance."

He was propped up in bed, in a private room in the Reading General Infirmary, and looked reasonably comfortable.

"I've brought you some grapes," said Mr Calder. "And some news. The police are holding Major Porter, on a charge of shooting at you with intent to kill. It's a very serious charge. It's his gun, registered in his name. If there are any prints on it, they'll be his. And they found it in the drawer of his desk."

"Of course they did. I saw you put it there."

"I told them," said Mr Calder, without taking any notice of this interruption, "that I was a guest at the club. That I happened to be in the corridor, heard the sound of a violent quarrel, followed by shots and looked in. You were slumped in a chair with the blood dripping down your arm on to the floor. I saw the major hurriedly stowing the gun away in the drawer of his desk. His idea being, no doubt, to hide it before the police burst in."

"And that's your story?"

"That's my story," agreed Mr Calder. "I'd be interested to know what yours was."

"I haven't told my story yet," said Martin with a grin. "Too shocked to answer any questions. Anyway, as one professional to another, I thought I'd have a word with you first."

"And what made you think that I was a professional?"

"When a man takes care to hit you in the one spot that doesn't signify a lot, *and winks at you when he's doing it*, I say to myself, he's a pro. He's planning a set-up. So I wait to see what it is."

Mr Calder said, "I'm relieved that I didn't misjudge you. Here it is. If you tell the same story as I do, the major's got no chance. He'll get seven to ten years. And I'll get the charge against your brother withdrawn."

"I thought they were all bloody incorruptible."

"So they are. But it's sometimes possible to persuade the authorities that a certain course would be in the public interest."

"You were taking a quite unjustifiable risk," said Mr Fortescue coldly.

"No risk, really, sir. I understand people like Martin Croft perfectly. We've got a lot in common, actually. Offer him a bargain which looks sensible all round and he'll take it every time. Debit side, a bullet in the arm. Credit, his brother let off the hook. Credit for us, the major put away for a long stretch."

"What will Martin do when he comes out of hospital?"

"I understand that he and his brother have been offered a job by a gambling syndicate in Mexico. Martin has already accepted. He says he finds England too dangerous."

JUNO'S SWANS

Celia Dale

So: THE LAST of England. But I am not one of Mr Ford Madox Brown's hollow-eyed consumptives, nor do I have some pallid virgin clinging to my arm, the very picture of wan defeat. Leaning on the rail of this P and O steamship, I confess to a singular satisfaction as I watch the murky shores of my homeland recede. I have done with her, with everything that held me there. I have no ties. I shall occupy my time on shipboard very tolerably. No doubt there will be whist; I shall make my regular perambulations round the deck morning and afternoon; I shall, if requested, contribute a dramatic monologue to the ship's concert; I shall devote my civilities to mature ladies travelling under the protection of their husbands and to young ladies travelling under that of their mamas. A man of intelligence—and I flatter myself I am far from being a fool—will hardly put his head into the same noose twice.

So here I am, ensconced in the solitude of the Writing Room, feeling the ship begin its slow plunge and rise as we move into open water, hearing the footsteps and voices of the other passengers as they bustle up and down the passageways, exploring the mighty monster that will be their home and haven for so many weeks before we reach Bombay. In an hour or two the dinner bell will sound. Until then it amuses me to sit here undisturbed and to commit to the thick sheets of steamship notepaper, handsomely embossed with pennants and anchors, the singular events which led me to leave my native shores. England, farewell! To paraphrase Cardinal Wolsey, Farewell, a long farewell to all my weakness!

I first met Emmeline at the house of mutual friends in Portman Square. It was a musical evening and I had been prevailed upon, after the tenors and sopranos had been heard, to give my rendering of Mr Irving's famous soliloquy from "The Bells". I confess I do it well—I was a leading light in my University theatricals, and no doubt it was my histrionic bent which led me to read for the Bar, although happily I have never been required to earn my living from it. The Bar or the pulpit are the only alternatives to a gentleman with a talent for drama, and I had no taste for the pulpit.

When my recitation ended I was surrounded by a host of cooing ladies: So powerful, so tragic, so thrilling, quite blood-curdling! And when the tide of lace, ribbons and flounces had receded I found my hand encased by the small kid-gloved fingers of a girl, fair and pale as a fairy, small as an elf, who stared up at me with great violet eyes. "You will haunt my dreams," she said in a sighing sort of voice.

An elderly gent, fat and purple of jowl, thrust up behind her. "Capital, capital! Better than the Lyceum, I assure you!"

"You're too kind," I said, or something of the sort.

"Not a bit of it, sir. Capital, quite striking!"

The young lady had released my hand and stood now with downcast eyes, playing with her fan.

"I trust I shall not seriously disturb this young lady's dreams," I said. "I have no desire to be a bogeyman."

"What? Bogeyman? Nonsense, sir, nonsense! Too fanciful, Emmeline—my daughter, sir, and I am Colonel . . ." well, it doesn't matter who. Within six months he was dead, struck down by an apoplexy, which was not surprising considering his size and the amount of brandy he poured into himself. A decent old codger, though, who took me to his heart for dual reasons: firstly, he had no son and, like all military men, regretted it. Although I am far from being the kind of fellow such a man might be thought to have admired (for I abhor your bluff, hard-drinking Service type whose only talk is whores and horses) I was in fact, I surmise, what he would secretly have liked as a son. I am tall, elegant, handsome— no need for false modesty here. I do not bluster or guffaw, my control is perfect yet my histrionic talent shows that I am capable of feeling.

His second reason, without doubt, was the desire to see his daughter safely married and to someone in whom he had perfect confidence. She was something of an heiress; but that, he soon found out, was immaterial to me, since I have ample means of my own. She was also delicate; her mother had died a few years after her birth (which had no doubt accelerated an inevitable decline) and Emmeline had inherited a constitutional weakness which made her frail as a flower and sometimes as beautiful. Her father, good old man, was anxious that she should not wed some coarse-grained fellow who would wear her out with child-bearing but someone who would cherish and encourage her frail energies and bring her the tranquillity she needed.

Such a man was myself. I am not a sensual man. I won't deny that I have, from time to time in my youth, patronized the better houses of Mayfair or kept a dollymop for a month or two in some discreet Kennington villa; but the gross beauties of the Haymarket were not for me, I have ever been far too fastidious, too elevated in spirit to wallow, as my fellow students did, in the stews and taverns of the metropolis.

There was something about Emmeline to which this delicacy in my nature responded. She was small and frail as a fairy, with fair hair that curled and fronded over her white brow and those great violet eyes. Her skin was pale and gauzy, like the wings one almost thought to see at her shoulders as, when she was in health, she flitted here and there about the house and grounds of . . . let us call it Haylett Hall. She was like some fragile flower that too easily wilts and fades, but, like them, she could revive and bloom again after some days of rest, her light, breathless voice trilling once more through the panelled rooms and passages of the house.

She aroused in me a singular mixture of emotions: a masculine instinct to protect and dominate, a curiosity as to the essence of her charm, something of a collector's pleasure in a rare and delicate piece, the pleasure of possession. Her white and childlike beauty attracted me strongly.

I had asked the Colonel for her hand two months after our meeting. He had embraced me, the engagement was announced, the wedding date arranged, and then he died. Amidst our tears we decided to continue as had been planned, for it was what he would have wished and the wedding was in any event to be a quiet one in the village church close by the Hall.

Thus it was. A brief honeymoon at Broadstairs (we did not venture abroad, for Emmeline dreaded the sea) and we returned to Haylett Hall to start our new life together—as had been planned from the beginning, for we would have lived as son and daughter with the Colonel, had he been spared.

Haylett Hall is not large but it is commodious and it is beautiful.

Built in the reign of Charles the Second, it has undergone various additions and enrichments, mainly in the time of George the Fourth. It has been in Emmeline's family for some two hundred years and the gardens, parkland and the strange wild area known as the Workings have been enlarged and beautified over that period. It was a property to be proud of and I was proud of it—indeed, it is perhaps the only single thing that I regret leaving behind me.

We settled in. It seemed a perfect life. I did not regret relinquishing my barrister's chambers, since I had hardly practised. We had an ample circle of acquaintances within the neighbourhood, a well-trained staff of servants—and Sybil.

Sybil. I confess I have paused in my narrative a while after writing that name. Sybil. As dark as Emmeline was fair, almost as tall as I, slender and swift as a sword. Sybil.

Of course I had known about Sybil. I had met her whenever I visited Haylett Hall to pay my addresses to Emmeline, and had escorted the two of them on their calls about the county. The two girls had been friends from childhood, had grown up together under the Colonel's care when Sybil's parents were tragically murdered by tribesmen near Kabul—the two men were brother officers and friends. It was Sybil who ran the household, who cared for Emmeline when she was ill, who nursed the old man through his final days. Something between an elder sister and a companion, she was as much a part of the house, I soon came to understand, as the panelling itself or the dark portraits on the stairs; and like them she did not obtrude herself, but seemed to be always there should she be needed, discreetly absent so that Emmeline and I could be alone during our courtship, present again for a hand of whist, a tramp over the countryside, an evening's laughter and song round the piano in the large, log-lit drawing-room. As strong as Emmeline was weak, she was an ever-present part of life at Haylett Hall, watchful for our comfort, a smile ever hovering on her lips, her dark eyes ever alert.

When the old man had died, and Emmeline lay prostrate in her room, tear-stained and weak with grief, Sybil had come to me as I sat before the fire in the library, musing on the enigma of mortality. Her eyes were red but there was no weakness in her manner. Direct as always, she said, "Lewis," she said, "I hope you will not postpone the wedding."

I murmured that I had not so intended.

"I'm glad," she said, clasping her long hands nervously so that the chatelaine she wore at her belt swung and tinkled against her skirt. "It will be best for Emmeline. With the Colonel gone, she may so easily decline. She needs a man's authority to order her affairs, to hold her grasp on life. My care for her is not enough."

"I swear solemnly that mine shall be."

"Yes." She looked at me, direct and dark. "Yes, that is what I believe. It is for her sake, you see. It is what is best for her." She turned and left the room. We never spoke of it again.

So we were man and wife, Emmeline and I. My flower, my fairy was mine, we talked and ate, played music and cards together, walked a little if the weather were fine, not too far and not too fast, drove out in the carriage, well wrapped up with rugs, went to London for a few weeks in the season if she were up to it, leaving Sybil at home. We shared a life together, Emmeline and I; but it was not a married life.

I need not be too delicate. Who, after all, will read this tale but I? That fairy, that gossamer girl who had so entranced and intrigued my senses, was no more a woman than is a whiting upon the fishmonger's slab. I am not, as I have said, a sensual man. I can forgo the pleasures of the flesh without inconvenience if circumstances order it. But marriage postulates certain activities, certain rights, and these not only was my poor Emmeline quite ignorant of but cringed from when the facts were known.

For some months I persevered, but although I conquered her resistance I never overcame her horror of this natural act—no doubt her terror of childbirth played some part in this, one must be charitable. Whatever the causes, connubial life with Emmeline soon became at first a mockery, then a penance, finally nothing. I moved out of the matrimonial bedroom into a handsome room the other side of the house, drawing on all my resources of fortitude and self-sufficiency to build a tolerable life of my own, as indifferent as I could make myself to the twittering, childish ninny I had somehow married and who was rapidly (due, no doubt, to the lengthening periods spent bed-ridden or lying upon sofas in a perhaps unconscious retreat from her obligations) growing fat.

I will not dwell upon that period of my life. Schooled in self-discipline though I am, even now I can scarce control the bitter anger, the resentment of those days, denied the comforts to which

I had the right, including that of children. All men desire a son. I won't pretend I care much for children, with their squalls and squabbles (I trust there aren't too many aboard this ship) but I had the right to expect my name, my talents and my handsome figure to be perpetuated. Well, no matter . . .

I lived sufficient to myself, affable to my neighbours, courteous to my wife, cold behind a mask of polite indifference. But slowly, more and more—Sybil.

My eyes were drawn to her when she was present, my thoughts when she was absent. Slowly she possessed first my waking reveries, then my dreams—dreams such as I had never experienced before. In them she was half naked, her slender body maddeningly revealed through torn or opened garments, shameless, lewd . . . In my dreams she spoke words from the gutter, made gestures from the stews. She drew me on, shuddering, wild . . . and in the morning I would look at her, neat and bright in her sensible country clothes, pouring the coffee, passing the kedgeree, adjusting Emmeline's rug, putting the slippers on those useless feet, holding the cup while she drank, gently brushing back that frizzing hair—and my eyes would burn at her over that mockery and she would meet my gaze, direct, bright, then turn aside to tend yet further the soft pale slug our fairy had become.

Sometimes, if Emmeline were well enough to come downstairs, I would find Sybil's gaze fixed upon me over the couch where my wife lay. Sometimes our hands would touch, she withdrawing hers with a swift movement and averted eyes. She kept more and more to Emmeline's rooms, but when we encountered one another her eyes sought mine again, dark, burning, questing. Once, when the doctor had just taken his leave after Emmeline had suffered one of her collapses, we stood at the foot of the stairs together, she almost as tall as I, her pale red-mouthed face lamp-lit, her eyes brilliant. She laid a hand on my arm and said, her voice trembling, "She is suffering, Lewis."

I covered her hand with mine and dared to say, "We are all suffering here."

"Yes. Yes, that's true." She withdrew her hand, glancing nervously at the parlourmaid who passed down the hall after seeing the doctor out. So low I could hardly hear her, she said, "I can't bear to see her suffer."

She turned and went swiftly up the stairs, back to Emmeline's side, holding her long skirts in one delicate hand, the white neck bent under the dark knot of hair that in my dreams had been so wild, so tangled. Watching her go, I said in my heart, You shall not, dearest. We will suffer no more.

I don't propose to go in detail into what followed. The practicalities are tedious and unimportant. Suffice it to say that it is uncommonly easy to obtain arsenic in sufficient quantities to kill an army, if you declare it is an army of rats, that no name I ever gave any chemist astute enough to desire one was ever verified, and that if one's purchases are made sufficiently far afield there is singularly little chance that anyone will ever recognize one. Add to all this a trusting domestic staff, a show of concern and husbandly attention, patience and common sense, and you will readily understand how Emmeline's illness, slight at first following that collapse, increased to a distressing and ultimately fatal conclusion. She was only twenty-eight.

Sybil was prostrated. We all were. The maids crept about red-eyed and snivelling, the butler and my own man looked grave as undertakers, the neighbours called dripping crape and condolences. I kept to my room for twenty-four hours, for truth to tell the event had taken its toll of me. When I issued forth again I was astonished at my haggard appearance, pale and distinguished like the Commendatore in *Don Juan.* I went about the sad business attendant upon death, mourned with the doctor over madeira and biscuits in the darkened library, accepted his regrets that medical skill, alas . . . and was afire for Sybil. Her maid told me she was prostrated still. The doctor prescribed sleeping draughts. I paced the silent house and empty gardens, wild with impatience to see that lovely form appear, haggard and tear-stained though she needs must be, sad too at the passing of a childhood friend, but looking at me with that clear bright gaze, the dark hair burning from the high brow, the slender figure vibrant . . .

Behind my grave composure I was mad with longing. My dreams mingled with my yearning till I felt I must rush and beat upon her door, throw myself in upon her, on her . . . I held myself rigid, schooled and disciplined to the outside world, a flawless performance. I sat, I waited; I walked, and waited. At last she came.

It was at the Workings, that strange wilderness of wood and quarry, of tangled bushes and treacherous paths where they say ancient Britons delved for flint, thick with trees and undergrowth now down its steep sides, with the glimpse of stagnant water at the bottom where once men had hacked at the rock. There is a path along the top, heavy with blackberries and foxgloves in their season, and at its curve a wooden seat, for the prospect opens out just there and you can see across the quarry to the hills beyond the village, the far side of the valley. It was the afternoon before the funeral and I had fled the house and my intolerable waiting, had taken a walking-stick and slashed my way through the wood to the Workings path and the bench, and there Sybil was sitting. She was weeping, her head in its simple bonnet bent into her hands, the veil thrown back. She started to her feet as I appeared.

"Lewis!"

"My dearest!" It burst from me in a groan and I held out my arms to her. She came into them like a bird, quivering and sobbing. I felt her slender body against mine, strong and smooth and so wonderfully alive. I took the bonnet gently from her head and dropped it on the bench, smoothed the hair from her wet cheeks. "Sybil," I said, "Sybil . . ."

"Oh Lewis . . ." She lifted her head and looked at me, eyes drenched in tears. "Oh Lewis, what shall I do? How can I bear it?"

"Hush, my dearest, we will bear it together. It is my burden rather than yours."

"No, no, it is mine." She pushed herself free and took a few steps away. "You don't know—you can't know. What can my life be now?"

I stepped forward and took her hand. "Your life will be with me, Sybil. In a little while, when a decent interval has passed. With me, Sybil, with me . . ." I covered her hand with kisses.

"What?" She stared at me and stepped backwards, pulling her hand away. "What are you saying?"

"That I love you, Sybil. I have longed to say it for months, years, to shout it aloud, to breathe it in your ears. I have longed to say it with my lips, to hear you say it with yours rather than with your eyes, your burning, brilliant eyes . . ."

"You are mad!" she cried.

"With love, with longing! Sybil . . ." I seized her hand again, striving to draw her to me once more and kiss at last that red, red mouth.

With violent strength she thrust me from her. "You are mad!" she repeated. "Mad! What fantasy is this?"

"No fantasy but a dream dreamed by us both. I saw it in your voice, your eyes. While she lived we were mute, but now . . . My dearest, my only passionate love . . ."

With all her strength she struck me across the face. She was breathing fast, her eyes wildly blazing, her voice shrill. "You fool!" she cried. "You mad, evil fool! I never loved you, I could never love you! It was she I loved, she, she, my silver flower, my gentle, tender woman—only she, only she . . ." She began to weep again.

I stared at her. "You loved my wife?"

"Yes, yes, always! It was only she . . ."

"You loved her—as I love you?"

"More, much more. What can men know of love . . ."

I struck her. She was near the edge, and she fell. After a while the bushes were silent again, the stagnant water still. I threw her bonnet after her.

Well, that's how it was. I returned to the house. Eventually there was a hue and cry. Eventually she was found. By the time the search party had trampled the path there was a plethora of footprints. And fortunately the marks where she had struck my cheek were hidden by my beard.

It was not quite possible to hold a double funeral; and I saw to it that they lay in different parts of the churchyard. No one else should lie down with what I had thought to be my Sybil. I saw to it that, unlike Juno's swans, they should not any longer be coupled and inseparable.

Ah, there's the dinner bell. This narrative is nicely timed. It has done me good to write it—confession is good for the soul, they say, but I have been more concerned to lay the facts on paper as a study into the singularly odd delusions that can ensnare the human heart. I must, as Sybil said, have been mad.

I am not mad now. I am extremely in possession of myself and ever shall be. I shall make my way to the stern of this vessel, drop this narrative page by page into its creaming wake, then go below to the Saloon and have my dinner. The first night out to sea one does not dress.

THE LAZARUS LIST

Peter Godfrey

IN OFFICE ARGOT we always refer to headquarters as Heaven, but the brass plate at the front door of the building in Ave Maria Lane near St Paul's declares publicly that its real title is The Ecumenical Foundation. This is the main entrance—the one we call Salvation—leading to a suite of rooms towards the gloomy rear of the building.

To get anywhere at all, one has to pass through a general reception-cum-typing area to a smaller room to be scrutinized and checked by the Keeper of the Gate. Peter—real name Esme Munro—sits in an office with four doors. Most inconspicuous of these is a green one, marked as the way to the fire stairs. It isn't. It opens into another room in the rear of a back-to-back building. From here, twisting passages and a rickety stair lead finally to a street door on Old Bailey, fifty yards up the road from the famous courts.

I had better introduce myself: My name is Joe Ferris and I am an Angel.

I came to Heaven that day through the Old Bailey entrance—called Damnation by way of contrast—straight from Heathrow to Peter's office. "You'd better go in right away," she said, and then—almost as an afterthought—kissed me. If she'd omitted this little routine of affection I'd have been sure the urgent call waiting for me at the airport had been at least a Penultimate Trump.

Archangel Gabriel was, as usual, well behind his paper-cluttered desk. He was a small man, and only his head and the horizon of his narrow shoulders were visible. As always, I saw him from the top down—sparse, untidy grey hair crowning a lined but full-lipped ruddy face, a long scrawny neck haloed by a snow-white clerical collar.

High-level government legerdemain had transposed him from

Canon Williams to Gabriel. But the metamorphosis from the practising clergyman chairman of Christian Sanctuary, a charitably financed body for the succour of African political refugees, to the head of a secret counter-intelligence unit concentrating on the activities of BOSS (the South African Bureau of State Security), had in no way altered his appearance or personality. I often thought of his collar as the symbolic link between the two sides of his life.

Characteristically, he wasted no time. "Here, Joe," he said, and handed over that morning's copy of the London *Times*. "Two announcements on the back page I want you to look at. First, the one I've ringed."

It was about midway down the third column of small advertisements. It read:

JOHN AND JUNE: Eleven. Come Forth.

"Today," said Gabriel, "is the tenth of June. Tomorrow—June 11—is the first session of the Commonwealth Heads of State conference."

"And John?"

"The Gospel according to St John, chapter 11, tells the story of the resurrection of Lazarus. 'Come forth' are the words Jesus used to draw Lazarus from the tomb." Gabriel shivered. "Listen, Joe. The advertisement together with the cost of one insertion was handed in at *The Times* yesterday afternoon by a taxi driver. We've traced him. He was hired for the assignment by an official at South Africa House, who hailed him as he cruised in the Strand. This morning every known BOSS official, including their chief, your old schoolmate Colonel Thorsen, left London openly and obviously on holiday, and each one for a different destination outside Britain."

He shivered. "I fear tomorrow, Joe. I feel the breeze from the wings of Azrael on my neck."

I agreed. "It has the smell of trouble." Then: "You said there were two advertisements?"

"Yes. There's nothing specific about the other, except one or two of the names have a South African ring . . . But see for yourself. Same column, fourth from the top."

It reads:

EDITOR anxious to contact any or all of the following
writers: Edgar Minshull, Frank Barker, Philip Ambrose,
Brett Mason, Oswald van Erkom, Gert Jansen. Box
7867.

This time, it was along my neck that the hair crawled. "I can't
think of anyone alive who would bracket all those names
together."

"Why not?" asked Gabriel.

"In South Africa at one time I wrote fiction under several
pseudonyms. This is the entire list. It looks like someone wants to
make very sure of contacting me."

"And you don't know anybody who would associate those
names with you?"

"Nobody alive," I said.

Gabriel looked at me from under lowered lids. "We haven't
been idle. Some—uh—influence provided one or two further
points. The advertisement was placed for three insertions. The
advertiser lives at the Migrant Club in Earls Court. Her name is
Mary Latimer. Mean anything to you?"

I shook my head.

"Strangely enough, it rings a muted bell with me. Somehow, I
associate it with Sanctuary . . . I'll do what I can to find out, while
you go and see the woman."

The late afternoon London rush hour had already begun. To use a
car or a taxi would be devastatingly slow and nerve-racking. I
decided to risk the crush on the underground, but before leaving I
asked Peter to make two enquiries over the telephone. She had to
wait for a return ring on the first call, but it came in not more than
five minutes.

"Mary Latimer," she told me, "called at *The Times* about half
an hour ago, asking for replies to her advertisement. There weren't
any. She was on foot, but was seen to catch a bus going to King's
Cross. My guess is that she changed there to the Piccadilly Line,
and should certainly be home by the time you get there. Her room
at the Migrant Club is 334. Any more you want from me?"

"Nothing except your love," I said. This time I left through
Salvation, tossed a mental coin, and decided that the slightly
longer walk to Blackfriars had the edge over the necessary change

of line at Holborn should I enter the Underground system at St Paul's. Ten minutes later I made a sardine of myself and forced an entry into an overcrowded District Line carriage.

It took fifteen minutes to Earls Court, another five to clear the ticket barrier, about seven minutes brisk walking to the Migrant Club. Twenty-seven minutes in all, which was about eight minutes too late.

The foyer of the club is like the lobby of an hotel. I walked straight past the desk clerk, to a self-service elevator. The door of room 334 was open, but the light was out. Cautiously, I groped to the wall on the right, found the switch and pressed it.

The body of Mary Latimer lay on its face immediately inside the entrance. Her key was still in the door. What had happened was obvious from the angle her head made. As she had opened her door someone lurking in the corridor—someone strong and highly trained in unarmed combat—had chopped down ferociously from behind her, cleanly breaking her neck.

The killer's confidence in his own skill was frightening. Almost certainly he had not bothered to investigate or even gain time by closing the door. He had made that one fierce lethal spasm, then continued calmly down the corridor to the elevators and safety.

I shivered. Gently I moved the body so that I could see the face. Whatever tic of shock had momentarily distorted the features at the instant of death, the muscles had now relaxed. The face was soft, almost reposeful.

Once again I felt a primordial fear of the inexplicable, prickling the tips of my hair. I knew her well. Correction: I had known her well. Correction: I knew her well when she used to type all my freelance fiction manuscripts. I *had* known her well—for the first time—when I attended her funeral in Johannesburg twelve years ago.

I felt my mind stumble. Alive once, dead once, then alive again, now dead again. Damn it to Hell. Lazarus? Could Lazarus be a woman?

Half an hour later Gabriel shot this first tentative theory down in flames. "The text quoted in the advertisement," he said, "was quite specific: John 11. That Lazarus was a man. If it had been a woman, I would have expected the text to be Luke 9: 49. That describes how Christ raised a girl from the dead. Let's deal with the problem more specifically. What do you say her real name was?"

"Anna Stern," I said.

"Right. First let me tell you everything I've discovered about Mary Latimer. Then you tell me about Anna Stern. Maybe something positive will emerge."

Gabriel shuffled papers in front of him. "Mary Latimer", he said, "was born in Britain, and emigrated to South Africa in 1950, at the age of eight. Her parents were both teachers, and both were killed in an automobile accident near Cape Town in 1961. Mary at the time had just left home to share an apartment with two other girls in Sea Point. She was employed as a typist in a legal office in the city.

"About the same time, Christian Sanctuary's representative in South Africa told us the girl had become very friendly with a young student in whom BOSS had become too interested. Sanctuary said Mary had been advised to leave the country and, if it became necessary, she would be placed on Jacob's Ladder."

I nodded. Jacob's Ladder was the code name for the transfer of South African political dissidents to more hospitable points of reception beyond the borders of the Republic.

"In fact," said Gabriel, "Mary applied for and obtained a British passport early in 1962. Later that year, she left Cape Town for Johannesburg, ostensibly on holiday. Apparently, she got on the ladder, because her docket was closed in London in 1963, after she had arrived at Heathrow via Nairobi, and Sanctuary had successfully negotiated a job for her at the Tanzumibian High Commission, where she has apparently been working ever since."

I said: "But of course it wasn't Mary Latimer who arrived here. Any indication where the substitution took place?"

"Almost certainly in Johannesburg. Just at that time we lost a vital rung in the Ladder there. A girl was killed in an explosion. Her name was Anna. Your Anna?"

"My Anna," I said heavily. "Strange, she always seemed so apolitical. I'd never have guessed she was an active helper of Christian Sanctuary . . . things are a bit clearer now. Mary must have contacted Anna and been in her Greenside cottage when a bomb exploded there. No doubt Mary was killed and mutilated beyond normal recognition. There must have been some similarity in looks, because Anna was able to use Mary's passport. And

Anna must have recognized the explosion as a deliberate attempt on her life to make her take the drastic step of mounting the Ladder herself."

Gabriel asked: "Was the explosion an attempt on her life?"

"At that time, I didn't think so. I thought the target was really her husband, Max. He was a lecturer in physics at the Witwatersrand University, and rather well-known for his views. Not political opinions, really. It was just that he had an intellectual contempt for certain personalities in the government at the time, and made them quite clear on every conceivable occasion."

"Even so, a bomb explosion seems an exaggerated way of shutting him up."

"Oh, I don't think that was the motive at all. The bomb went off at a time when he was certain to be in college. My own opinion was that it was an attempt to frame him. The police seemed strangely disconcerted when Anna's body was found. Anyway, Max was immediately arrested—not for suspected homicide, as you might imagine. No, he was detained under the Emergency Regulations for 'hoarding explosives for use by terrorists'. That enabled the Specials to dispense with usual arrest procedures, and keep him incommunicado in a cell at their headquarters. He must have suffered more than the usual hell at their interrogations.

"I saw him two days later, at Anna's funeral. Max was a man who always prided himself on erectness of bearing. I saw him from behind, handcuffed to a burly man in plain clothes. He seemed so bowed and dispirited I would never have recognized him as Max until the pair in front moved forward a few paces.

"Let me explain. As a nine-year-old lad, Max lost his two smallest toes and part of the ball on his right foot in an accident. He limped badly for a long time, but learned how to compensate for the imbalance as he grew older. As an adult, from the front his walk appeared perfectly normal. But from behind, the compensatory tensions and relaxations of his muscles and tendons gave him a sort of inhibited roll, a slight leaning to one side that was unmistakably and characteristically Max.

"So at the funeral, as soon as I realized who he was, I stepped up next to him to try at least to give him some words of consolation. He looked at me. We had always been friendly, had often laughed together, but this time only pain and ice peered out of his eyes. Neither of us spoke."

Gabriel asked: "Did you ever hear of him again?"

"Yes. A week later. I went to his inquest. Nobody gave any evidence of bruises or electric burns or other injuries. Nothing like that, no. Merely a warder describing how he had found Max, the morning after his wife's funeral, hanging in a cell."

Peter brought coffee, black and strong. Gabriel said to her: "Pull up a chair. Join the conference."

She sat down, but obviously some previous verbal passage of arms still rankled. She said, sweetly: "Of course you realize I'm only a woman, and therefore have no capacity for logic. All I will be able to do is slow you down by asking questions."

Gabriel grunted. "That's our greatest need at the moment. Questions. Women's questions."

"If you can ask the right questions," I said, "chances are that we can produce the right answers. You've heard everything we've said up to now?"

Peter nodded. It was office routine that all Gabriel's interviews be taped and that, whenever possible, she should herself monitor the recording.

Gabriel said: "And does nothing we've discussed prompt a query?"

"Several things," said Peter. "But one point in particular. Who was murdered? I mean, who did her killer think she was? Anna Stern or Mary Latimer?"

Both of us straightened with renewed interest. "Now that," said Gabriel, "is a very good question. Joe?"

I thought about it. "Mary Latimer, as far as we know, has led a blameless life since she returned to Britain. She had no obvious links with the past. Obviously, Anna had nothing to fear in her guise of Mary Latimer. But she might have had much to fear as Anna Stern.

"Something suddenly prompted Anna to re-open her closed past, and seek the aid of an old South African contact—me. I think she recognized someone or something—no, definitely someone— whose very presence in Britain indicated danger. I'm also certain this person *recognized her*. I even know where it must have happened. At her work."

Gabriel said: "How can you know that?"

"Let's go back for a moment to my discovery of her body.

There's one thing I didn't mention. She was carrying an envelope which she'd picked up at the desk. It simply carried the name Mary Latimer and the words, 'care of Migrant Club'. Inside was advertising matter for coach tours. Several copies of the same pamphlet were scattered on tables in the entrance lounge."

Peter asked: "What's the significance of all this, Joe?"

"It's an old stratagem for finding out a person's room number at an hotel without making unnecessary enquiries. You address an envelope to the person and drop it on the reception clerk's desk. Then you watch him to see which pigeonhole he places the letter in. That's what the killer must have done. He knew what name Anna was using. No doubt he had found out somehow where she stayed. But he still had to find the number of her room.

"Anna picked up the letter when she called at the desk for her key. But the killer was before her, and made himself inconspicuous in the corridor. It was gloomy there.

"Long drapes cut out the light from the window, and the bulb had been removed from the nearest electrical fitting."

Peter said: "I still don't understand. You say the killer knew her as Anna Stern. How could he know she was calling herself Mary Latimer?"

"Simple. He saw her at work. She was a receptionist at the Tanzumibian High Commission. All the receptionists there have their names prominently displayed on their desks. So when the killer looked at her, he not only recognized Anna Stern, he also knew immediately what she was calling herself."

"Do you think," asked Gabriel, "that Anna knew she'd been recognized?"

I shook my head. "No. Obviously she thought the man she had seen was dangerous to her in some way. If she thought she wanted anything more than advice from someone she trusted, she'd have acted more urgently than merely placing a cryptic advertisement in *The Times*. She'd have probably gone straight to Christian Sanctuary and asked for direct aid. But one thought now haunts me. I think the killer probably did not know she had recognized him. I think he is Lazarus. I think that when he read the column, as he must have done every day, he saw the other advertisement."

Peter said: "Why should he have bothered to read that notice?"

"Only if it had some significance for him," I said, grimly. "And that implies that he knew Anna had placed it as a plea for help, and from this he deduced *he* had been recognized."

"Why does the idea haunt you?"

"Can't you see? Anna's cry to me for aid was a call for Lazarus to strike."

Gabriel was impatient. "No guilt can possibly apply to you, Joe. Time is short, time is very short. We must get back to the point." To Peter: "Any more questions?"

"Only one," said Peter. "Why was Lazarus hanging round the Tanzumibian High Commission?"

The effect was gratifying. Gabriel slumped back, the tension obviously drained from all muscles. His mouth relaxed into a broad beam of contentment.

I stood up impulsively to hug and kiss her. "That's it, love," I said. "That's what I call highly developed female intuition."

Peter tried valiantly to look unflappable but curiosity overrode prudence. "Explain," she said. "What did I do?"

Gabriel said: "You leapt over the laws of logic as though they were inch-high hurdles, and came up with the solution to our problem."

"I'm very glad," said Peter, acidly. "But will someone now make my solution clear to me?"

I tried to be placatory. "Your question suddenly put in perspective the obvious nature of the Lazarus coup—and who the projected victim has to be. Listen . . .

"Dr Tiko Naziwambe, the President of Tanzumibia, is a key man today in Africa. Not only is he popular with his own people, he is also respected and honoured in other African countries as an Elder Statesman. As an old friend and ally of Britain, he has reconciled many of the smaller African states with their former colonial masters, and has kept them following the British lead in pan-African policy. If he were to be assassinated while he is here as the guest of and under the protection of the British government, it would certainly be to the benefit of South Africa."

Peter said: "Why?"

"At the moment there is complete solidarity among all the African states on the question of South Africa and its policy of *apartheid*. World opinion generally is hostile to South Africa's racial policies. Britain, the United States—in fact, the whole of both Western and Eastern blocs and the Third world—looks on South Africa, in the words of one of its own ministers, as 'the skunk of the western world.'

"Strongest ingredient holding together this massive wall of hostility faced by South Africa is Dr Naziwambe. If he dies in circumstances under which Britain can be accused of not providing him with sufficient protection, the result would inevitably be some crumbling of unity. Arguments or dissent on any grounds among the African states would obviously take some of the pressure off South Africa."

"And," added Gabriel, "South Africa is highly skilled at exploiting disagreements among its enemies. Ironically, if Dr Naziwambe were killed in London at this psychologically ripe time—while on a visit of good will—the obvious and only beneficiary of such violence will not even be suspected. Every known BOSS agent is safely outside Britain."

Peter objected: "But Lazarus surely is a BOSS agent."

"I said *known* agent. Lazarus is clearly a 'sleeper'. Any trail connecting him with BOSS must have been well hidden years ago. Almost certainly, BOSS's only connection with him is through an advertisement in a pre-selected newspaper. Remember: tomorrow is June 11."

My voice sounded unexpectedly grim: "And Lazarus will come forth from the dead to deal out death."

Peter shivered. "What can we do?"

"First thing," said Gabriel, "is to give Dr Naziwambe every protection. You know him, don't you, Joe?"

I nodded. "Spent a month with him in 1963 doing a series of articles on Tanzumibia. We got on very well."

"Then you can renew your friendship tomorrow. I'll alert Special Branch to take extra care along the route, and arrange for you to be at the President's side from the moment he leaves from the High Commissioner's house in Hampstead. And Peter: issue a penultimate trump. I want every available Angel strategically placed at the conference and along the route. Every possible Angel, d'you hear?"

I said, softly: "But no Azrael."

"Dear God," said Gabriel, "with Your help, no Azrael."

I managed a deep sleep for five hours on the truckle bed kept in a side office before the Special Branch car called for me. On the way to the Hampstead home of the High Commissioner for Tanzumibia where Dr Naziwambe was staying, Detective Inspector Jackson outlined the special precautions that were being taken. I raised one or two tentative questions, heard the answers and gave a conditional approval.

"We're dealing with a whole set of intangibles," I said. "We don't know what Lazarus looks like, where he will strike from, or even how he will strike. You say there is no cover for a sniper anywhere within range of the house? Right. Then I don't see you can do more than you've done—a bullet-proof automobile, and escorting cars before and behind."

Jackson added: "And you in the car with the President. If an attempt is going to be made, it will have to be on the journey. There is absolute security at the Commonwealth Centre."

Dr Naziwambe greeted me like an old friend. "Good to see you, Joe. The years have been kind to you. You look as though I'd last met you a week ago."

"And you haven't changed an hour, Mr President," I said.

We both smiled in appreciation of each other's diplomatic lying. In reality Tiko Naziwambe was a frail and brittle husk of the forceful personality of 1963. His hair, his shaggy eyebrows were a dull grey; only his eyes reflected internal fires. He motioned to the man at his side: "Joe, meet John Carew, my chief economic adviser. He'll be with us in the car." He cackled unexpectedly. "That'll be a change—to have a man I can trust on either side of me."

Carew shook hands firmly and spoke pleasantly with a soft accent, the origins of which eluded me, although I have an ear for that sort of thing. He was tall and fair and carried himself erect, like a former soldier. I had seen newspaper pictures of him. Now I realized why his left profile always faced the camera. An old puckered scar distorted the right lower lip, and trailed down the chin.

Dr Naziwambe consulted an old-fashioned pocket watch. "Time for us to be going," he said.

Carew took the President's left arm to help him down the path to the waiting car. I lingered a moment to check the positions of the security guards and then stepped forward to follow.

The men were now a few yards in front of me. Dr Naziwambe

from the rear looked even older and frailer, but the strong hand on his arm held him comparatively steady. Carew, his left hand in his pocket, walked slowly but firmly at his side.

Steady, reliable, but a gait that had an incipient sailor's roll, a sort of *leaning*, compensation for an old injury . . . the *Lazarus list*.

And with that thought, another: *Max Stern was left-handed.*

I dived forward, my sheer momentum knocking Carew to the ground. I grabbed his left wrist with both hands, twisting fiercely. The hand came out of the pocket gripping then dropping a hypodermic filled with a sickly yellow liquid. On the periphery of my vision I saw a security man helping a shaken Dr Naziwambe to his feet.

Lazarus now lay helpless, face down, arms twisted behind him. I knelt on the small of his back. He gasped: "What gave me away, Joe?"

"The same thing Anna spotted. It's ironic, Max. Plastic surgeons, elocutionists, years of practising the habits of a new personality, training in unfamiliar skills of 'sleeping' and burrowing for position in another country—none of these could affect one simple give-away: the way you walked. Why did you do it, Max?"

"They had me, Joe. Pressure . . . I preferred to live in comfort. More than that—I preferred to live . . ."

"And Anna?"

"Anna. Ah, yes. I *had* to kill her, Joe." He ground his teeth so fiercely there was an audible *crack*.

"I know," I said. "For the second time . . ."

But I spoke into an unlistening ear. Azrael, the Angel of Death, comes swiftly when summoned with cyanide.

"HOOCH, MON!"

Herbert Harris

SINCE MY UNCLE Leo (who was a small-time crook like the rest of the family) quit Britain for America in the late twenties to better himself, and got accidentally shot in a brief altercation between (if I remember rightly) Big Jim Florrio and Dutch Schmaltz, I have never had the slightest connections with the bootlegging or moonshining side of the underworld, perhaps because I had never run across it until recently.

This might surprise you when I tell you that when my Uncle Leo got shot scotch whisky in Britain cost about eight shillings a full bottle, whereas today in this year of disgrace 1983 that same bottle of amber ecstasy, even the legal kind, costs somewhere between six and seven quid a bottle, and the mean sons-of-bitches in Whitehall keep adding new bits of tax to it.

I offer these figures merely to underline the fact that the field has been wide open in these sceptred isles for years for somebody to produce large quantities of hooch or rotgut and put it on the market, the black one of course, at half the legitimate price.

If I had only had the proper facilities, maybe I should have embarked upon such a project myself. But if the business initiative was lacking in yours truly, it was certainly not lacking in Angus Maconochie, the only initiator of an illicit still who ever actually crossed my path.

However, I am tripping ahead rather too fast. To understand how I came to hear of this hooch-merchant in a land where hooch-merchants are astonishingly thin on the ground, it is necessary for you to make the acquaintance of "Matilda" Loveless.

I put Matilda in quotes there because it is only her nickname, she being Australian (you know, Waltzing Matilda) and descended, with all the undesirable features, from some digger who was once transported to New South Wales in a convict ship. Matilda is not loveless either. In fact, the reason why they keep a set of towels with Matilda's name on them in Holloway Prison is because she *will* go around trying to share her warm, affectionate nature with complete strangers of the opposite sex.

I renewed acquaintance with Matilda Loveless in the Blue Monkey one autumn evening, when the leaves fluttered down from the Soho strippers and smoke curled up from the bonfires of a hundred filter-tips. The advantage of a place like the Blue Monkey is that you do occasionally meet up with people who can do you some good and pick up the odd scrap of information that can be turned to profit. When Matilda said to me conspiratorially, "I can tell you something about *him* that will make your ears sizzle!" my ears did, in fact, become rigid like those of a well-trained pointer.

Everything about Matilda was on the large side, including her eyes, fastened on me like glowing orbs across the top of her pink gin. I had not seen her for ages and had rather missed her. She has a definite appeal for the full-blooded male, but we need not go into that.

Earlier on, after we had chatted our way through the well-fancy-meeting-you stage and settled down to some dedicated drinking in an intimately secluded corner of the club, I had asked her, "Is it really true about you going straight?"

"Oh, sure," Matilda confirmed, nodding her blonde head vigorously. "I mean, the worst part of prison is not having any men around. It makes being in the nick absolute torture for a girl like me."

I made sympathetic sounds. "And since you came out?"

"Well, some geezer took me to this dance out in the country. And I met this gorgeous man—a Scotsman called Angus Maconochie—who had this sort of hypnotic way with him. A girl sort of became putty in his hands."

Matilda smiled reminiscently. "Somehow or other I found myself telling him everything about me . . . just everything! He listened with tremendous interest, and then he says, all sudden like, 'You want a job working for me?'

"So I says, a bit cautious, 'And what as exactly?' So he tells me, and in no time at all I am working for him. He looked a really lovely hunk of manhood to begin with, but he's turned out to be a bit of a cold fish."

I encouraged her to go on talking.

When Matilda spoke of "going straight," the term was a trifle misleading.

It was true that she had not been helping herself to the bulging notecases of her gentlemen guests, or emerging from a department store, as she once did, with a pouch full of lingerie masquerading as an advanced pregnancy. Nevertheless, working as an assistant to Angus Maconochie can hardly be described as "going straight" by any stretch of the imagination, as you will shortly see.

"Mr Maconochie Senior—Angus's father—was sort of an amateur scientist," Matilda explained. "He had this beautifully equipped place built on the back of his house—a kind of research laboratory, you know—and the house was tucked away in a wood in the most beautiful countryside, miles from anywhere. And, of course, when Mr Maconochie handed in his chips, young Angus was left the place. . . ."

Matilda switched on one of her wicked grins that could be highly dangerous to the more susceptible.

At this point she decided to go the whole hog and tell me something about her employer that was going to make my ears sizzle.

"Angus Maconochie was no scientist like his Dad," she went on, "but he certainly had some bright ideas. He reckoned he could put that laboratory of his old man's to real good use. Well, I mean . . . all those lovely glass tubes and retorts and things all going begging . . ."

I swallowed painfully, suddenly remembering all those nasty things that crazy scientists keep in test-tubes, and I said uneasily, "Er—what does this geezer do exactly?"

Matilda's robust laugh revealed an expanse of pink gums.

"Look," she said, "see that up there?" She nodded her citrus-honey head in the direction of some bottles on an upper shelf behind the bar. "You see that bottle of Rabbie Burns?"

Well, of course I saw it. A bottle of scotch whisky called "Rabbie Burns." It had a most attractive blue label with what I imagined was a portrait of the Scottish national poet, plus the words "Fine Old Matured Whisky, 100° proof."

"It looks all right," I said. "What about it?"

"That's Angus Maconochie's masterpiece," said Matilda. "He makes it."

As I said earlier, since my Uncle Leo died with his boots on in what my Aunt Rose described as "some unspeakable speakeasy," I had never heard of anyone actually operating an illicit still, and I regarded the blonde with unconcealed surprise.

"Of course," she explained, "Maconochie doesn't have to charge any Government Tax or anything, so he can sell the stuff at half the usual price and still make himself a handsome profit. And with all these private drinking and gambling clubs around—like this one—he never has to go short of customers."

"Holy cow," I said in a reverent whisper, "he must be making a bomb!"

The blonde head nodded energetically again. "He sure is," she said, "and, what's more, he stacks all the dough away in an old steel cupboaid and doesn't even bank it. I guess the poor boy's just scared of the tax-men asking a lot of awkward questions."

I swallowed again, harder this time. Perhaps I even drooled a little. I glanced right, left, up, down, and asked with a slight croak, "Matilda, my love, you're joking, aren't you?"

"No, on the level, straight up," Matilda assured me earnestly. "Of course, Maconochie never actually *revealed* to me that he was hoarding all this beautiful mazuma, but one day I happened to get a peep at this cupboard when he had the door open. And, boy . . ."

"Go on?" I prompted, rolling a tongue round my lips.

"There were dirty great bundles of five-pound notes in there! Boy, oh boy, did the sight make little Matilda's mouth water! I reckon just about half the contents of that cupboard would have set me up for years!"

"But this is very interesting, darling," I said, leaning so far towards her that I could feel the draught from her eyelashes. "Very interesting indeed. And does Angus Maconochie ever go away?"

Her answer was as sweet as the music of an angel's harp. "Oh, sure. He's away right now as it happens. He won't be coming back until the day after tomorrow."

"Have another drink, love," I said. "Something really expensive. Me . . . I'll try the Rabbie Burns."

"I admire a man with guts," Matilda said.

If Matilda had not been such an unscrupulous little tramp, she would never have dropped this white-hot tip-off straight into my lap. But, as I had always suspected, Matilda was a bit stuck on me. We were kindred spirits, as you might say.

This looked about the cushiest pushover that had ever come my way. A sitting duck. The blonde even had a key to the Scotsman's place, so that it wasn't even necessary to case the joint and do a breaking and entering job.

"If you only had a small van," she suggested helpfully, running the tip of a forefinger up and down my wrist, "you could go along there and help yourself any time, day or night. I mean, quite apart from the fact that this house of his is buried away in the back of beyond, with not a soul anywhere near it, Maconochie himself has a small van that visits the house every so often and takes away the customers' supplies. So a van wouldn't be at all conspicuous. Are you with me?"

"I'm way ahead of you, love," I said. "And I have to admire your cheek. It's more brazen than that dress you're wearing."

"Saucy!" she said, giggling and giving me a shove.

I could have kissed Matilda from sheer joy just then. Later I could have wrung her goddam neck, but at that moment it looked so good, so promising . . .

However, I will be quite frank. I made the one great tactical error of taking Taffy Thomas with me when I went to do the Maconochie job.

Taffy Thomas had a very big frame and a very big heart. He had not been getting too many jobs just lately, and I thought I would do him a good turn out of sheer magnanimity. Another consideration was that Taffy happened to be the owner of a small van. Unfortunately he possessed a brain in complete contra-distinction to his large body, which was why, I suppose, he hadn't been getting many jobs lately.

I did ask Matilda if she would like to come along too, but she said "Not flaming likely!"—or words to that effect—"I don't want to get thrown into clink again, at least not until they've got integrated prisons." (I often wonder where she picks up these big words.)

Anyway, it was just myself and Taffy Thomas and a van not quite as old as the Model T Ford.

As my blonde friend had said, the Scotsman's place was beautifully hidden away miles from anywhere. The older Maconochie had wanted a laboratory where he could work in complete quiet and without interruption.

His son Angus now had a similar desire, only the product was something totally different—"Rabbie Burns, Fine Old Matured Whisky 100° proof."

"Do you think, bach," Taffy Thomas said in his green Welsh valley accent, "we might knock off a few bottles of the luffly hard stuff as *well* as the bundles of fivers?"

"Never mind that," I said severely. "You concentrate on the ackers. Forget the gut-destroyer—you can buy all you want of that with your rake-off. It's lousy, anyway. Rabbie Burns would have spat it in Maconochie's face."

Taffy Thomas, who was driving (driving!), succeeded in losing his way three times, but we eventually found the house, and we let ourselves in with Matilda's doorkey and followed the little plan she had drawn for us. As luck would have it, the steel cupboard was in a room on the ground floor, and if you are wondering why I say this was lucky, you will find out very shortly.

The steel cupboard was strong-looking, one might say nearly impregnable, and, naturally, Maconochie had locked it and taken the key with him.

"By Gor, I fancy we'll 'ave a spot of trouble with that, bach," Taffy observed uneasily. "Looks like Fort Knox, don't it?"

"Well, we're going to have to force it, of course," I said crossly. "Get a jemmy."

"I didn't bother to bring a jemmy," Taffy said. "You said you had a key."

"I meant the key of the front door!" I shouted. "Anyway, we'll have to make do with something else. Look in your tool-bag!"

Taffy shifted awkwardly from one foot to the other and tried to screw off one forefinger. "I'm sorry, bach, but I . . . I left the tool-bag in the garage back 'ome."

"Oh, no!" I bellowed, beating my temples with my fists. "You couldn't be *that* thick, mate . . . not *that* thick!"

The Welsh nut hung his head for a while, then his round moon-face brightened.

"We could shift it, look you!"

"Shift *this*? It must weigh a flipping ton!"

Taffy expanded his bullfrog chest and flexed his massive biceps. "God save us," he said, "I could pick this thing up, bach, and shake it like my young Blodwen's money-box!"

"Then let's see you do that!" I said sourly.

He very nearly did, although I doubt that Taffy Thomas will ever be quite the same man again.

"Come on," I said with a gruff reluctance, "we shall have to carry it out to the van together!"

This is exactly what we did. Luckily, it was not so very far from the room in which the steel cupboard stood to the courtyard where we had parked the van, although it felt like a hundred miles.

Manoeuvring the cupboard into Taffy's van was, I think, even more exhausting than getting it out of the house, by way of two absurdly narrow doorways, but we did finally make it.

I draped myself across the bonnet of the van to get my breath back. "Holy cow," I panted, "I thought this job was going to be a soft touch!"

I think Taffy was gasping even more loudly than I, and we were both drenched to the skin in perspiration.

Finally he closed the doors of the van and climbed back behind the wheel. "Well, we did it, boyo! And now let's get to hell out of 'ere!"

"I go along with that," I said, glaring at him.

We had only travelled about two miles when a policeman on a motor-cycle flagged us down and nudged us into the kerb.

He shoved his head through the window on my side. "You must be the one we're looking for!" he said briskly.

I felt as if all my joints had turned suddenly to plasticine. "Er—what about?" I asked, hoping I wasn't going to be sick.

"You Cattermole's Chemicals?" he barked officiously.

"No," I answered, "we're Steelware Office Furniture."

He marched to the back of the van and peered through one of the small windows in the doors. Then he returned.

"Yeah, okay," he said. "Only your van's the same colour as Cattermole's Chemicals, see. The stupid nits picked up the wrong carboy of acid. Could be very dangerous. Keep an eye open for them as you go along, and tell 'em what's happened if you see 'em."

"Sure, sure, a pleasure," I said with a big beam.

The cop went roaring up the road. I took out a handkerchief and wiped the sweat off my face.

"I feel as sick as a dog," Taffy confessed, his moon-face whiter than usual. "Sometimes I feel, bach, as if a life of crime doesn't suit me."

I felt like that too, but wouldn't have dared admit it.

We drove straight back to Taffy's place. He had a decrepit shed which he called his "garage," and in which he kept his van and a few other things which I suspect he had knocked off.

When we had gone through the enervating process of unloading the steel cupboard from the van, Taffy Thomas rubbed his hands together gleefully.

"Now for it, bach!"

He produced the bag of tools which he had left behind and launched such an assault on that cupboard that you might suspect he was demolishing Tower Bridge.

Finally the doors burst open and a veritable cascade of mouth-watering bundles poured out on to the floor.

Taffy's eyes almost fell out of his head. "Praise be to St David!" he cried in awe. "Oh, boyo, look at all those banknotes . . . all those beautiful blue fivers. . . ! Are *we* in the money or are we in the money!"

"In the WHAT?" I screamed at him. I picked up one of the bundles that looked like fivers and hurled it at Taffy's head with some violence.

I suppose I have no right to blame Matilda Loveless.

They certainly *did* look remarkably like five-pound notes.

Unfortunately, they consisted of thousands of labels in an attractive shade of blue, bearing not the likeness of Her Majesty Queen Elizabeth II but that of the boyishly good-looking Scottish bard and carrying the words "Rabbie Burns, Fine Old Matured Whisky, 100° proof."

THE ADVENTURE OF THE SUFFERING RULER

H. R. F. Keating

IT WAS IN the early autumn of 1896 that, returning one day from visiting by train a patient in Hertfordshire and being thus in the vicinity of Baker Street, I decided to call on Sherlock Holmes, whom I had not seen for several weeks. I found him, to my dismay, in a sad state. Although it was by now late afternoon he was still in his dressing-gown lounging upon the sofa in our old sitting-room, his violin lying on the floor beside him and the air musty with cold tobacco smoke from the neglected pipe left carelessly upon the sofa arm. I glanced at once to the mantelpiece where there lay always that neat morocco case which contained the syringe. It was in its customary place, but, when under pretence of examining the familiar bullet-marked letters 'VR' on the wall above, I stepped closer, I saw that it lay upon the envelope of a letter postmarked only two days earlier.

"Well, Holmes," I said, jovially as I could, "I see that your bullet holes of yore are still here."

"It would be strange indeed, Watson, had they disappeared," my old friend answered, with somewhat more fire than he had earlier greeted me.

He laughed then in a melancholy enough fashion.

"Yet I could wish that they had vanished between one night and the next morning," he added. "It would at least provide my mind with some matter to work upon."

My spirits sank at the words. Holmes had always needed stimulation, and if no problem was there to arouse his mind a seven per cent solution of cocaine awaited.

"But have you no case on hand?" I asked.

"Some trifling affairs," Holmes replied. "A commission for the Shah of Persia, a little question of missing securities in Pittsburgh. Nothing to engage my full attention. But, you, my dear Watson, how is it that you have been visiting a patient in Hertfordshire?"

I turned to my old friend in astonishment. I had said nothing of the reason for my being in the vicinity.

"Oh, come, doctor," he said. "Do I have to explain to you once again the simple signs that tell me such things? Why, they are written on your person as clearly as if you carried a newspaper billboard proclaiming them."

"I dare say they may be, Holmes. But beyond the fact that Baker Street station serves that particular county and that I nowadays visit you chiefly when I chance to be in the locality, I cannot see how this time you can know so much of my business."

"And yet the moment you removed your gloves the characteristic pungent odour of iodoform was heavy in the air, indicating beyond doubt that your excursion had been on a professional matter. While your boots are dust-covered to the very tops, which surely means that you travelled for some little time on a country lane."

I glanced down at my boots. The evidence was all too plain to see.

"Well, yes," I admitted. "I did receive this morning a request to visit a gentleman living near Rickmansworth whose condition was causing him anxiety. An unhealed lesion on the abdomen complicated by brain fever, but I have high hopes of a good recovery."

"My dear Watson, under your care who can doubt of that? But I am surprised to hear that your practice now extends to the remote Hertfordshire countryside."

I smiled.

"No, no. I assure you none other of my patients necessitates any journey longer than one performed easily in a hansom."

"And yet you have just been down to Hertfordshire?"

"Yes. I was called on this morning by the manservant of a certain Mr Smith, a trusted fellow, I gathered, though of European origin. He told me that his master had instructed him to seek out a London doctor and to request a visit as soon as possible. Apparently, Mr Smith has a somewhat morbid fear of any of his close neighbours knowing that he is ill and so prefers a physician from a distance, even if the visit means a considerably greater financial outlay."

"You were well remunerated then?"

"I think I may say, handsomely so."

"I am not surprised to hear it."

"No, there, Holmes, you are at fault. My services were not asked for because of any particular reputation I may have. In fact, the manservant happened to be in my neighbourhood upon some other errand and, so I understand, simply saw my brass plate and rang at my door."

Holmes raised himself upon one elbow on the sofa. His eyes seemed to me to shine now with a healthier light.

"You misunderstand me, Watson. You had already indicated that your services were called upon more or less by chance. But what I was saying was that the size of your fee did not surprise me, since it is clearly evident that you were required for a quality quite other than your medical attainments."

"Indeed?" I answered, a little nettled I must confess. "And what quality had you in mind?"

"Why, distance, my dear fellow. The distance between medical adviser and patient, and the complete discretion that follows from that."

"I am by no means sure that I understand."

"No? Yet the matter is simple enough. A person living in a remote country house, a gentleman for whom monetary considerations have little weight, sends a trusted servant to obtain the immediate services of a London doctor, of any London doctor more or less, and you expect me to be surprised that you received a fee altogether out of the ordinary?"

"Well, Holmes," I replied, "I will not disguise that my remuneration was perhaps excessive. But my patient evidently is a wealthy man and one prey to nervous fears. He trusts, too, to receive my continuing attentions from week to week. The situation does not strike me as being very much out of the ordinary."

"No, Watson? But I tell you that it is out of the ordinary. The man you attended this afternoon is no ordinary man, you may take my word for that."

"Well, if you say so, Holmes, if you say so," I replied.

Yet I could not but think that for once my old friend had read too much into the circumstances, and I quickly sought for some other subject of conversation, being much relieved when Holmes too seemed disinclined to pursue a matter in which he might be thought to have me at a disadvantage. The remainder of the visit passed pleasantly enough, and I had the satisfaction of leaving

Holmes looking a good deal more brisk and cheerful than he had done upon my arrival.

I went down to Hertfordshire again a week later and found my patient already much better for the treatment I had prescribed. I was hopeful enough, indeed, to feel that another two or three weeks of the same regimen, which included plenty of rest and a light diet, would see the illness through.

It was just as I stepped back from the bed after concluding my examination, however, that out of the corner of my eye I detected a sharp movement just outside the window. I was so surprised, since there was no balcony outside, that something of my alarm must have communicated itself to my patient who at once demanded, with the full querulousness of his indisposition, what it was that I had seen.

"I thought I saw a man out there, a glimpse of a face, dark brown and wrinkled," I answered without premeditation, so disturbed was I by an aura of malignancy I had been aware of even from my brief sight of that visage.

But I quickly sought to counteract any anxiety I might have aroused in my already nervous patient.

"Yet it can hardly have been a man," I said. "It was more likely a bird perching momentarily in the ivy."

"No, no," Mr Smith said, in sharp command. "A face. A burglar. I always knew this house was unsafe. After him doctor, after him. Lay him by the heels. Catch him. Catch him."

I thought it best at least to make pretence of obeying the peremptory order. There would be little hope of calming my patient unless I made an excursion into the garden.

I hurried out of the room and down the stairs, calling to the manservant, who, I had gathered, was the sole other occupant of the house. But he evidently must have been in the kitchens or elsewhere out of hearing since I had no reply. I ran straight out of the front door and looked about me. At once, down at the far side of the garden, I detected a movement behind a still leaf-clad beech hedge. I set out at a run.

Holmes had been right, I thought, as swiftly and silently I crossed a large, damp-sodden lawn. My patient must be a man of mystery if he was being spied upon by daylight in this daring fashion. His cries of alarm over a burglary must, then, be false. No ordinary burglar, surely, would seek to enter a house by broad day.

My quarry had by now gone slinking along the far side of the beech hedge to a point where I lost sight of him behind a dense rhododendron shrubbery. But I was running on a course to cut him off, and I made no doubt that before long I would have the rogue by the collar.

Indeed, as soon as I had rounded the dense clump of rhododendrons, I saw a small wicket gate in the hedge ahead with the figure of the man who had been spying on my patient only just beyond. He appeared from his garb to be a gypsy. In a moment I was through the gate, and in another moment I had him by the arm.

"Now, you villain," I cried. "We shall have the truth of it."

But even before the man had had time to turn in my grasp I heard from behind me the sound of sudden, wild, grim, evil laughter. I looked back. Peering at the two of us from the shelter of the rhododendrons was that same brown, wrinkled face I had glimpsed looking in at my patient's window. I loosened my grip on the gipsy, swung about and once more set out in pursuit.

This time I did not have so far to go. No sooner had I reached the other side of the shrubbery than I came face to face with my man. But he was my man no longer. He wore the same nondescript clothes that I had caught sight of among the brittle rhododendron leaves and his face was still brown-coloured. But that look of hectic evil in it had vanished clear away and in its place were the familiar features of my friend, Sherlock Holmes.

"I am sorry, Watson, to have put you to the trouble of two chases in one afternoon," he said. "But I had to draw you away from that fellow before revealing myself."

"Holmes," I cried. "Then it was you at the window up there?"

"It was, doctor. I knew that it was imperative that I myself should take a good look at this mysterious patient of yours, and so I took the liberty of following you, knowing that this was your day for visiting the case. But you were a little too quick for me in the end, my dear fellow, and I had to beat a more hurried retreat than I altogether cared to."

"Yes, but all the same, Holmes," I said. "You cannot have had any good reason to suppose that it was necessary to spy upon my patient in that manner."

"No good reason, doctor? Why, I should have thought the third finger of his right hand was reason enough, were there no other."

"The third finger of his right hand?"

"Why, yes, my dear fellow. Surely you are not going to tell me that you noticed nothing about that? Come, I was at that window for little more than three or four minutes and I had grasped its significance long before you turned and saw me."

"Now that I think about it," I replied, "my patient does wear a finger-stall on the third finger of his right hand. Some trifling injury, I suppose. It certainly could in no way contribute to his condition."

"I never suggested that it did, doctor. I am sure you know your business better than that. Trust me, then, to know mine."

"But does his concealing that finger have some significance?" I asked.

"Of course it does. Tell me, what does a man customarily wear upon his third finger?"

"A ring, I suppose. But that would not be upon the right hand, surely?"

"Yes, Watson, a ring. You have arrived at the point with your customary perspicacity. But why should a man wish to conceal a particular ring? Tell me that."

"Holmes, I cannot. I simply cannot."

"Because the ring has a particular meaning. And who is it who would wear a ring of that nature? Why, a monarch, of course. I tell you that man in bed there is a king, and he is hiding for some good reason. There can scarcely be any doubt about that."

To my mind, there was at least room for a measure of disagreement with this conclusion. Smith was perhaps a name that anyone wishing to live anonymously might take, but certainly my patient had shown not the least trace of a foreign accent, as he was surely likely to do if he were the ruler of one of the lesser European states whose appearance, especially since he wore a full beard, might be unknown to me. Yet he did have a manservant of European origin, though here again this was not an altogether uncommon circumstance for a single English gentleman who might be something of a traveller. I would have liked to put all these doubts and queries to my friend, but from the moment that he had told me what he had deduced from my patient's concealed finger he lapsed into one of those moods of silence well familiar to me, and for the whole of our journey back to London he uttered scarcely a word, little more than to say to me at the station in Hertfordshire that he had a number of telegrams which he needed urgently to despatch.

I was curious enough, however, to find an opportunity of visiting Baker Street again next day. But, though I found Holmes fully dressed and a great deal more alert than on my last visit, I was unable to obtain from him any hint about the direction of his inquiries. All he would do was to talk, with that vivacity of spirit which he could display whenever the mood took him, about a bewildering variety of subjects, the paintings of the Belgian artist, Ensor, the amorous adventures of Madame Sand, the activities of the Russian nihilists, the gravity of the political situation in Illyria. None was a matter on which I felt myself particularly informed, yet on each Holmes, it seemed, had a fund of knowledge. At length I went back to my medical round not one whit better able to decide whether my Hertfordshire patient was no more than the nervous Englishman, Mr Smith, whom he seemed to be, or in truth some foreign potentate sheltering under that pseudonym in the safety of the Queen's peace.

The following morning, however, I received a telegram from Holmes requesting me to meet him at his bank in Oxford Street at noon "in re the hidden finger." I was, you can be sure, at the appointed place at the appointed hour, and indeed a good few minutes beforehand.

Holmes arrived exactly to time.

"Now, my good fellow," he said, "if you will do me the kindness of walking a few yards along the street with me, I think I can promise you a sight that will answer a good many of the questions which I have no doubt have been buzzing in your head these past few days."

In silence we made our way together along the busy street. I could not refrain from glancing to left and right at the passers-by, at the cabs, carriages and vans in the roadway and at the glittering shopfronts in an endeavour to see what it was that Holmes wished to show me. But my efforts were in vain. Nothing that I saw roused the least spark in my mind.

Then abruptly Holmes grasped my arm. I came to a halt.

"Well?" my companion demanded.

"My dear fellow, I am not at all clear what it is to which you are directing my attention."

Holmes gave a sigh of frank exasperation.

"The window, Watson. The shop window directly before you."

I looked at the window. It was that of a photographer's establishment, the whole crowded with numerous likenesses of persons both known and unknown.

"Well?" Holmes demanded yet more impatiently.

"It is one of these photographs you wish me to see?" I asked.

"It is, Watson, it is."

I looked at them again, actors and actresses, the beauties of the day, well-known political figures.

"No," I said, "I cannot see any particular reason for singling out one of these pictures above any of the others. Is that what you wish me to do?"

"Watson, look. In the second row, the third from the left."

"The Count Palatine of Illyria," I read on the card below the portrait which Holmes had indicated.

"Yes, yes. And you see nothing there?"

Once more I gave the photograph my full attention.

"Nothing," I answered at last.

"Not the very clear likeness between the ruler of that troubled state and a certain Mr Smith at present recovering from illness in Hertfordshire?"

I examined the portrait anew.

"Yes," I agreed eventually. "There is a likeness. The beards have a good deal in common, and perhaps the general cast of the countenances."

"Exactly."

From an inner pocket Holmes now drew a newspaper cutting.

"*The Times*," he said. "Of yesterday's date. Read it carefully."

I read, and when I had done so looked up again at Holmes in bewilderment.

"But this is a report of the Count Palatine appearing on the balcony of his palace and being greeted with enthusiasm by a vast crowd," I said. "So, Holmes, how can this man in the photograph be my patient down in Hertfordshire but two days ago?"

"Come, Watson, the explanation is childishly simple."

I felt a little aggrieved and spoke more sharply than I might have done in reply.

"It seems to me, I must say, that the sole explanation is merely that my patient and the Count Palatine of Illyria are not one and the same person."

"Nonsense, Watson. The likeness is clear beyond doubt, and nor is the explanation in any way obscure. It is perfectly plain that the man glimpsed at a distance by the crowd in Illyria is a double for the Count Palatine. The situation there, you know, is decidedly grave. There is the most dangerous unrest. If it were widely known that the Count was not at the helm in his country, the republican element would undoubtedly make an attempt to seize power, an attempt, let me tell you, that would in all likelihood be successful. However, you and I know that the Count is seriously ill and is living in Hertfordshire, under your excellent care, my dear Watson. So the solution is obvious. With the connivance of his close circle the Count has arranged for a substitute to make occasional public appearances in his stead in circumstances under which he will not easily be identified."

"Yes, I suppose you must be right, Holmes," I said. "It certainly seems a complex and extraordinary business though. Yet your account does appear to connect all the various elements."

"It connects them indeed," Holmes replied. "But I think for the time being we can assure ourselves that all is well. Do me the kindness, however, doctor, to let me know as soon as there is any question of the Count becoming fit enough to resume his full powers."

It was, in fact, no later than the following week that I was able to give Holmes the reassuring news he had asked for. I had found my patient very far along the road to recovery, and though, not wishing to let him know that Holmes had penetrated his secret, I had not said to him that quite soon he would be ready to travel, I had left his bedside with that thought in my mind. In consequence I went from the station at Baker Street on my return directly to our old rooms.

"He is distinctly better then?" Holmes asked me.

"Very much so, I am happy to say. The lassitude that originally gave me cause for anxiety has almost completely passed away."

"Bad. Very bad, Watson."

"But surely, Holmes . . ."

"No, Watson, I tell you if the Count's enemies should gain any inkling of the fact that he is likely to be able to return to Illyria in the near future, they will stop at nothing to make sure that he never crosses the Channel."

"But, Holmes, how can they know that he is not in Illyria? You yourself showed me that extract from *The Times*."

"I dare say, Watson. Yet an illusion of that sort cannot be kept up indefinitely. No doubt the conspirators watch every appearance the supposed Count makes upon the Palace balcony. At any time some small error on the part of the substitute may give the game away. Very possibly that error has been already made and suspicions have been aroused. Remember that I myself was not the only spy you caught down in Hertfordshire a fortnight ago."

"The gipsy, Holmes? But I thought he was no more after all than a passing gipsy."

"Quite possibly he was, Watson. Yet did it not strike you as curious that the fellow was skulking in the grounds of the house?"

"Well, I had supposed that he had in fact never penetrated the garden itself."

"Indeed, Watson? Then it is perhaps as well that I have taken an interest in the matter. We should not wish the Count Palatine to fail to reach his homeland in safety. You have said nothing of his rapid recovery to anybody but myself?"

"Of course not, Holmes. Of course not."

Yet just one week later as, making what I hoped might be my last visit into Hertfordshire, I approached my mysterious patient's residence I was reminded with sudden shame that I had in fact spoken about his recovery outside the house the previous week when I had been talking to the manservant who had driven me back to the station in the dog-cart, and I recalled too that I had spoken in tones deliberately loud and clear so as to make sure that I was understood by this foreigner. I was debating with myself whether those words of mine could perhaps have been overheard then by some lurker, when my eye was caught by just such a person within some fifty yards of the gate of the house itself, an individual who seemed by his dress to be a seaman. But what was a seaman doing here in Hertfordshire, so far from the sea?

I decided that it was my duty now at least to deliver an oblique warning to the Count Palatine's faithful manservant, even though I still did not wish to disclose that I knew through Holmes whom he served. I succeeded, I hope, in giving him some general advice about the dangers of burglars in the neighbourhood, advice which I hoped would alert him without betraying what Holmes and I alone knew. I was relieved, too, when my patient, having declared his intention of visiting a Continental spa now that he felt so much better, asked if his servant could collect from me a supply of a nerve tonic I had prescribed sufficient to last him for a number of weeks. I gladly arranged for the man to come to me next day for the purpose, thinking that I could in this way get the latest tidings before the Count Palatine—if indeed this were the Count Palatine—left our shores.

My anxieties over the lurking seaman I had noticed by the house gate proved fully justified when the manservant called on me the day afterwards. He reported that he had encountered this very fellow in the garden at dusk the night before, and that he had given him a thorough beating before chasing him from the premises. I decided it would be as well to visit Holmes and report on the favourable turn to the situation. It ought, I believed, to assuage any fears he might have. Instead therefore of returning home to lunch I called in at my club, which lies between my house and Baker Street, to take some refreshment there.

It was while I was hastily consuming a boiled fowl and half a bottle of Montrachet that the place next to me at the table was taken by an old acquaintance, Maltravers Bressingham, the big-game hunter. I enquired whether he had been in Africa.

"Why, no, my dear fellow," he replied. "I have been shooting nearer home. In Illyria, in fact. There is excellent sport to be had in the wild boar forests there, you know."

"Indeed?" I answered. "And were you not disturbed by the state of the country? I understand the situation there is somewhat turbulent."

"Turbulent?" Bressingham said, in tones of considerable surprise. "My dear fellow, I assure you that there are positively no signs of unrest at all. I spent a week in the capital, you know, and society there is as calm and as full of enjoyment as one could wish."

"Is it indeed?" I said. "I believed otherwise, but it must be that I have been misinformed."

Sadly puzzled, I left the club and took a hansom for Baker Street. I found Holmes in bed. I was more dismayed at this than I can easily say. A fortnight before, when I had first called on him after a period of some weeks, he had been lying on the sitting-room sofa certainly and in a condition I did not at all like to see. But his state now seemed a good deal more grave. Was that indomitable spirit at last to succumb totally to the sapping weakness which lay for ever ready to emerge when there was nothing to engage the powers of his unique mind? Was the world to be deprived of his services because it held nothing that seemed to him a worthy challenge?

"Holmes, my dear fellow," I said. "What symptoms affect you? Confide in me, pray, as a medical man."

In response I got at first no more than a deep groan. But I persisted, and at length Holmes answered, with a touch of asperity in his voice which I was not wholly displeased to hear.

"Nothing is wrong, Watson. Nothing. This is the merest passing indisposition. I do not require your professional services."

"Very well, my dear fellow. Then let me tell you of events down in Hertfordshire. I trust they will bring you not a little comfort."

But even as I spoke those words, my heart failed me. Certainly I had what had seemed glad tidings from Hertfordshire. But my news was of the foiling of an apparent attempt on the Count Palatine of Illyria, a ruler whom I had believed, on Holmes's authority, to be needed urgently in a country prey to severe unrest. Yet I had heard not half an hour before from an eye-witness of impeccable antecedents that there was no unrest whatsoever in Illyria, and if that were so was not the whole of Holmes's view of the situation a matter for doubt?

Yet I had broached the subject and must continue.

"I happened on my final visit to our friend, Mr Smith, the day before yesterday to notice lurking near the gates of the house a person dressed as a seaman," I said.

Holmes in answer gave a groan yet louder than any before. It caused me to pause a little before continuing once more, in an altogether less assured manner.

"I considered it my duty, Holmes, to warn Mr Smith's manservant of the presence of that individual, and to hint in general terms that the fellow might be some sort of burglar intent on the premises."

Another deep groan greeted this information. Yet more falteringly I resumed.

"This morning, my dear chap, the manservant called to collect from me a quantity of nerve tonic that I had prepared for his master, and he told me that he had surprised just such a mysterious seaman in the grounds of the house last evening and that he had—"

Here my hesitant account abruptly concluded. Holmes had given vent to yet another appalling groan, and I was able to see, too, that he was holding his body under the bedclothes in an altogether unnaturally stiff position.

A silence fell. In the quiet of the bedroom I could hear distinctly the buzzing of a bluebottle fly beating itself hopelessly against the window panes. At last I spoke again.

"Holmes. My dear old friend. Holmes. Tell me, am I right in my guess? Holmes, are you suffering from the effects of a thorough thrashing?"

Another silence. Once more I became aware of the useless buzzings of the fly upon the pane. Then Holmes answered.

"Yes, Watson, it is as you supposed."

"But, my dear fellow, this is truly appalling. My action in warning that manservant resulted in your suffering injury. Can you forgive me?"

"The injury I can forgive," Holmes answered. "The insult I suffered at the hands of that fellow I can forgive you, Watson, as I can forgive the man his unwitting action. But those who were its cause I cannot forgive. They are dangerous men, my friend, and at all costs they must be prevented from wreaking the harm they intend."

I could not in the light of that answer bring myself to question in the least whether the men to whom Holmes had pointed existed, however keenly I recalled Maltravers Bressingham's assertion that all was quiet in Illyria.

"Holmes," I asked instead, "have you then some plan to act against these people?"

"I would be sadly failing in my duty, Watson, had I not taken the most stringent precautions on behalf of the Count Palatine, and I hope you have never found me lacking in that."

"Indeed I have not."

"Very well then. During the hours of daylight I think we need not fear too much. They are hardly likely to make an attempt that might easily be thwarted by a handful of honest English passers-by. And in any case I have telegraphed the Hertfordshire police and given them a proper warning. But it is tonight, Watson, that I fear."

"The Count's last night in England, Holmes, if indeed . . ."

I bit back the qualifying phrase it had been on the tip of my tongue to add. Common sense dictated that the terrible situation Holmes foresaw was one that could not occur. Yet on many occasions before I had doubted him and he had in the outcome been proved abundantly right. So now I held my peace.

Holmes with difficulty raised himself up in the bed.

"Watson," he said, "tonight as never before I shall require your active assistance. We must both keep watch. There is no other course open to me. But I fear I myself will be but a poor bruised champion should the affair come to blows. Will you assist me then? Will you bring that old Service revolver of yours and fight once more on the side of justice?"

"I will, Holmes, I will."

What else could I have said?

The hour of dusk that autumn evening found us taking up our watch in Hertfordshire in that same thick rhododendron shrubbery where Holmes had hidden in the disguise of an old, wrinkled, brown-faced fellow at the beginning of this singular adventure. But where he had from deep within that leafy place of concealment looked out at the mellow brightness of afternoon, we now needed to step only a foot or two in among the bushes to be quite concealed and we looked out at a scene soon bathed in serene moonlight.

All was quiet. No feet trod the path beyond the beech hedge. In the garden no bird hopped to and fro, no insect buzzed. Up at the house, which beneath the light of the full moon we had under perfect observation, two lighted windows only showed how things lay, one high up from behind the drawn curtains of the bedroom where I had visited my mysterious patient, another low down, coming from the partly sunken windows of the kitchen where doubtless the manservant was preparing the light evening repast I myself had recommended.

Making myself as comfortable as I could and feeling with some pleasure the heavy weight of the revolver in my pocket, I set myself to endure a long vigil. By my side Holmes moved from time to time, less able than on other such occasions in the past to keep perfectly still, sore as were his limbs from the cudgel wielded, with mistaken honesty, by that European manservant now busy at the stove.

Our watch, however, was to be much shorter than I had expected. Scarcely half an hour had passed when, with complete unexpectedness, the quiet of the night was broken by a sharp voice from behind us.

"Stay where you are. One move and I would shoot."

The voice I recognized in an instant from the strength of its foreign accent. It was that of Mr Smith's loyal servant. Taking care not to give him cause to let loose a blast from the gun I was certain he must be aiming at our backs, I spoke up as calmly as I could.

"I am afraid that not for the first time your zeal has betrayed you," I said. "Perhaps you will recognize my voice, as I have recognized yours. I am Dr Watson, your master's medical attendant. I am here with my friend, Mr Sherlock Holmes, of whom perhaps you have heard."

"It is the doctor?"

Behind me, as I remained still as a statue, I heard the crunching of the dried leaves underfoot and a moment later the manservant's face was thrust into mine.

"Yes," he said, "it is you. Good. I was keeping guard because of the many rogues there are about here, and I saw in the bushes a movement I did not like. But it is you and your friend only. That is good."

"You did well," Holmes said to him. "I am happy to think that the Count has another alert watcher over him besides ourselves."

"The Count?" said the servant. "What Count is this?"

"Why, man, your master. There is no need for pretence between the three of us. Dr Watson and I are well aware that the man up in the house there is no Mr Smith, but none other than the Count Palatine of Illyria."

Holmes's voice had dropped as he pronounced the name, but his secrecy was greeted in an altogether astonishing manner. The gruff manservant broke into rich and noisy laughter.

"Mr Smith, my Mr Smith the Count Palatine of Illyria?" he choked out at last. "Why, though my master has travelled much, and though I began to serve him while he was in Austria, he has never so much as set foot in Illyria. Of that I can assure you, gentlemen, and as to being the Count Palatine . . ."

Again laughter overcame him, ringing loudly into the night air.

I do not know what Holmes would have done to silence the fellow, or what attitude he would have taken to this brazen assertion. For at that moment another voice made itself heard, a voice somewhat faint and quavering coming from up beside the house.

"What is this? What is going on there? Josef, is that you?"

It was my patient, certainly recovered from his nervous indisposition enough to venture out to see why there was such a hullabaloo in his grounds.

"Sir, it is the doctor and, sir, a friend of his, a friend with a most curious belief."

At the sound of his servant's reassuring voice my patient began to cross the lawn towards us. As he approached, Sherlock Holmes stepped from the shrubbery and went to meet him, his figure tall and commanding in the silvery moonlight. The two men came together in the full middle of the lawn.

"Good evening," Holmes's voice rang clear. "Whom have I the honour of addressing?"

As he spoke he thrust out a hand in greeting. My patient extended his own in reply. But then, with a movement as rapid as that of a striking snake, Holmes, instead of taking the offered hand and clasping it, seized its third finger, covered as always with its leather finger-stall, and jerked the protective sheath clean away.

There in the bright moonlight I saw for the first time the finger that had hitherto always been concealed from me. It wore no heavy royal signet ring, as indeed was unlikely on a finger of the right hand. It was instead curiously withered, a sight that to anyone other than a medical man might have been considered a little repulsive.

"You are not the Count Palatine of Illyria?" Holmes stammered then, more disconcerted than I had ever seen him in the whole of our long friendship.

"The Count Palatine of Illyria?" Mr Smith replied. "I assure you, my dear sir, I am far from being such a person. Whatever put a notion like that into your head?"

It was not until the last train of the day returning us to London was at the outskirts of the city that Holmes spoke to me.

"How often have I told you, Watson," he said, "that one must take into account all the factors relevant to a particular situation before making an assessment? A good many dozen times, I should say. So it was all the more reprehensible of me deliberately to have imported a factor into the Hertfordshire business that was the product, not of the simple truth, but of my own over-willing imagination. My dear fellow, I must tell you that there were no reports of unrest in Illyria."

"I knew it, Holmes. I had found out quite by chance."

"And you said nothing?"

"I trusted you, as I have trusted you always."

"And as, until now, I hope I have been worthy of your trust. But inaction has always been the curse of me, my dear fellow. It was the lack of stimulus that drove me to deceit now. You were right about your patient from the start. He never was other than a man with a not unusual nervousness of disposition. You were right, Watson, and I was wrong."

I heard the words. But I wished then, as I wish again now with all the fervour at my command, that they had never been uttered, that they had never needed to be uttered.

SOMETHING EVIL IN THE HOUSE

Celia Fremlin

LOOKING BACK, I find it hard to say just when it was that I first began to feel anxious about my niece, Linda. No—anxious is not quite the right word, for of course I have been anxious about her many times during the ten years she has been in my care. You see, she has never been a robust girl, and when she first came to live with me, a nervous, delicate child of twelve, she seemed so frail that I really wondered sometimes if she would survive to grow up. However, I am happy to say that she grew stronger as the years passed, and I flatter myself that by gentle, common-sense handling and abundant affection I have turned her into as strong and healthy a young woman as she could ever have hoped to be. Stronger, I am sure (though perhaps I shouldn't say this) than she would have been if my poor sister had lived to bring her up.

No, it was not anxiety about Linda's health that had troubled me during the past weeks; nor was it simply a natural anxiety about the wisdom of her engagement to John Barlow. He seemed a pleasant enough young man, with his freckled, snub-nosed face and ginger hair. Though I have to admit I didn't really take to him myself—he made me uneasy in some way I can't describe. But I wouldn't dream of allowing this queer prejudice of mine to stand in the way of the young couple—there is nothing I detest more than this sort of interference by the older generation.

All the same, I must face the fact that it was only after I heard of their engagement that I began to experience any qualms of fear about Linda—those first tremors of a fear that was to grow and grow until it became an icy terror that never left me, day or night.

I think it was in September that I first became aware of my uneasiness—a gusty September evening with autumn in the wind—in the trees—everywhere. I was cycling up the long gentle hill from the village after a particularly wearisome and inconclusive committee meeting of the Women's Institute. I was tired—so tired that before I reached the turning into our lane I found myself getting off my bicycle to push it up the remainder of the slope—a thing I have never done before. For in spite of my fifty-four years I am a strong woman, and a busy one. I cycle everywhere, in all weathers, and it is rare indeed for me to feel tired. Certainly the gentle incline between the village and our house had never troubled me before. But tonight, somehow, the bicycle might have been made of lead—I felt as if I had cycled fifteen miles instead of the bare one and a half from the village; and when I turned into the dripping lane, and the evening became almost night under the overhanging trees, I became aware not only of tiredness, but of an indefinable foreboding. The dampness and the autumn dusk seemed to have crept into my very soul, bringing their darkness with them.

Well, I am not a fanciful woman. I soon pulled myself together when I reached home, switched on the lights and made myself a cup of tea. Strong and sweet it was, the way I always like it. Linda often laughs at me about my tea—she likes hers so thin and weak that I sometimes wonder why she bothers to pour the water into the teapot at all, instead of straight from the kettle to her cup!

So there I sat, the comfortable old kitchen chair drawn up to the glowing stove, and I waited for the warmth and the sweet tea to work their familiar magic. But somehow, this evening, they failed. Perhaps I was really *too* tired; or perhaps it was the annoyance of noticing from the kitchen clock that it was already after eight. As I have told you, I am a busy woman, and to find that that tiresome meeting must have taken a good two hours longer than usual *was* provoking, especially as I had planned to spend a good long evening working on the Girls' Brigade accounts.

Whatever it may have been, somehow I couldn't relax. The stove crackled merrily; the tea was delicious; yet still I sat, tense and uneasy, as if waiting for something. And then, somehow, I must have gone to sleep, quite suddenly; because the next thing I knew I was dreaming. Quite a simple, ordinary sort of dream it will seem to you—nothing alarming, nothing even unusual in it, and yet you will have to take my word for it that it had all the quality of a nightmare.

I dreamed that I was watching Linda at work in the new house. I should explain here that for the past few months Linda has not been living here with me, but in lodgings in the little town where she works, about six miles from here. It is easier for her getting to and from the office, and also it means that she and John can spend their evenings working at the new house they have been lucky enough to get in the Estate on the outskirts of the town. It is not quite finished yet, and they are doing all the decorations themselves—I believe John is putting up shelves and cupboards and all kinds of clever fittings. I am telling you this so that you will see that there was nothing intrinsically nightmarish about the setting of my dream—on the contrary, the little place must have been full of happiness and bustling activity—the most unlikely background for a nightmare that you could possibly imagine.

Well, in my dream I was there with them. Not with them in any active sense, you understand, but hovering in that disembodied way one does in dreams—an observer, not an actor in the scene. Somewhere near the top of the stairs I seemed to be, and looking down I could see Linda through the door of one of the empty little rooms. It was late afternoon in my dream, and the pale rainy light gleamed on her flaxen-pale hair making it look almost metallic—a sort of shining grey. She had her back to me, and she seemed absorbed in distempering the far wall of the room—I seemed to hear that suck-sucking noise of the distemper brush with extraordinary vividness.

And as I watched her, I began to feel afraid. She looked so tiny, and thin, and unprotected; her fair, childlike head seemed poised somehow so precariously on her white neck—even her absorption in the painting seemed in my dream to add somehow to her peril. I opened my mouth to warn her—to warn her of I know not what—but I could make no sound, as is the way of dreams. It was then that the whole thing slipped into nightmare. I tried to scream—to run—I struggled in vain to wake up—and as the nightmare mounted I became aware of footsteps, coming nearer and nearer through the empty house. "It's only John!" I told myself in the dream, but even as the words formed themselves in my brain, I knew that I had touched the very core of my terror. This man whose every glance and movement had always filled me with uneasiness—already the light from some upstairs room was casting his shadow, huge and hideous, across the landing . . . I struggled like a thing demented to break the paralysis of nightmare. And then, somehow, I was running, running, running. . . .

I woke up sick and shaking, the sweat pouring down my face.

For a moment I thought a great hammering on the door had woken me, but then I realized that it was only the beating of my heart, thundering and pounding so that it seemed to shake the room.

Well, I have told you before that I am a strong woman, not given to nerves and fancies. Linda is the one who suffers from that sort of thing, not me. Time and again in her childhood I had to go to her in the night and soothe her off to sleep again after some wild dream. But for *me*, a grown woman, who never in her life has feared or run away from anything—for *me* to wake up weak and shaking like a baby from some childish nightmare! I shook it off angrily, got out of my chair and fetched my papers, and, as far as I can remember, worked on the Girls' Brigade accounts far into the night.

I thought no more about it until, perhaps a week or so later, the same thing happened again. The same sort of rainy evening, the same coming home quite unusually tired—and then the same dream. Well, not quite the same. This time Linda wasn't distempering; she was on hands and knees—staining the floor or something of the sort. And there were no footsteps. This time nothing happened at all; only there was a sense of evil, of brooding hatred, which seemed to fill the little house. Somehow I felt it to be focused on the little figure kneeling in its gaily patterned overall. The hatred seemed to thicken round her—I could feel giant waves of it converging on her, mounting silently, silkily till they hung poised above her head in ghastly, silent strength. Again I tried to scream a warning; again no sound came; and again I woke, weak and trembling, in my chair.

This time I was really worried. The tie between me and Linda is very close—closer, I think, than the tie between her and her mother could ever have been. Common-sense sort of person though I am, I could not help wondering whether those dreams were not some kind of warning. Should I ring her up, and ask if everything was all right? I scolded myself for the very idea! I mustn't give way to such foolish, hysterical fancies—I have always prided myself on letting Linda lead her own life, and not smothering her with possessive anxiety as her mother would have done.

Stop! I mustn't keep speaking of Linda's mother like this—of Angela—of my own sister. Angela has been dead many years now, and whatever wrong I may have suffered from her once has all been forgotten and forgiven years ago—I am not a woman to harbour grievances. But, of course, all this business of Linda's approaching marriage was bound to bring it back to me in a way. I couldn't help remembering that I, too, was once preparing a little house ready for my marriage; that Richard once looked into my eyes as John now looks into Linda's.

Well, I suppose most old maids have some ancient—and usually boring—love story hidden somewhere in their pasts, and I don't think mine will interest you much—it doesn't even interest me after all these years, so I will tell it as briefly as I can.

When I fell in love with Richard I was already twenty-eight, tall and angular, and a school-teacher into the bargain. So it seemed to me like a miracle that he, so handsome, gay and charming, should love me in return and ask me to marry him. Our only difficulty was that my parents were both dead, and I was the sole support of my young sister Angela. We talked it over, and decided to wait a year, until Angela had left school and could support herself.

But at the end of the year it appeared that Angela had set her heart on a musical career. Tearfully she begged me to see her through her first two years at college; after that, she was sure she could fend for herself.

Well, Richard was difficult this time, and I suppose one can hardly blame him. He accused me of caring more for my sister than for him, of making myself a doormat, and much else that I forget. But at last it was agreed to wait for the two years, and meantime to work and save for a home together.

And work and save we did. By the end of the two years we had bought a little house, and we spent our evenings decorating and putting finishing touches to it, just as Linda and John were doing now.

Then came another blow. Angela failed in her exams. Again I was caught up in the old conflict; Richard angry and obstinate, Angela tearful, and beseeching me to give her one more chance, for only six months this time. Once again I agreed, stipulating that this time was really to be the last. To my surprise, after his first outburst, Richard became quite reasonable about it; and soon after that he was sent away on a series of business trips, so that we saw much less of each other.

Then, one afternoon at the end of May, not long before the six months were up, something happened. I was sitting on the lawn correcting exercises when Angela came out of the house and walked slowly towards me. I remember noticing how sweetly pretty she looked with her flaxen hair and big blue eyes—just like Linda's now. The spring sunshine seemed to light up the delicacy of her too-pale skin, making it seem rare and lovely. She sat down on the grass beside me without speaking, and something in her silence made me lay down my pen.

"What is it, Angela?" I said. "Is anything the matter?"

She looked up at me then, her blue eyes full of childish defiance, and a sort of pride.

"Yes," she said. "I'm going to have a baby." She paused, looking me full in the face. "Richard's baby."

I didn't say anything. I don't even remember feeling anything. Even then, I suppose, I was a strong-minded person, who did not allow her feelings to run away with her. Angela was still talking.

"And it's no use blaming *us*, Madge," she was saying. "What do you expect, after you've kept him dangling all these years?"

I remember the exercise book open in front of me, dazzling white in the May sunshine. One of the children had written "Nappoleon"—like that, with two p's—over and over again in her essay. There must have been half a dozen of them just on the one page. I felt I would go mad if I had to go on looking at them, so I took my pen and crossed them out, one after another, in red ink. Even to this day I have a foolish feeling that I would still go mad if I ever saw "Nappoleon" spelt like that again.

I felt as if a long time had passed, and Angela must have got up and gone away ages ago; but no, here she was, still talking.

"Well, *you* may not care, Madge," she was saying. "I don't suppose you'd stop correcting your old exercises if the world blew up. But what about *me*? What am I to *do*?"

I simply had to cross out the last of the "Nappoleons" before I spoke.

"Do?" I said gently. "Why, Richard must marry you, of course. I'll talk to him myself."

Well, they were married, and Linda was born, a delicate, sickly little thing, weighing barely five pounds. Angela, too, was poorly. She had been terribly nervous and ill during her pregnancy and took a long time to recover; and it was tacitly agreed that there should be no more children. A pity, because I know Richard would have liked a large family. Strange how I, a strong, healthy woman who could have raised half a dozen children without turning a hair, should have been denied the chance, while poor, sickly Angela . . . Ah well, that is life. And I suppose my maternal feelings were largely satisfied by caring for poor delicate little Linda—but it seemed only natural that when first her father and then Angela died the little orphan should come and live with me. And indeed I loved her dearly. She was my poor sister's child as well as Richard's, and my only fear has been that I may love her too deeply, too possessively, and so cramp her freedom.

Perhaps this fear is unfounded. Anyway, it was this that prevented me lifting the telephone receiver then and there on that rainy September night, dialling her number, and asking if all was well. If I had done so, would it have made any difference to what followed? Could I have checked the march of tragedy, then and there, when I woke from that second dream? I didn't know. I still don't know. All I know is that as I sat there in the silent room, listening to the rain beating against my windows out of the night, my fears somehow became clearer—came to focus, as it were. I knew now, with absolute certainty, that what I feared had something to do with Linda's forthcoming marriage. Her marriage to John Barlow.

But what could it be? What *could* I be afraid of? He was such a pleasant, ordinary young man, from a respected local family; he had a good job; he loved Linda deeply. Well, he seemed to do so. And yet, as I thought about it, as I remembered the uneasiness I always felt in his presence, it occurred to me that this uneasiness—this anxiety for Linda's safety—was always at its height when he made some gesture of affection towards her—a light caress, perhaps—a quick, intimate glance across a crowded room. . . .

Common sense. Common sense has been my ally throughout life, and I called in its aid now.

"There is nothing wrong!" I said aloud into the empty room. "There is nothing wrong with this young man!"

And then I went to bed.

It must have been nearly three weeks later when I had the dream again. I had seen Linda in the interval, and she seemed as well and happy as I have ever known her. The only cloud on her horizon was that for the next fortnight John would be working late, and so they wouldn't be able to spend the evenings painting and carpentering together in the new house.

"But I'll go on by myself, Auntie," she assured me. "I want to start on the woodwork of that front room tonight. Pale green, we thought, to go with the pink . . ." So she chattered on, happily and gaily, seeming to make nonsense of my fears.

"It sounds lovely, dear," I said. "Don't knock yourself up, though, working too hard."

For Linda *does* get tired easily. In spite of the thirty years' difference in our age, I can always outpace her on our long rambles over the hills, and arrive home fresh and vigorous while she is sometimes quite white with exhaustion.

"No, Auntie, don't worry," she said, standing on tiptoe to kiss me—she is such a little thing—"I won't get tired. I'm so happy, I don't think I'll ever get tired again!"

Reassuring enough, you'd have thought. And yet, somehow, it didn't reassure me. Her very happiness—even the irrelevant fact that John would be working late—seemed somehow to add to the intangible peril I could feel gathering round her.

And three nights later I dreamed the dream again.

This time, she was alone in the little house. I don't know how I knew it with such certainty in the dream, but I did—her aloneness seemed to fill the unfurnished rooms with echoes. *She* seemed nervous, too. She was no longer painting with the absorbed concentration of my previous dreams, but jerkily, uncertainly. She kept starting—turning round—listening; and I, hovering somewhere on the stairs as before, seemed to be listening too. Listening for what? For the fear which I knew was creeping like fog into the little house? Or for something more?

"It's a dream!" I tried to cry, with soundless lips. "Don't be afraid, Linda, it's only a dream! I've had it before, I'll wake up soon! It's all right, I'm waking right now, I can hear the banging . . ."

I started awake in my chair, bolt upright, deafened by the now familiar thumping of my heart.

But was it my heart? Could that imperious knocking, which shook the house, be merely my heart? The knocking became interspersed with a frantic ringing of the bell. This was no dream. I staggered to my feet, and somehow got down the passage to the front door and flung it open. There in the rainy night was Linda, Linda wild and white and dishevelled, flinging herself into my arms.

"Oh, Auntie, Auntie, I thought you were out—asleep—I couldn't make you hear—I rang and rang. . . ."

I soothed her as best I could. I took her into the kitchen and made her a cup of the weak thin tea she loves, and heard her story.

And after all, it wasn't much of a story. Just that she had gone to the new house as usual after work, and had settled down to painting the front room. For a while, she said, she had worked quite happily; and then suddenly she had heard a sound—a shuffling sound—so faint that she might almost have imagined it.

"And that was all, really, Auntie," she said, looking up at me, shamefaced. "But somehow it frightened me so. I ought to have gone and looked round the house, but I didn't dare. I tried to go on working, but from then on there was such an awful feeling—I can't describe it—as if there was something evil in the house— something close behind me—waiting to get its hands round my throat. Oh, Auntie, I know it sounds silly. It's the kind of thing I used to dream when I was a little girl. Do you remember?"

Indeed I did remember. I took her on my lap and soothed her now just as I had done then, when she was a little sobbing girl, awake and frightened in the depths of the night.

And then I told her she must go home.

"Auntie!" she protested. "But Auntie, can't I stay here with you for the night? That's why I came. I *must* stay!"

But I was adamant. I can't tell you why, but some instinct warned me that, come what may, she must not stay here tonight. Whatever fear or danger might be elsewhere, they could never be as great as they would be here, in this house, tonight.

So I made her go home, to her lodgings in the town. I couldn't explain it to her, nor even to myself. In vain she protested that the last bus had gone, that her old room here was ready for her. I was immovable. I rang up a taxi, and as it disappeared with her round the corner of the lane, casting a weird radiance behind it, I heaved a great sigh of relief, as if a great task had been accomplished; as if I had just dragged her to shore out of a dark and stormy sea.

The next morning I found that my instinct had not been without foundation. There *had* been danger lurking round my house last night. For when I went to get my bicycle to go and help with the

Mother's Outing, I found it in its usual place in the shed, but the tyres and mudguard were all spattered with a kind of thick yellow clay. There is no clay like that anywhere between here and the village. Where could it have come from? Who had been riding my bicycle through unfamiliar mud in the rain and wind last night? Who had put it back silently in the shed, and gone as silently away?

As I stood there, bewildered and shaken, the telephone rang indoors. It was Linda, and she sounded tense, distraught.

"Auntie, will you do something for me? Will you come with me to the house tonight, and stay there while I do the painting and—sort of keep watch for me? I expect you'll think it's silly, but I *know* there was somebody there last night—and I'm frightened. Will you come, Auntie?"

There could be only one answer. I got through my day's work as fast as I could, and by six o'clock I was waiting for Linda on the steps of her office. As we hurried through the darkening streets, Linda was apologetic and anxious.

"I know it's awfully silly, Auntie, but John's still working late, and he doesn't even know if he'll finish in time to come and fetch me. I feel scared there without him. And the upstairs lights won't go on again—John hasn't had time to see the electricity people about it yet—and it's so dark and lonely. Do you think someone really *was* there last night, Auntie?"

I didn't tell her about the mud on my bicycle. There seemed no point in alarming her further. Besides, what was there to tell? There was no reason to suppose it had any connection . . .

"Watch out, Auntie; it's terribly muddy along this bit where the builders have been."

I stared down at the thick yellow clay already clinging heavily to my shoes; and straight in front of us, among a cluster of partially finished red brick houses, stood Linda's future home. It stared at us with its little empty windows out of the October dusk. A light breeze rose, but stirred nothing in that wilderness of mud, raw brickwork and scaffolding. Linda and I hesitated, looked at each other.

"Come on," I said, and a minute later we were in the empty house.

We arranged that she should settle down to her painting in the downstairs front room just as if she was alone, and I was to sit on the stairs, near the top, where I could command a view of both upstairs and down. If anyone should come in, by either front or back door, I should see them before they could reach Linda.

It was very quiet as I sat there in the darkness. The light streamed out of the downstairs room where Linda was working, and I could see her through the open door, with her back to me, just as she had been in my dream. How like poor Angela she was, with her pale hair and her white, fragile neck! She was working steadily now, absorbed, confident; reassured, I suppose, by my presence in the house. As I sat, I could feel the step of the stair behind me pressing a little into my spine—a strangely familiar pressure. My whole pose indeed seemed familiar—every muscle seemed to fall into place, as if by long practice, as I sat there, half leaning against the banisters, staring down into the glare of light.

And then, suddenly, I knew. I knew who it was who had cycled in black hatred through the rainy darkness and the yellow mud. I knew who had waited here, night after night, watching Linda as a cat watches a mouse. I knew what horror was closing in even now on this poor fragile child, on this sickly, puny brat who had kept *my* lovely, sturdy children from coming into the world—the sons and daughters *I* could have given Richard, tall and strong—the children he should have had—the children *I* could have borne him.

I was creeping downstairs now, on tiptoe, in my stockinged feet, with a light, almost prancing movement, yet silent as a shadow. I could see my hands clutching in front of me like a lobster's claws, itching for the feel of her white neck.

At the foot of the stairs now—at the door of the room—and still she worked on, her back to me, oblivious.

I tried to cry out, to warn her. "She's coming, Linda!" I tried to scream: "I can see her hands clawing behind you!" But no sound came from my drawn-back lips, no sound from my swift light feet.

Then, just as in my dream, there were footsteps through the house, quick and loud, a man's footsteps, hurrying, running, rushing—rushing to save Linda, to save us both.

EVERYBODY'S BIRTHDAY

Jeffry Scott

SOME PARTS OF London have more hard luck to the square yard than seems fair or reasonable.

Detective Constable Archie Grigg was often struck by that thought.

Grigg worked the triangle bounded by Rosetta Street, Great Northern Prospect and Cap-a-Pie Lane. Last-gasp respectability, drudgery treading water inches above the sharks of financial ruin, and a great deal of glumly matter-of-fact, little-league villainy flourished inside that triangle.

Yet when young Archie turned his back on Great Northern Prospect and strolled westwards, within minutes he would be passing parked Rolls Royces and Lamborghinis. Set off from Cap-a-Pie Lane, heading north, and there frowned the glass and concrete or Victorian fortresses of shipping, banking and insurance.

Archie Grigg found it odd and vaguely depressing. Where he worked, people were known to live in parked cars for weeks at a stretch. Close by were cars costing as much as a modest house. While not a political animal, DC Grigg couldn't help wondering what his clients made of it all.

"What this place needs," he muttered, "is a birthday."

Inspector Patsy Hanlon gave him a sharp glance. Both men wore jeans and sweaters; neither had shaved that morning. They seemed scruffy and aimless, as policemen should when keeping observation in a slum area.

A fish van was expected at the car park they decorated, and whatever the labels on its crates, the contents would be silver bullion stolen from City vaults the previous day. So they sat on the car park wall, smoking dog ends, scratching, and alternately swigging from and squabbling over an anonymous, gummy bottle holding nothing headier than cold tea. A touch theatrical, admittedly, but they awaited men as wary and observant as themselves, and needed to blend with the scenery.

"You keep rambling on about birthdays," Hanlon commented. "What's it in aid of, son?"

Caught out musing aloud, Grigg coloured. "I dunno, Boss. Just . . . well, there's a chronic shortage of smiles round here. If I ever come up on the Pools, I'll bung a few quid through every letterbox on the patch. What'd it cost, ten thousand, top whack? Worth every penny, startle a few sods into being happy."

Hanlon stared at him, a spark of humour in the unforgiving grey eyes. "Ah, a philanthropist. We get all kinds at Rosetta Street these days. You're a Pig, son, a mindless tool of the Fascist Establishment, so stop talking dirty."

A nervous hour crawled away, dragging anti-climactic minutes behind. Hanlon, eyes bleak again, ducked behind a derelict lorry and appeared to be relieving himself against the rear wheel. When he came out, his personal radio was in open sight, along with his temper.

"It's a stumer. That blasted van's still at Walthamstow, they must have split the stuff and taken it by cars. My pet grass has got a lot to answer for." DC Grigg pitied the Inspector's informer.

But Hanlon shook off the black mood as they walked back to the police station. "Mass birthday, eh? Quite a thought."

Grigg was never quite sure how to take his master. "Leave off, sir. I was only talking to pass the time."

Bristles rasped as the older man dragged a thumbnail along his jawline. "Rest easy, son—your secret's safe with me. Hey-up! *He's* had a birthday!"

A genuine tramp was approaching the pair of fakes, and even his shambling was jaunty. Several new ties adorned his collarless neck and his grimy wrist was loaded with cheap expanding-link watch straps.

Hanlon and DC Grigg exchanged speaking glances. The Inspector grimaced. "Sure he nicked 'em, no danger. But life's too short . . . and I want a shave."

Bell jingling jubilantly, a West Indian boy cycled past. Gaudy, pristine neckties streamed in the wind of his passage. An alarm clock, polished tin case molten in the sunlight, had been taped to his handlebars like a speedometer and its twin, slung from a bootlace lanyard, bumped against his chest.

Patsy Hanlon turned, breath indrawn to shout after the lad, and then thought better of it. Now he was frowning as they walked.

Nellie Wasserman has dispensed newspapers, magazines and simple-minded cheer from her stall opposite the Rosetta Street nick, ever since being orphaned by a V2 in 1945. The stall is a little nightmare of kipper boxes and the skeleton of a deckchair, ever under construction, never completed. It is illegal as hell. England can be like that.

Passing the stall, DC Grigg dug his superior officer in the ribs. "Bloody hellfire," Hanlon groaned, leaving spaces between the syllables.

Each shelf bore a brand new alarm clock, varying styles of tin and plastic, and the ticking suggested a positive infestation of death watch beetles. Inspector Hanson scrubbed his bristles in a frenzy.

Nellie being deaf and dumb, compounded the problem. Hanlon thrust his face close to the old girl's, shaping his lips to the words. "I'll be back for the *Sun* in ten minutes, gel. I don't want to see any clocks, then. Twig?"

She nodded solemnly, incuriously, already starting to stow the things away. Archie Grigg noticed that her layers of coats were decorated with a new artificial silk belt designed to adorn a male neck. . . .

Hanlon took the stairs to the CID office, three at a time. "Find out which shop's been done," he commanded. "Somewhere selling clocks and ties."

"And ballpens," Grigg added diffidently. "That tramp had a row of them in his top pocket, and I happen to know he can't write."

Hanlon's battery powered shaver hesitated in its buzzing. "Pens," he repeated neutrally. "Dear me. Gets better and better all the time."

The Inspector was less philosophical when Grigg reported that no local shops nor market stalls had been robbed. Decently attired by then in multiple tailor's blue pinstripe, Patsy Hanlon glared at him.

"Ruddy birthdays! You've wished this on us, Griggy-boy." Inspector Hanlon groped for a phrase. "Something's not right and it . . . offends me. Put yourself about, son. Find out what's happening, where that stuff's coming from. Poor old Nellie won't make any sense, but somebody must know. Find out, and I mean pronto."

Illogical as it was, Archie Grigg went on his way feeling that it was all his fault. . . .

The tramp could not be found and the West Indian cyclist had pedalled off the map. Grigg strode hither and thither across his triangular patch, eye cocked for a glint of metal, a flutter of colour—anything or nothing, he would know what when he saw it.

Eventually he found Samantha, nude to the waist, sitting on her front doorstep and pensively winding a wisp of auburn hair around a forefinger. At five years of age one can get away with wearing only navy blue knickers in the street.

Samantha had taken an old shoebox and balanced a shiny new alarm clock on top. The lid of the box, roughly folded into a peaked roof, surmounted the clock.

Archie Grigg squatted beside her. He had a niece about Samantha's age, and his own childhood was not so distant as to be beyond recall. "Model of Big Ben?" he hazarded.

"Nah, it's that big clock in the tower, Westminster way. I seen it once. We was in a bus as went past, Mum'n me. It's on telly a lot, too."

"Ah. Where'd you get the lovely clock, darlin'?"

"Present mine," Samantha replied laconically. "I gotter toy bus, see. Only it's lost itself just for the present, like. When I find it I'll run it past this—here and then it'll be me and Mum up West. Cor, Mister, it *was* Big Ben, I remember now."

"What's a present mine?"

Ask a silly question . . . "A mine with presents in." The girl sighed pettishly. "You go there and dig for your prezzies, like gold or . . . or . . ." Great intellectual effort. "Coal," she squeaked triumphantly.

"I bet you could show me where it is, this mine."

Samantha laughed shortly. "Gotter be joking." Reaching behind her, she pressed the doorbell.

Samantha's mother had the build and the instincts of a good welterweight. "Dirty old man trying to chat me, Mum," was Samantha's bland introduction.

Blushing and tangle-tongued, Archie Grigg fumbled his warrant card out in the nick of time. Half an hour later, chaperoned by Mrs O'Rourke, Samantha led him to a dankly hopeless entry within sound if not sight of busy Cap-a-Pie Lane. Developers had bought an arcade of shops and demolished most of them before running out of money. A supermarket, four-year-old prices still white-washed on fragments of shattered window, was the only undamaged building. Samantha took the adults down the side, to the goods entrance.

Grigg knew it was the place. Out of the wind, just right for a tramp dossing down. A mountain of empty boxes likely to attract Nellie, who was always reconstructing her ramshackle stall. Marks on the concrete of the yard, tucked beyond sight of passers-by in Cap-a-Pie Lane, showed that children had been using the space as a cycle speedway track.

Samantha trotted to a rank-smelling corner and a rubbish bin twice the height of a man. Working with the thoughtless speed and skill of habit, the girl built crates into a pyramid. Mounting it, she leaned into the bin, groped blindly, and came out with a handful of ties.

"I'll have those, my love." Archie Grigg secured the evidence. Samantha returned the crates to their heap.

"No sense letting everybody find my present mine."

"But you told Nellie?"

"Well, Nellie's my Gran. Not the real 'un, she's dead, but I've, like, adopted her."

Samantha's mother nodded over the girl's head. "That's right, sir. She takes Nellie sandwiches and that. There's no harm in it."

DC Grigg was studying the waste bin. "D'you think anyone else knew about your mine, Samantha?"

Pondering the question, she nodded. "There's an old tramp what kips down here, he prolly saw me getting stuff out. And there's Royston. He's gotter bike. I told him where to come, so as I could get a ride."

"Just like her Dad," Mrs O'Rourke confided. "General dealer, him—always swapping this for that and a share of something else. Dealt himself right into the Scrubs, so he has, reckless pig."

Hastily Archie Grigg took them home before returning to Rosetta Street nick.

Inspector Hanlon had been joined by the quiet and saturnine Detective Sergeant Sainte. "So it *was* birthday time all round." Hanlon was addressing the sergeant, and to Grigg's bafflement, Sainte was nodding, grinning, sharing a rueful joke.

"All that gear, brand new, tucked away," said Sainte, agreeing with a conclusion that had not been voiced. He sniffed consideringly. "Chummy will be long gone by now, though. His sort don't linger."

"I don't get it, Boss." DC Grigg was plaintive. "I can imagine kids nicking stuff and slinging some away. But nothing's been reported stolen, certainly not so much. It's . . . well, senseless."

"Shall I tell him, sir?" Evidently relishing the scene, Sergeant Sainte's thick lips were curling ever so slightly at the corners.

Patsy Hanlon grinned openly. "This is where experience tells, son. I'll even do the Sherlock Holmes number for you. When we check the contents of that bin, nothing there will have cost more than a couple of quid, and most of it will be around the 99 pee mark. Stand on me, Grigg, that's what we'll find."

Of course! But before Grigg could prove that he wasn't entirely slow on the uptake, Sainte had struck in. "Funny money, counterfeit money," he said sadly. "You set out with a bag of it and hit a district, as it might be ours. Then you keep buying items, breaking a fiver or a tenner every time. Just dear enough to make sense of offering a biggish note, but cheap enough to get a worthwhile amount of real money back."

Inspector Hanlon was tiring of the game. "Of course you have to keep stashing the stuff you buy, and that's how present mines are made. Any minute now that phone'll ring and the bank—the *first* bank, there'll be more—will be screaming blue murder. As the local traders pass the stuff back.

"Tasty, I don't think. Checking the shops, trying for a description of Chummy, getting Forensic on that bin, which is a laugh for a start, the way your mates have been mauling it about, Griggy-boy. Still, you did well, running it down sharpish."

Archie Grigg's pleasure lasted for at least a quarter of a second—until Sergeant Sainte cleared his throat.

"There's no rush about turning out the contents of the bin," Sainte mused aloud. "Chummy just might use it again. Good place. All right, he's shot his bolt in our manor, if he's got any sense. And funny money blokes aren't stupid. But he might be working the general area, far side of the railway line for instance. In which case . . . well, he might slip across to his old hidey-hole and dump some more gear."

Inspector Hanlon shrugged, lifted an eyebrow. "Gawd, you're

an optimist, Sainty. Why not, though? Grigg, you've done so well, you get the plum job."

Those who lust after promotion, learn to be satisfactory straight-men to comics with rank. "What job would that be, sir?" Archie Grigg heard himself asking, innocently.

Patsy Hanlon clicked his tongue. "You know, deep in your heart, son. Obbo on that supermarket yard—just in case."

It started to rain while Detective Constable Grigg was picking his observation point, and he was damp and chilled to the bone surprisingly soon thereafter. Shivering and solitary, Archie Grigg started to become a former potential philanthropist.

After three hours, he decided that he *hated* birthdays. . . .

TERROR RIDE

Berkely Mather

REG CARTER SAID, "Seventy acres. Too much for one man to work, not enough for two. Six inches of topsoil and it slopes the wrong way. Eight miles from the nearest village and perched on the edge of the moor. I'm going to sell the damned place."

"Yes, dear," said Ella dutifully.

"Sure, you'd like that, wouldn't you," snarled Reg. "Well, I'm *not* going to sell—see?"

"No, dear," said Ella.

"Can't you say anything but bloody 'yes, dear' and 'no, dear'?" demanded Reg; but she'd fallen into that trap before, so now she said nothing. She just refilled his cup of tea from the brownstone pot and moved the marmalade a tentative inch closer to him, and brushed an incipient tear from the corner of her eye with the back of her hand.

He gulped down the tea, scalded his mouth, cursed, and jumped to his feet. At the kitchen door he turned and scowled at her, and said in tones of deepest contempt, "That's right, snivel! No guts—that's your trouble."

She sat, shoulders drooped and hands folded limply in her lap, sniffling miserably until she heard the truck being coaxed into reluctant life in the shed across the farmyard, sputtering jerkily because of the trouble the starter always gave and which he was constantly swearing he was going to fix once and for all with a sledgehammer. She got up and went out into the soft but steady rain. He backed the truck out of the shed, swung around, and headed for the road, gunning the motor impatiently. She pattered through the mud and opened the gate.

"When will you be back, dear?" she asked timidly.

"How the hell do I know?" he shouted above the roar of the engine. "Six o'clock, seven o'clock or maybe eight. What difference does it make? It's market day—or had you forgotten that too?" He drove through, stopped, and added, "And shut the gate this time or you'll have the sheep in the bloody vegetables again."

She went back into the kitchen and took a cigarette from the pack she kept hidden behind the flour bin. He didn't like to see her smoke. It wasn't "farmer's-wifely," he said. She shivered and stood looking down at the glowing stove. Three years of it, she reflected. How much more could she take? She'd have left him long ago had it not been for Louise. Or would she?

He still had his good moments, when things were going reasonably well with the small, ill-paying farm—moments which if not exactly tender were at least amiable. She remembered their earlier days here, when he had given up his job in the land surveyor's office and put his savings and a small legacy from his mother into the farm. The work had been desperately hard but their hopes had been high and they had been happy. But now these recurring moods of his—

The waking whimpering of the baby in the bedroom above brought her back to the present. She dragged out the bathtub and spread towels on the rug in front of the stove, then poured hot water from the blackened iron kettle, added cold and tested it carefully with her bared elbow. She went up the narrow stairs and lifted the baby from her cradle, crooning over her and burying her face in the soft warmth of her woolly night clothes. The whimpering stopped and the baby crowed contentedly.

Ella undressed her and lowered her gently into the water, and then there was a knock at the door. She looked round, surprised. The postman was not due for an hour yet.

"Come in," she called. "It's not locked."

The door opened and two men entered, carefully closing it behind them. The one in the lead was short and tubby, with a round cherubic face and greying hair plastered flat with the rain. The other was tall and angular, younger, but with a deeply lined face and mean little eyes that didn't seem to focus properly. The older man was dressed in the mudstained ruins of what had once been a smart city suit; the other, more serviceably in jeans and a leather coat. The older man beamed at her delightedly.

"My dear!" he gushed. "What a picture of maternal beatitude. Would that I had the brush of a Rembrandt or a Botticelli." His voice was rich and plummy.

"I'm sorry," said Ella, confused. "My husband has just gone—"

"To market—like the little piggy in the nursery rhyme, while t'other one stayed at home," supplied the man. "So we heard from our hiding place, behind the shed." He sniffed ecstatically, his nostrils flaring. "Bacon? Do I smell bacon? Of your gentle charity, dear lady, just a dozen rashers, crisp but not frizzled, with four gloriously fresh farm eggs on top—*each*."

He yelped as the other man pushed past him and grabbed a piece of toast from the table. "Mind my wrist, you clumsy clod!" he swore, and Ella saw for the first time the handcuffs that linked the older man's right wrist to the other's left. "Forgive my language, my dear," he went on. "This fellow is a trial. An average prison population of thirty-seven thousand, so the statistics say, and unkind Fate has to pair me with this moron."

Ella had risen from her knees beside the bathtub and had wrapped the baby in a towel. Her eyes slid sideways toward the door. The older man smiled gently, chidingly, at her and waggled a finger of his free left hand.

"Ah, no, my dear," he admonished. "It would be highly inadvisable to take the little darling from a warm bath out into the cold rain. Give her to me." He held out his left arm. Ella backed away quickly, her eyes widening. The thin man lurched forward and gripped her by the arm, hard. Ella bit back a moan and clutched the baby tighter.

"Do as you're told, stupid," he snarled. "Unless you want to get hurt."

"Please—please—" whispered Ella. "Let me put her back in her cradle upstairs. I'll get you anything you want then—food—"

"Of course you will," cooed the older man. "Could a mother's heart be anything but compassionate? But I'll take little ducksie-wucksie." He eased the baby away from her. "And now get on with the breakfast. *I* have the patience of a saint, but I fear for my friend."

He lowered his voice confidentially. "His fourth conviction for grievous bodily harm, you know. He's in—*was* in—for fourteen years." He smiled gently and backed away to a rocking chair by the stove, drawing the thin man with him. The baby started to wriggle, and then to wail. He made soothing noises and pulled the other man's arm toward him as he wrapped the towel more comfortably about her.

Ella stood looking at them in an agony of indecision. The thin man snarled again like a vicious animal and raised his free right arm threateningly. Ella hurriedly got bacon and a bowl of eggs from a shelf by the window, poked up the fire, and put on a big frying pan. The baby's wailing had ceased for the moment and she lay in the crook of the older man's arm, looking up at him with wide eyes.

"*That's* better," he said with deep satisfaction. "Dogs and children—they take to Uncle Robert like magic." He looked up at the clock on the mantelpiece. "The news," he said. "Make a long arm for the radio, Grotters."

The other man reached out to the old-fashioned set on a side table and switched on the radio. A burst of pop music filled the room. "Not that, you idiot," said his companion.

The other made adjustments of the dial and an announcer's voice came up: "—as the motor coach conveying them from the Ilchester Assizes skidded off the road and overturned. The thirty convicts, who were being taken to the County Gaol after sentence, were linked in pairs by handcuffs. Six pairs made a break, but five have been recaptured. The remaining pair is still at large. They are Robert Finsome, sentenced to five years for false pretences, and Thomas Grottersley, sentenced to fourteen years for robbery with violence and grievous bodily harm. The public are particularly warned of the latter. He is described as being a man of enormous physical strength but of very low mentality and—"

The thin man swore filthily and switched off.

"Oh, come now," chuckled the other. "You mustn't be oversensitive, Grotters. We can't *all* be members of the criminal intelligentsia. Anyhow, that enormous physical strength of yours is going to be useful in removing this wretched jewellery from our lily-white wrists."

"Shut your damn mouth," Grottersley said savagely, and added to Ella. "Get a move on with that grub, you."

Half an hour later, fed and replete, they sat in front of the fire on adjoining chairs, the baby in a carry-cot beside them, while Ella prepared the baby's food in a saucepan.

Finsome said, "And now, my dear, let us discuss tactics. Who normally calls here during the day?"

"Only the postman," she answered dully. "He's due about now." She glanced over her shoulder at the window through which could be seen a stretch of the lonely moorland road, running arrow-straight for half a mile until it disappeared into a dip between the low surrounding hills. Finsome stood up and peered out through the driving rain.

"Admirably sited," he said approvingly. "It couldn't be better. And how does the postman actually deliver your mail?"

"He drives the post-office van," she answered. "He usually comes in here for a cup of tea."

Grottersley leered meaningfully at her, and Finsome regarded him with disapproval.

"Really, Grotters," he said severely. "That's most uncalled for." He turned to Ella. "At the same time, my dear, that's the way this cynical old world is inclined to jump to conclusions. Especially in regard to such a young and pretty woman as yourself—and in such a lonely place."

"My husband is always here," she said, flushing. "Well, most days."

"But not *this* day," said Finsome. "You must discourage the postman, kindly but firmly, and in a manner not likely to arouse his suspicions. Do you understand?"

"She'd better understand, unless she wants a belt on the ear," growled Grottersley. "Make him shove the letters under the door, and tell him to buzz off. Tell him your old man's suspicious, and he's looking for him with a pitchfork. And make it real convincing, because we'll be holding the baby—out of sight."

"No—please—" she gasped. "Don't take her out of the kitchen. I promise you I won't say anything to him."

"Of course you won't," Finsome said soothingly. "We trust you implicitly. But there's no need for you to be as coarse as my friend has suggested. Tell him you're just about to give the baby a bath."

Grottersley looked past him through the window. "Here he is now," he said tensely. Down the rainswept road a red van had appeared. Finsome picked up the carry-cot and made for the stairs, but Grottersley held him back.

"There's two of 'em," he said, pointing. "Look—the other's a cop. You can see his helmet through the windshield. The pig!"

The van rolled up to the gate and stopped, and two figures in oilskins got out. Finsome passed the carry-cot to Grottersley, awkwardly by its twin handles, nearly dropping the baby on to the stone floor. He shouldered the frantic Ella to one side and shot the bolt on the kitchen door.

"Watch it!" he whispered. "I'm warning you. Grottersley is holding the baby. Fourteen years—life—what's the difference? Don't try anything."

They went quickly through the door leading to the stairs. There was a peremptory rap at the other door.

"Sorry, Arthur," Ella called shakily. "You can't come in. I'm—I'm just going to give the baby a bath."

"Two of us here," said the postman. "I've got the Law with me."

"Sergeant Hunt, Mrs Carter," said another, more formal, voice. "Just doing the rounds of the outlying farms. There's a couple of escaped prisoners on the run. You may have heard it on the radio—"

"I did," she said breathlessly.

"Nothing to worry about really. They wouldn't be fools enough to make for the moors in this weather," the policeman went on. "But it's best to be on the safe side. Keep your eyes open for any strangers hanging around, and warn Mr Carter to do the same. If you do see anybody you don't recognize, get the station on the phone immediately. All right?"

"I'll do that," she answered, and some letters slid in under the door.

"Three bills and a circular," said the postman. "Read 'em myself on the way up. So long."

"So long," Ella replied. She leaned against the door, her knees shaking under her. Squelching footsteps receded on the other side, then came the sound of the motor starting up, and the van bumped slowly along the rutted farm road.

The two men came back into the kitchen. The baby, hungry, had started to wail complainingly. Ella flew at them and snatched the carry-cot from Grottersley, her eyes blazing hate. Finsome beamed.

"Splendid, my dear," he said enthusiastically. "A perfect performance. Now, a mite more of your willing co-operation and we'll be on our way. Tools—we need tools. Anything your husband has in the way of strong metal shears, files, that sort of thing—"

But she wasn't listening. She had the carry-cot beside her on a chair and she was once more heating the baby's food. Grottersley stepped up to her and gripped her arm cruelly. She winced, but continued to stir the contents of the saucepan.

"We're talking to you, beautiful," he said. "Pay attention."

"They're in the shed outside," she told him.

"Well, go and get 'em." He started to push her toward the door, but she shook free and returned to her task. He swung, backhanded, knocking her across the room. She came hard up against the wall and slid down on to her knees. A thin trickle of blood appeared at the corner of her mouth. Finsome tut-tutted reproachfully.

"There's no need for that sort of thing—we hope," he said. "Run along and get them, there's a good girl."

She dragged herself to her feet, shaking her head slowly from side to side as if to clear it.

"The baby," she mumbled. "Let me take her with me. I'm not leaving her with—with him—"

"Now that's silly, isn't it?" Finsome chided her. "*I'll* look after the baby. Off you go. Hurry, dear, for your own sake. The sooner we're rid of these things, the sooner we'll be gone."

She hesitated a moment longer. Grottersley stepped toward her. She moved to the door, stifling a sob, and slid back the bolt and went out. The men moved to where they could keep her in view. They could see her in the open-fronted shed groping round the shelves inside and collecting what she found in a gunny sack.

She returned to them and Grottersley grabbed the sack and tipped the contents on to the floor. Ella went back to the stove. She wiped the blood from her mouth with her apron and taste-tested the heat of the food, then knelt beside the baby, coaxing her with the spoon.

"Pliers, two wrenches, a hammer, a bloody blunt saw, and two wood files," Grottersley raged at her. "Do you mean to say this is all you've got?"

"Not very promising," gloomed Finsome. "Are you sure there's nothing more there?" he asked over his shoulder.

"That's the lot," she said listlessly.

They toiled for over an hour, ruining the saw and rubbing the files smooth without any noticeable effect on the tough steel of the chain connecting the two handcuffs.

"Give us the hammer," Grottersley said at last. "You can spring the lock sometimes, if you know where to hit."

They laid their wrists together on the hearthstone.

"Careful," quavered Finsome anxiously.

Grottersley struck a half dozen cautious blows on his own handcuff without success, then turned the heavy hammer on to that of Finsome's, with considerably more force. The fourth blow glanced off the steel and there was a spurt of blood from the older man's wrist. He bellowed and overbalanced, writhing on the floor in agony, and pulling Grottersley over with him.

Ella, nursing the baby to sleep in the rocker, slipped her quickly into the carry-cot and dived for the hammer, but Grottersley had regained his feet. He kicked her, catching her in the ribs. She gasped and tried to rise. He kicked again, harder, and she collapsed and lay still. . . .

Reg Carter stopped at the gate and sounded the horn. Through the rain he could see the warm glow of the lamp in the kitchen window, but there was no answering movement inside. He sounded the horn again, waited, then got out, cursing, and opened the gate himself.

He drove through and garaged the truck in the shed, then gathered up some bundles and ploughed through the mud to the kitchen door. He opened it and went in, shaking water from himself like a wet poodle.

"Why the hell didn't you open the gate for me?" he yelled angrily. Then a stone pickling jar hit his skull and he went down like a log. Grottersley grabbed him by the collar and pulled him across the kitchen and up the stairs. Finsome, his injured hand bound in a bloodstained towel, walking beside them, whimpering and moaning.

They went into the bedroom. Ella, trussed and gagged on the bed, turned the whites of her eyes toward them. One-handed, Grottersley heaved Reg's inert body on to the bed beside her.

"Company for you," he grunted. "He ain't dead. The jerk ought to be—keeping a stinking set of tools like that around the house." He took the loose end of the clothesline that was binding Ella, and with his right hand and Finsome's left they managed to tie Carter securely. Then they returned downstairs. Grottersley doused the oil lamp and they went out to the truck. He opened the door on the passenger's side and grunted, "Get in first and move over to the wheel. What the hell are you waiting for?"

"How on earth do you expect *me* to drive?" snuffled Finsome. "One hand injured and the other shackled to you."

"You'll have to manage. Come on, get a move on. We haven't got all night."

"But I can't, you fool!" howled Finsome. "Don't you see—if I'm on the right our linked hands will be crossing in front of us. If you're behind the wheel our linked hands will be between us, and we can move the gearshift together—"

"But I can't drive," Grottersley told him, and the other man stared at him in dismay.

"You—you mean you don't know *how* to drive?" he gasped.

"'S'right. Never had the chance to learn," Grottersley mumbled. "In quod when most kids of my age was getting their licences— and I been in and out ever since. You know what it's like—"

"Oh, my God," moaned Finsome. "What a time to tell me this." He thought for some moments, then said, "Only one thing for it. The girl will have to drive."

"What if she makes a squawk, or jumps out or something when we get into traffic?" questioned Grottersley doubtfully.

"She won't—not if we've got the brat in the back with us," Finsome said positively, and the other gaped at him admiringly.

"Why the hell didn't we think of that in the first place?" he said, "Come on, let's get her."

They hurried back through the darkness, into the house and up the stairs.

"A little drive for you," Finsome explained as Grottersley untied her bonds. "And baby comes too—and nothing will happen to her as long as you behave sensibly."

She was screaming incoherently even as Grottersley untied the silk stocking that was gagging her. "I won't—I won't, I tell you!"

Grottersley slapped her hard across the face. "All right then, stay here. But the kid goes with us, see?"

She rolled to the edge of the bed and tottered to her feet, biting back a moan as the circulation started again in her cramped limbs.

Five minutes later they were in the truck. Ella in front behind the wheel and the men in the back, with the baby warmly wrapped in everything woollen that Ella could find, crying complainingly in the carry-cot between them.

"Shove something over her mouth, for God's sake," Finsome said irritably and Ella screamed again.

"No—no—you'll smother her," she cried out. "Let her ride in front with me—I'll keep her quiet—"

"Get on with it or I'll go to work on her," Grottersley threatened.

The faulty starter jammed and under her inexpert directions they had to climb out again and rock the truck into second gear to free it. The motor started finally and she backed out, swung around, and headed for the gate.

"You'll have to get out and open it," she shouted to them. "If I take my foot off she'll stall."

Raging and cursing they climbed over the tailboard again, but they took the carry-cot with them, and her half-formed plan to make a dash for it was stillborn.

"We're going to Portsmouth," Finsome told her as they climbed in again. "There's an all-night diner there called Jack's Snackery, just outside town."

"Portsmouth?" she gasped. "But that's over a hundred miles away."

"Then you'd better step on it," Grottersley said. "And listen—if we're stopped tell 'em your old man has had an accident and you're going for the doctor."

"That might send them to the farm," Finsome said. "No—a sick animal. You're going to the vet for some medicine."

A light swung slowly from side to side signalling them to halt as they turned on to the main road six miles farther on. Grottersley, on his knees behind her, chattered with terror. Finsome pulled him down beside him on to the floor of the truck, under some empty wheat sacks.

"Tell them," he ground out. "And make it convincing. I'm warning you—if they look inside the kid's done for."

It was the police, but represented only by a very wet Sergeant Hunt. He came up to the truck and raised his lamp.

"Oh, it's you, Mrs Carter?" he said, surprised.

"Don't stop me," she begged. "The stud ewe—sick. Medicine from the vet. My husband is sitting up with her—"

He stepped back and waved her on. From the back came vague noises of approval and relief as the truck sped down the main road.

"Keep it like that," Grottersley said, "and nobody's going to get hurt."

But ten miles farther on she fumbled a gear change; the truck stalled and the starter jammed again. She put it into reverse and let it run backward down the rear slope, slipping her clutch as she had seen her husband do; but she misjudged and the rear wheels finished in the roadside ditch.

Screaming obscenely, the men got out, taking the carry-cot with them and putting it over the hedge into a field; but nothing they could do would rock the starter free this time. The rain was coming down in a solid sheet now, and Ella was sobbing frantically. "The baby! The baby! She'll catch her death of cold! Please—please put her back inside. I'll do anything—anything—"

"Then *do* it!" Grottersley shouted, punching her hard.

She remembered then in her extremity. "It's a thing called the bendix drive," she said. "My husband puts a screwdriver in and pushes against something and—"

"Don't talk about it! Get on with it!" yelled Finsome.

She fumbled in the toolbox and ran round to the front of the truck and raised the heavy, rear-hinged bonnet, propping it up on its strut. She made ineffectual jabs at the flywheel casing—and then, like a blinding flash of light, the idea came to her. She straightened and turned to the two men crowding close in on her.

"It's no good," she said. "My hand's not strong enough. I'll show you where it is. If one of you—"

"Give me the bloody thing," snarled Grottersley, and snatched the screwdriver from her.

"There," pointed out Ella. She guided his free right hand down into the dark cavern of the engine space. "If you'll hold it—"

She jumped back, sweeping the strut away, and the heavy hood clanged down, and her whole weight was on it, and Grottersley was screaming and trying to push her away with his other hand; but Finsome was shackled to that one, and he wasn't co-operating—and the night was being split with their concerted howls of pain when the police car swept up. . . .

Ella was crooning over the baby in the back seat of the police car. In front a policeman was talking into a microphone.

"The woman and the baby are all right, but one of the blokes has got his hand just about chopped off, and the other seems to have gone nuts. Hurry with that ambulance. Over."

"There, there, my precious," whispered Ella. "*Silly* men shouting and making all that fuss about nothing—and frightening Mummy's little darling."

SETTLED OUT OF COURT

Cyril Donson

I'D NEVER SEEN Jack Ledger in such an affable mood. My first thought was that my favourite copper must be sickening for something. When he welcomed me like a long lost brother into his office, I was sure of it.

"I guessed you'd be along sooner or later. I reckon we must have the biggest part of the Fleet Street Press in town. You here on duty this time? . . . not visiting your sister?"

"Business," I confirmed. "But having my sister living close will save me having to fight for a room at one of the local hotels. So you finally nailed those two Maltese bastards?"

"Yes. They'll be in court tomorrow morning for the first hearing, and this time they won't wriggle out of it. Not even their shyster lawyer is going to do them any good."

"That's great news. Coming so soon after your promotion, it can't do you any harm with the powers above. Is there anything in it for me . . . I mean. . . ?"

"I know what you mean," he said, giving me a disapproving look, not as harshly critical as usual, probably because he was feeling good. "And the answer this time is no. You'll take what all the others take. It's all sewed-up. You'll be in court tomorrow?"

"Of course. Maybe I'll nose around a bit. You never know. I might come up with some angle nobody else will have."

"You never give up do you? Christ, the slating we sometimes get in your papers, seems to me you crime reporters in the city make us look like angels of mercy."

I grinned at him. "Oh but you *are*, Jack. You shouldn't believe everything you read in the papers. Come on, I'll buy you a drink."

"It won't do you any good," he said darkly. "Like I said—"

"Okay, okay. Come on Jack, let's forget the case and talk over old times. You'n me were at school together."

When we left the station together he was still eyeing me with suspicion. We looked in at the Mason's Arms. You couldn't shift in there for reporters. I steered him back out and we finished up in the quieter Miner's Welfare.

"Anybody would think you can't stand the company of your own breed," said Jack.

"I was only thinking of you," I lied glibly. "You don't want all that lot round your neck. I'm going to have a pint, what will you have?"

"Whisky," he said with a leer. "A double."

I ordered and we found a table with no bother. He sipped his drink, set it down, and said:

"All right. What do you want to know, Russ?"

I drank some beer. It was a real treat to get Yorkshire ale again.

"Just a brief run-down and anything the opposition might not have been told . . . even if it's not for publication."

"Okay. Here it is. You're familiar with the background of the Hazeen brothers. They did a flit from London five years ago after the big clean-up there on porn, drugs, pimpery and gambling, when the Vittorio mob got big sentences. We had a tip-off to keep an eye on their activities when they moved to Sheffield."

"And you saw nothing suspicious. They set up legitimate businesses, and seemed to have given up their bad ways. But two years after they'd taken up residence in the West Riding, as it was before the conniving politicians changed it for their own reasons, the crime rate began to soar."

"Right . . . especially the incidence of drugs, porn . . . the whole shebang. We got very close to the Hazeens, but never had enough to take 'em to court. We pulled in a fair number of the smaller fry. None of them would talk. We've never given up trying. Finally, a week ago, we had a stroke of luck. We found a witness, somebody with enough on the brothers to put 'em away for a long time."

He went silent for a moment. Impatiently I prompted him:

"Well?"

"Oh . . . aye. It was one of those things, you know. We pulled in a pusher, feller called Fletcher. His name rang a bell, so we did some checking. When we were able to show him proof that his own daughter, a kid of seventeen, had been roped in by one of the pimps working for the brothers, Fletcher went berserk. When he found out that his daughter was working part-time as a prostitute . . ."

"Typical, eh?" I remarked with some cynicism. "The bastard had no conscience about helping other folk's youngsters become drug addicts, but when his own daughter is involved—"

"Right," said Jack. "But, bastard or not, he made a statement that is going to put the Hazeens where they belong. Seems Fletcher is one of the few trusted lieutenants who meet the brothers . . . and take a percentage of all their activities. We didn't even have to work on him, promise to put in a word for him if he turned State's evidence."

"I can imagine. Any response from the Hazeens' lawyer?"

"Naturally. The usual protests, questions, everything and anything to try to convince us we've backed another loser. Only I reckon he knows bloody well that this time, they're on a loser."

"I take it you've got Fletcher in custody?"

"He's on bail. That was part of the deal. But we've got him at a secret address, with a round-the-clock police guard outside." And before I could even put the question, he added: "No, I won't tell you where we've got him. And no, you can't talk to him."

We had another drink and before we'd finished these, we were joined by a man I didn't know, until memory started a half-forgotten train of thought. And then I recognized him. He was older, but I was certain it was the same man. When Jack introduced us, this was confirmed.

"This is Detective-Sergeant Olroyd. He's been with us a year. Mick, I'd like you to meet an old friend of mine, Russ Kidd."

We shook hands. "Hi," he said. "What's your line then?"

"He's a crime reporter, the best," said Jack. "Probably."

I grimaced at him good-naturedly. But watching Olroyd, I saw the freeze set in. After that he didn't look my way again, and pointedly ignored me.

He discussed some police business with Jack and then left. Jack looked at me wryly. "Olroyd doesn't like reporters."

"Funny you should say that," I said. "That was the feeling I got." I noticed a frown on Jack's face that hadn't been there before. Curious, I said:

"Correct me if I'm wrong, but I also get the feeling you're not too happy about him?"

His good mood suddenly evaporated, he said: "Too dam' right I'm not. He was sent to us from London—"

"Yes, I know," I said. "They moved him from the city."

"Then you know why?"

"Yes. The story goes that he duffed up some rapists in the cells. They transferred him to an office job because he was too rough. But I didn't know he'd been transferred up here."

Neither of us said much more about it after Jack had told me that he'd had quite a headache with Olroyd.

When I arrived at my sister's place later, they'd been half-expecting me. Her husband Maurice had just got in from work. We sat down to the typical gargantuan Yorkshire midday dinner.

"We thought you'd be coming, Russ," said Maurice. "This trial coming up has stirred quite a bit of interest locally. We all knew the Hazeen brothers were a right couple of bastards. Time they got their come-uppance. They ought to have let that new copper, Olroyd, loose on 'em. He's just what we need these days, a few really tough ones to dish out to these thugs a bit of what they like to hand out to defenceless old folk."

Gladys said: "Maurice is right. The trouble in this country today is we have too many crackpot psychiatrists and do-gooders. There's only one way to fight fire . . . and that's with fire."

After dinner I got Maurice talking, hoping to pick up maybe one or two fresh angles on the Hazeens, but he didn't know as much as I did. Later at the club, when we went for a drink, he introduced me to a smart-looking man I'd not seen on previous visits. He had the look of an executive type and I guessed he must be around fifty. But he looked ten years older.

I learned why, from Maurice, when the man moved on to join friends at another table.

"He's the new bank manager at the Yorkshire Bank, George Smith. And if anybody had cause to hate the guts of those Hazeens, he does," Maurice informed me.

"Tell me about it," I said.

"You notice he looks years older than he ought to? He's got good reason. He's a nice bloke, educated, tried to bring up his only son to be decent. The lad did well, went to university, and he was all set for a brilliant career, until . . ."

"He got on to drugs?" Maurice nodded, his homely face reflecting his inexpressible disgust.

"It happened on his long summer vacation. He got really hooked. He finished up a hospital case, a human wreck, his career gone for a burton."

Grimly, I said: "There's too many like him."

I'd never seen Maurice look so murderous when he said: "I'm telling you, Russ, all my life I've been a decent citizen, and you know I'm a quiet, peaceful kind of bloke, but if that had been my lad, I'd have killed those two bastards myself."

"I know how you feel," I said. "But you can't take the law into your own hands."

He exploded with a hard, sardonic laugh. "You're joking! The law today is a bloody farce. Just look what happened the other day—a bloke is fined £200 for doing a soccer match streak. A few days before that a youth who stabbed and nigh on killed another one was fined £25 and sent home. Don't talk to me about law. No wonder decent coppers get cheesed and go bent."

I decided to have an early night to be fresh for the court preliminary hearing next day. The court was in Sheffield which would mean a twelve mile drive in heavy traffic from my sister's place in Mexborough.

But it wasn't to be. Suddenly the whole Hazeen case blew up in Jack Ledger's face. He rang me just before nine p.m. to give me the shock news.

"Fletcher's been shot dead. The news hasn't got out yet. Thought you'd like to be in on it. I'll wait for you in my office."

When I arrived at the station, Jack was shattered. Olroyd was like a human volcano, all churned-up with a rage so excessive he was sending out warning signals. Jack was pulling rank and telling him in no uncertain manner to cool it.

He told me what had happened. "We had a man watching the hotel, front and back, and another in the main reception lobby. We warned Fletcher to keep his head down. The bloody fool must have been standing at the window. Somebody killed him with one shot."

"An expert job," I said. "Sounds like a contract shooting. But here?"

Olroyd cut in, plainly finding it difficult to hide his blazing fury. "Those two bastards knew their goose was cooked. It had to be them who brought in a hit-man. I think we should go bring them in."

Jack gave him a weary look. "Use your loaf. If the Hazeens planned this you can be dam' sure they had an alibi with plenty of witnesses."

"Aren't you even going to—?" demanded Olroyd.

"Olroyd, if you use that tone of voice to me just once more, I'll put you back in uniform. Don't teach me my job. The Hazeens are being checked out right now. And we already know what the result of that will be."

It proved to be exactly as Jack had predicted. The Hazeen brothers, at the estimated time of the killing, were having dinner with their lawyer and at least a dozen independent witnesses present.

I didn't sleep much that night, and I figured Jack didn't either.

The court hearing was even more brief than had been expected. Prosecuting counsel told the court that, the only witness for the prosecution now being deceased, he had no alternative but to withdraw. The case was dismissed and the Hazeens smugly left the courtroom, pausing on their way out to say to Jack and Olroyd at his elbow:

"No hard feelings, superintendent?"

Jack ignored them, but Olroyd, keeping his voice low, almost hissing the venomous words, said:

"You may be feeling spry now, you two bastards, but I'll get you both before long, I promise you."

Jack pulled Olroyd away and glared at him. We waited until the Hazeens had had time to get away before we all trooped out dismally.

I drove back to Mexborough doing some heavy thinking. I knew most of the villains in the district, but they were petty crooks and unlikely to get mixed up in any of the Hazeen brothers' rackets. I was looking for a possible lead to the killer, somebody with his ear to the ground who might owe me a favour, and come up with some information.

I'd almost given up the notion. Then I remembered Bill Barwell. He'd done time but was going straight, almost. He ran a rooming house for characters passing through or staying, who were ex-cons. I knew Jack would check all the obvious places. I decided to check this one myself.

I was too late. Barwell informed me that he'd had a man there, a feller he thought was a musician. But only half an hour earlier Olroyd had called.

"He went up to the man's room, was up there maybe fifteen

minutes then came down and left. You didn't miss him by much. He just told me to keep my nose clean."

"The man is still in his room?"

"Yeah. I've been here all the time and I'd have seen him if he'd gone out. I think Olroyd was looking for somebody but this feller ain't the one."

I agreed it looked that way, thanked Barwell and left. But I couldn't shake off a feeling that there was something not just right. The feeling persisted all through dinner at my sister Gladys's place. Finally, after dinner, I went to see Jack.

He was up to his neck in it. He had men out checking every possible place the hit-man might have stayed. He'd had the reporters clamouring for news. His nerves were frayed and he didn't look at all pleased to see me.

But he took another two tablets and fixed me with a glazed look. "I suppose you've been doing some checking. You come up with anything?"

"No. Have you had somebody check out Barwell's lodging house?"

"Now you're starting to question the way I do my job. For Chris' sake. Of course I have. Olroyd was doing that one."

"Has he been back?"

"Not yet. You got some special reason for asking?"

"I don't really know, Jack," I said. "It's just a feeling I have in my bones . . ."

I told him I'd gone to Barwell's place and what the latter had told me. Jack gave me an odd look.

"So? Olroyd checked the man, found it wasn't the one we're looking for, and went on to his next routine call—"

"I suppose you're right. It was just a feeling, and knowing what Olroyd is like—"

Jack considered. "You and your bloody hunches. What are you trying to suggest?"

"It wouldn't hurt to check Barwell's place again—"

He went quiet for a couple of minutes, then, impulsively, he said: "You're a freak. You know that? But these peculiar hunches of yours have been right in the past . . . okay. Let's go take a look. And I warn you, if you've been wasting my time—"

But the phone rang before we were through the doorway.

The shock on Jack's face, when he took the call, transmitted itself to me. He replaced the receiver and looked at me, his stare even more glazed.

"That was Mayfield's secretary. She just got back to the lawyer's office and found three men shot dead . . . the Hazeen brothers and their lawyer . . ."

"Christ," I exclaimed. And the odd feeling was there again nagging at me even more urgently.

"Jack . . ." I began. He nodded, looking like death warmed up.

"Yeah. Let's go and check. And we'd better make it fast."

Driving him to the lodging house I knew what Jack must be thinking, how he must be feeling. I was hoping to God what I suspected wouldn't be true.

I parked away from the building. We went inside. It took Jack only two minutes to persuade Barwell to produce a spare key and open the door of the room Olroyd had gone to.

We found the man gagged and handcuffed to the bed-rail. Jack looked sick.

"Right," he said. "Leave him the way he is."

We all left the room and Jack locked the door. "We'll wait downstairs. Is there some place we can watch without being seen, Barwell? I want to see who comes in and goes up those stairs."

Barwell suggested we crouch behind the reception desk. We took up our positions, Jack cautioning Barwell to act naturally. Barwell assured us he would. But he looked puzzled.

Olroyd arrived twenty minutes later. He went straight up to the room we'd checked. Minutes later he came back down with the man in handcuffs.

"Get me a call through to the police station. I want to talk to Superintendent Ledger."

We waited, let him make his call. When told Jack wasn't available he said: "Get word to him I've caught the hit-man. Tell him I went after the suspect and was too late to stop him shooting the Hazeens and their lawyer. I overheard enough to work it out they refused to pay him what he was asking for the job he'd done."

That was the moment Jack showed himself. Grimly he said: "Olroyd, you're under arrest."

I never felt more sorry for Jack. Nothing worse could have dropped into his lap than a bent copper. Olroyd was suspended and his statement taken, then he was formally charged with three murders.

The news was not given out at once, Jack issuing only a statement that Olroyd had been suspended from duty and that a police inquiry was being made.

My hunch had been right, but Jack never thanked me. I didn't expect him to. I saw Olroyd's statement. He admitted that after finding the hit-man he had "lost his cool" and his hatred of the Hazeens had got the better of him. He admitted taking the hit-man's gun, intending to kill the brothers and their crooked lawyer, and make it look like the hit-man had done the job. But . . . he swore, he did not kill them, because when he arrived at the office he'd found all three already dead.

Jack was certain that Olroyd had finally gone too far, and so was I, until the forensic report came through.

The bullets which had killed the Hazeens and their lawyer didn't match bullets fired from the hit-man's gun.

This news was small comfort to Jack. Olroyd might be innocent of the killings but he was guilty as hell on intent. And it now meant the hunt was on again for the real killer.

I remembered what Maurice had told me about the bank manager. It seemed to me anyone with a good motive for killing the Hazeens must now be suspect.

I told Jack and, without any real enthusiasm, he had the bank manager brought in for questioning. A gun was found at his home. The pistol had been recently cleaned. The bank manager claimed that he had fired it recently but only at a local club of which he was a member. He had no alibi for the estimated time of the murders. His gun fired the same calibre bullets as those found in the three bodies.

"Book him," said Jack. The manager's gun was sent for tests and a report. If sample bullets fired from it matched up with those taken from the three murdered men, Jack had his man.

Still protesting his innocence, the bank manager was held on suspicion.

I'd been present when the man made his statement, and I had a strong feeling he was telling the truth. But things looked black for him.

It was suddenly remembering something else that sent me out looking for a prostitute. I found her easily enough. She took me to a room—where else?—at Barwell's lodging house. When she started to undress, I stopped her.

"I just want to talk," I said.

She must have thought I was barmy, the way she looked at me. I plied her with the questions that had been hammering away and which had finally prompted me to see the girl. She proved more sophisticated and worldly-wise than I'd anticipated, and I was getting nowhere at all.

She finally broke when I looked inside her handbag and found the gun. She sobbed out her story, begged me to let her go, and I would have liked to do that, knowing she'd rid the world of three men who had been responsible for God knew how much pain and misery, perhaps even death.

But I took her in. The bank manager was released. Off the hook for the murders, Olroyd had to await his fate. He was finished as a copper. About the girl, Jack said:

"Maybe they'll go easy on her when they know the whole story. Christ, what a stinking rotten world we live in!"

"Yes," I said. I left him. I'd got myself a new angle for my story. But for once I got no pleasure out of sending it.

TARANTELLA

Ella Griffiths

DETECTIVE SERGEANT Edwin Fossdal gazed distastefully about him. He wasn't very happy at being surrounded by batteries of cages containing fluttering birds, swinging monkeys, and scampering rodents. It was not that he didn't like animals and pets. What put him off was the non-stop chattering, maniacal screaming, and snuffling and grunting—not to mention the assorted odours, sweet and sour, that assailed his nostrils. This was the second petshop he'd been in that morning. Both had been broken into, the intruders having carefully chipped away the putty surround of the glass in the door, removed the retaining tacks, and simply lifted out the pane. When they left they had taken the trouble to replace the glass and nail strips of wood across at top and bottom to hold it in place. They must have been fond of animals, the sergeant reflected; didn't want any to escape or catch a chill. Well, it was a nice thought. A more down-to-earth explanation was that they'd hoped the burglary would go longer undetected.

Both shops were owned by the same couple, Gustav Lund and his wife. Lund was in his early sixties, his wife, Lina, much younger: how much, the sergeant was not prepared to hazard a guess. The couple managed only one of the shops themselves, Boutique I, Boutique II being looked after by Lund's cousin, Victor Friberg, a man of about fifty.

Gustav Lund had been injured in a railway accident in France some five years previously. He could get about a bit on crutches, but generally made use of a wheelchair. He had a staccato way of speaking, the words tumbling out in a veritable torrent. Fossdal had the impression that he was possessed of a violent temper which he had to make a constant effort to keep under control. He wouldn't have been surprised had Lund suddenly lunged at him with one of his crutches, had he been sufficiently provoked, so simmering with suppressed rage did he appear to be. He hadn't been talking to him for very long, however, before he began to feel profoundly sorry for him. The name Gustav Lund rang a bell in his mind, something to do with sport, he thought, but at thirty-two the sergeant was too young to be able to place him offhand. The main thing was that an active man in his prime had suddenly been rendered incapable, confined to a wheelchair, and was obviously —and understandably—having difficulty in coming to terms with his cruel fate.

"If I'd had my way the police would never have been called in in the first place," Lund had said. "Said," thought the sergeant. "He'd damn' near snarled!" "Far too many people in our business have been suspected of being out for cheap publicity over things like this. Claim they've had a parrot or a snake stolen—*they*'re always good for a line or two in the paper. Gives us a bad name. I know the competition's hotting up, even here in Bergen, but we don't need to resort to that kind of thing."

"I wouldn't have reported it, either, Gustav, if they hadn't taken Pauline," Lina Lund declared defensively.

Without appearing to do so, the sergeant studied her more closely. If her nose had been a bit bigger and her mouth a bit smaller, she'd have been a beauty, he decided. Well, above average, at least. She had sparkling, intelligent eyes, and her skin was fresh and clear; only a telltale web of tiny wrinkles at the corners of her deep-blue eyes proclaimed that she was no longer in the first bloom of womanhood. She was tall, slim, and smartly dressed. On this hot July day she was wearing a close-fitting pale-green dress of coarse linen and white, high-heeled shoes. Her hair, jet black like a gypsy's, fell in soft curls to her shoulders. She was so tanned that Fossdal surmised that she had recently been South. "She never got that tan in Bergen, that's for sure," he told himself morosely.

"Pauline?" he said, forcing his mind back to the problem in hand.

"My favourite parrot," Lina Lund explained sadly. "She's an Amazon, Sergeant. Lovely she is, really lovely. Bright green and a cobalt-blue head and neck. She has dark-brown eyes with a bright orange ring round, and black legs and feet. And she's so affectionate—*and* she's a good talker. Picks up words and tricks in no time. She needs a lot of attention, love, you know. Well, caring for, anyway. If only my husband hadn't refused to let me keep her at home, she wouldn't have been stolen!" She shot a challenging glance at her husband, who returned it with a baleful look.

"I want peace and quiet when I'm home," he said. The sergeant nodded sympathetically; he felt the same way.

"These burglaries don't make sense," Lund went on in a more reasonable tone, turning his attention to the policeman. "Who'd want to break into a shop—only a small branch at that—just to steal a tarantula worth about two hundred and twenty-five kroner? If they'd wanted it all that badly, they could've nabbed it any time during the day. Easily done, too easily, in fact. Two or three of you, that's all you need, two to keep the assistants busy or talking while the other chap grabs the spider. The parrot's a different matter; she's worth eighteen thousand. And why take a black widow, too? That's what I can't understand."

"I don't know anything about insects at all," Edwin Fossdal said apologetically, "especially not spiders. But I do know black widows are dangerous. Bite can be fatal, can't it?"

"Spiders aren't insects," Gustav Lund answered, his tone betraying his pity at the sergeant's ignorance. "In fact, they *feed* on insects. All insects have six legs. Six. And when I say 'all', I mean all one and a half million species. There're about twelve thousand different species in Norway. Spiders have eight legs, and they're arachnids. There're about three hundred and fifty different kinds in Norway, and they live on insects, as I said."

"I can't see what anyone'd want a spider for," said the sergeant, who was again fast losing his recently found sympathy for Lund. He didn't like people who talked down to him as though he were an ignoramus of the first order. "Where could you keep it, for a start?"

"Most people use an aquarium," Lund explained. "Instead of filling it with water, you make a miniature landscape—sand, stones, twigs, moss, plants, that kind of thing. Need a little water, too, of course. Spiders don't cost much in the food line. One beetle's enough to keep them going for a week. Some people prefer to feed their spiders mealworms. You buy them in small quantities—well, measures, actually; a teaspoonful costs about ten kroner. We keep *our* spiders in a glass showcase near the door. That's where both the widow and the tarantula were."

"You didn't have an Amazon in *your* shop, then, Mr Friberg," Edwin Fossdal pursued, turning his attention to Victor Friberg, who looked as tanned and fit as Lina Lund. Suddenly he began to feel sorry for Gustav Lund again. It couldn't be very pleasant having to associate with two such good-looking and healthy specimens every day when you yourself were so badly disabled, he thought. Friberg's mane of snow-white hair was in startling contrast to his youthful features, which were dominated by a pair of the darkest brown eyes Fossdal had ever seen on a Norwegian of either sex.

"I?" Friberg exclaimed. "Good Lord, yes! I've two, in fact."

"We had five, counting the one that was stolen," Gustav Lund put in. "Strange that they should only have taken Lina's."

"Strange?" his wife burst out. "Tragic's more like it. It's a tragedy, a real tragedy. Poor little Pauline! She was only a baby, really. Nowhere near sexually mature. That takes five or six years. She was genuinely fond of me, you know. I used to give her sunflower seeds as an extra treat every now and again—she'd take them from my hand. And peanuts and hazel nuts. Raisins, too, sometimes. And lots of chopped meat. I was the one who taught her to talk, taught her all her tricks . . ."

"You talk as though she were dead, Mrs Lund," the sergeant said as her voice trailed away.

Lina Lund bit her lip: "As far as I'm concerned, she is," she said bitterly. "You'd be surprised how many people would like a parrot—only they can't afford to pay the price. You can bet your life the thieves had a customer ready and waiting, one who wanted my Pauline and no other. They'd let her go for half price, I expect, eight or nine thousand. If only I knew that she was in good hands . . ."

"Well, she would be, wouldn't she?" the policeman said reasonably. "If someone was prepared to shell out thousands of kroner for her, they'd not be likely to neglect her once they'd got her. Stands to sense. But I agree with you, Mr Lund: why take the spiders if they were after the parrot? How do you get spiders like that into the country in the first place, by the way?"

"No problem," Friberg answered, "no problem at all. There's no law against it, not if you import them through the proper channels. If that black widow had come in with a crate of fruit, say, it would have been destroyed. I don't mean someone'd have stamped on it, I mean the Pest Control people would have been called in and killed it. Officially, sort of."

"Do you keep a record of who buys what?" Edwin Fossdal asked.

"We keep books, of course, accounts of what we buy and sell, so's we know what we have in stock," Gustav Lund explained. "But we don't keep a record of purchasers' names and addresses."

"Not even when it's a matter of poisonous spiders like these?" the policeman asked. "So that you'd have some idea of who was interested in black widows and tarantulas and so on, I mean."

Gustav Lund grimaced, though it was probably an attempt at a smile. "Tarantulas—*Trocosa apuliac*'s the Latin name, by the way—don't very often bite human beings. They have to be provoked. And even if they do get bitten, people don't die as a result. Pain, yes, and a swelling, but that's all. In the Middle Ages they thought bites brought on cramp and they got people who were bitten to dance to sweat out the poison. The dancers used to wander about from town to town, picking up others on the way. That led to all kinds of trouble—it was an open invitation to hooliganism, I suppose. They used to work themselves into a frenzy, tarantism it was called—a kind of mass hysteria. Hadn't anything to do with the poor old tarantula, really, but there you are, the legend stuck. Same with the dance, you know, the tarantella. Actually both the spider and the dance were named after Taranto in southern Italy, where there was a lot of tarantism, apparently. The black widow's a different matter entirely. *Latrodecutus mactans*. A bite from that *can* be fatal. Only about four per cent of them are, though, if that—and there's an anti-serum nowadays. Agonizing pain, though, even if you don't die. Then there's the brown spider, *Loxosceles reculae*. That's a nasty one, if you like! You get it in the States, especially in the Deep South; extends a fair way north, too, right up to—"

"Come on, Gustav!" Friberg broke in irritably. "We accept that you know more about everything than us ordinary mortals, but I don't think the sergeant's come here to listen to a lecture on spiders!" He turned to Edwin Fossdal: "When do you think we shall be able to open the shops again?"

"Oh, give our chaps a couple of hours or so, that should do it," the policeman replied. "There're bound to be dozens of worthless fingerprints all over the place." He sighed. "Would you mind telling me where you all were last night?"

"You don't think it was one of us, surely?" Lina Lund burst out. She stared at him distrustfully, a frown furrowing her forehead.

The sergeant smiled: "Routine, Mrs Lund, pure routine," he reassured her. "Perhaps I can start with you?"

"We didn't do anything very special," she replied, somewhat mollified. "Watched television, that's all. Until they closed down, actually. My husband and I, that is. Then we said goodnight and started to get ready for bed. Only I didn't feel very sleepy, so I decided I'd have a breath of fresh air before calling it a day. I didn't go far, just to the park near where we live. It was still light, of course, and it was nice and quiet. I sat on a seat—for quite a long time, really. Never saw a soul."

"My wife and I have separate bedrooms," Gustav Lund put in by way of explanation. "On opposite sides of the house. I snore. That too. According to her, anyway."

"You don't know how long Mrs Lund was out, then?"

"No, Sergeant, I don't. Sorry. And she doesn't know how long *I* was out, either. I have difficulty in sleeping, too, you see. Not as much as my wife, of course: she spends half her life at the doctor's, getting sleeping tablets!"

"His name's Malo," Lina Lund said sourly. "Stefan Malo. He'll confirm it. Tell you I'm a hypochondriac, I expect. I know I look the picture of health, but I'm not. And I've had problems getting to sleep ever since the accident." She threw her husband a meaningful glance.

"Where'd you go, Mr Lund?" the sergeant asked quickly before another altercation could start.

"I drove round more or less at random," Gustav Lund replied. "Don't ask me where, though. I haven't the foggiest. My car's specially fitted out for wrecks like me. Practically drives itself. If you knew how much time I spent cruising the streets at night when it's quiet . . ."

"Don't be so dramatic, Gustav!" Victor Friberg broke in. "Sergeant Fossdal'll think we're a weird lot altogether, what with you two bickering away in front of him and telling him you spend half the night trailing around the town! Show a little consideration for how *I* feel, standing here. He'll think I'm the same."

"Where were *you*, then, Mr Friberg, yesterday evening and last night?" the sergeant asked before either of the others could reply.

"At home," Friberg said. "Alone," he added, giving Lina Lund a taunting look. "Or did I imagine it?" the sergeant wondered.

"It's only the three of us who have an interest in the shop," said Lund. "Egil, our son, is away on holiday—inter-railing together with a friend. Down on the Continent, you know. He couldn't care less about the business; wants to be a doctor. However, that's beside the point. What I'm getting at is that these shops are our bread-and-butter, so it stands to sense that we wouldn't do anything that'd harm the business. You can take my word for it that none of us would stoop to a lowdown trick like this . . ."

"I'm sure you wouldn't," the policeman said soothingly. "Don't you have to be pretty used to handling spiders to steal one?" he asked, going off at a tangent. "They move so fast, it beats me how you get hold of them."

"It's easy enough," Lina Lund answered. "Thick gloves, that's all you need. I use pigskin gauntlets. But what about our leaving? Can we go down to our cabin, or do we have to stay stuck here? It's so hot, and who knows how long it's going to last?" She looked at him appealingly.

Edwin Fossdal smiled despite himself: "No, Mrs Lund, you can go where you like." It had been on the tip of his tongue to say that she was as free as a bird, but he stopped himself just in time. What had caused him to smile was the knowledge that the police were currently investigating two nasty knifings, a bank robbery, and a tragic case in which an elderly man had been brutally assaulted in his own home and robbed of all his savings. And here he was listening to lectures on spiders and parrots! Wisely, he kept his thoughts to himself. Instead, he asked: "Will you all be going?"

"We're like Siamese triplets," said Gustav Lund, scowling at his cousin. "We enjoy one another's company."

"You could've fooled me," thought the sergeant. He could not help wondering what prompted them to stick together so. The business part he could understand, but in their leisure-time. . . Was Lina Lund the answer? It seemed by no means unlikely.

What actually kept the Lunds and Friberg together was the necessity of having to run the two shops. After his accident Gustav Lund had been unable to take an active part in day-to-day affairs and Lina had tended more and more to lean on Victor Friberg. A more enterprising personality would have cut loose long ago, but Friberg was painfully conscious of his lack of academic and professional qualifications, and also of the fact that he was too old to make a fresh start. Besides, he had long-term plans for himself and Lina. Plans or dreams. So he had carried on, putting a good face on things and getting deeper and deeper into the rut.

Had Gustav Lund had only himself to consider he would have sold Boutique I long ago and retained only the smaller shop. But it was silly to think along those lines: his main preoccupation was with keeping Lina.

But she had plans of her own. . . .

They didn't usually spend their weekends together, but this particular weekend it seemed a sensible thing to do. They needed not only to agree on a plan, but it had to be a good one. As soon as the press got hold of the story they knew they would be inundated with phone calls from frightened people wanting to know what they should do if they were bitten by a black widow! Then there'd be the other type, who'd say it was all a publicity stunt, as Gustav had pointed out. Whatever happened, they were going to have problems, that Lina didn't doubt.

Friday evening they had a light dinner of shrimps and white wine and afterwards took their whiskies-and-sodas out on to the terrace, where they sat enjoying the glorious weather. It was not often the citizens of Bergen, on Norway's west coast, saw the sun for more than a few hours at a stretch. But they failed to decide on a plan of action.

On Saturday morning Lina Lund and Victor Friberg went down to the sea for a swim before breakfast. As they swam, he turned towards her.

"When's it to be?" he asked in a low voice, although there was no one anywhere in sight.

"Today," she answered, also keeping her voice down.

When they got back to the cabin it was to find Gustav Lund sitting in a garden chair on the terrace. He looked well and seemed to be in a better mood than he had been for a long time. The reason was quite simply that for once he was not plagued by the terrible pain that generally held him in its grip. He couldn't help but wonder why Dr Malo was so reluctant to operate; plenty of other people had got rid of their duodenal ulcers that way. But the doctor had contented himself with making a series of tests—two series, in fact—and had afterwards assured him that he had nothing to worry about. Sometimes he couldn't help thinking that he was being used as a guinea pig, as he seemed to be getting so many different drugs and medicines. The last lot must have been much stronger than any of the others he'd taken; they subdued the pain, there was no doubt about that, but they made him feel drowsy. He couldn't go on taking them indefinitely, he realized, not unless things changed and he got used to them. He needed a clear head to drive his car. He had toyed with the idea of changing to another doctor. But Stefan Malo was considered to be an excellent doctor, and Lina just about idolized him, with his well-groomed appearance, deep voice, and dancing eyes.

"I wish *I* could have a swim," he couldn't help sighing.

"You can, Gustav, you can!" his wife said immediately. "Victor and I can manage, you'll see."

Gustav Lund permitted himself a wry smile: "No," he said, "I was only joking."

After breakfast they sat lazing in the sun. Lina and Victor Friberg walked about the garden and Gustav buried himself in the *Guinness Book of Records*.

"Now it's two hours since we ate, it must be!" Lina exclaimed. She was looking her best. Her body, beautifully tanned, was still firm and strangely youthful-looking compared with her face. Perhaps it was the tired look about her mouth that made her appear nearer her true age, her husband reflected. "Anyway," she continued gaily, "I don't think it's true what they say about having to wait two hours after a meal before having a swim. I don't think that's what gives you cramp at all."

"I think I'll have a cigarette first," Victor Friberg said. He seemed nervous and ill at ease. "You go on ahead, Lina."

"No, I'll wait," Lina said, settling herself more comfortably on her sun couch.

She lay staring up at the blue dome of the sky, thinking how strange life actually was. In a way it seemed that what she intended to do had been planned by someone else a long time ago. It had all started that day on the bus when she happened to overhear snatches of conversation between two youngsters, a boy and a girl, who were evidently into entomology. The girl had been so despairing because her mother couldn't seem to grasp that bees, for example, were such a rewarding object of study. "When I told her that there are tremendous differences between one strain and another as regards temperament, and that some of them are more aggressive than others, all she said was that that's the way it is with people, too, and why didn't I take up psychology instead," she complained. "And that day we made poison from bees . . . You weren't there, were you, Karl?"

"No, sore throat," the boy had replied.

"Amazing," the girl continued. "We got them to sting through a cloth impregnated with . . ."

At that moment the driver had had to slam on his brakes, and Lina and any of her fellow passengers who might have been listening had lost the rest of the story. But she was probably the only one sufficiently interested to eavesdrop; had she not been an entomologist, she wouldn't have bothered either, she reminded herself.

"Afterwards we extracted the poison . . ." the girl had continued. The boy nodded: "I heard the bees were made to sting by being given an electric shock," he said.

"Yes," the girl answered. "I've had two good bee stings in my life, two I shall never forget. Have you ever been stung?"

"*I've* been stung," Lina had thought. She'd been only eleven at the time. Dr Matsen had always kept bees, and it had been he who had attended to her swollen arm.

"It's only the queen and the workers that have stings and poison sacs, Lina," he'd explained, to take her mind off the pain. "And it's only the workers that sting people. They're females, actually, only the sex organs aren't properly developed."

Lina's mother had looked up quickly at the mention of sex organs and rather sharply had asked the old doctor if he didn't think the girl was too young for "that kind of thing". The doctor had merely smiled and patted her on the shoulder without answering.

"I was suddenly surrounded by bees," Lina had said, still trembling from the terror of her experience.

"Bees are just like people," the doctor had explained. "They react to different smells—perfume, sweat, all sorts of things. And once one's stung, the smell of the poison attracts the others, and they sting, too. It's a sort of chain reaction."

"Tell me, doctor," Lina's mother had said, "a bee's sting's serrated, isn't it? Serrated the wrong way, so to speak, so that once it's in, the bee can't get it out again. The bee dies, doesn't it, but what happens if the sting's left in? Can somebody who's been stung die?"

The doctor had smiled reassuringly, Lina remembered: "I doubt it very much," he'd said, "very much indeed. I've lots of books on bees, Lina, so if you'd like to know more about the little creature that stung you, just say so and you can borrow some."

"Thank you," her mother had said decisively before Lina had time to answer, "but I think Lina's had enough of bees to last her for a long time to come."

But her mother had been wrong. In point of fact, Lina's abiding interest in bees and other insects dated from that moment in the doctor's surgery, though several years were to pass before she realized it.

If she hadn't been pregnant with Egil at the time, she would never have married Gustav, she reflected. But Gustav had been so determined, and marriage was the be all and end all in a family like hers. In those days Boutique I had simply been Hans Lunde & Son, a name Gustav had changed when he took over the business from his father. And she had been needed in the shop. At the time it hadn't seemed such a sacrifice to have to give up the plans for research she had nurtured as a student, but when she began to grow restless and their financial situation continued to improve, Gustav had had a small laboratory built on to the house where she could spend her leisure hours. Now, thanks to her research and reading, she knew that what really stimulated worker bees was not the poison they carried in their poison sacs, but isoamyl acetate, produced and secreted just before or at the moment a bee stings, and that it was this secretion which, if the bees were of a naturally aggressive strain, brought others to the scene.

A few days after overhearing that interesting conversation on the bus she had gone to bed with Stefan Malo for the first time. It was the first time she had had sex since Gustav had been injured in the train crash, and the doctor had been celibate for six months, ever since his wife died.

"Come on, Lina, let's have that dip!" Victor's voice jerked her back to reality as he stubbed out his cigarette and got to his feet.

"Shan't be long, Gustav," Lina said, as she prepared to follow Friberg down to the shore.

"Don't worry about me, dear," her husband replied. "I'll be all right. I'm finding this book most interesting. You run along and enjoy yourself!"

Her heart went out to him. He couldn't help but feel inferior, both as a human being and as a man. His love for Egil was about the only thing that kept him going, she thought. All he lived for was to give the boy a secure future. How lucky I've been, she mused, not for the first time, touching her husband lightly on the forehead with her fingertips, as, eyes closed, he leant back in his chair.

"Why can't we get it over?" Victor Friberg hissed when they were safely out of earshot. "As long as the police . . ."

But she wasn't listening. Her thoughts went back to that time, years ago, when she'd been young and naïve, but not so young as to think that she could escape responsibility for her actions. She'd been completely captivated by Victor, an irresponsible Casanova who'd left her in the lurch as soon as she told him she was going to have a baby.

Shortly afterwards she had met Gustav, without having the faintest idea that he was Victor's cousin. There was no excuse for what she'd done, she knew that, but she consoled herself with the knowledge that she wasn't the first and was hardly likely to be the last to resort to such an expedient. Gustav had taken it for granted that the child was his and had insisted on marrying her. It was not until many years later that Victor had come back into her life after having been abroad ever since he'd absconded. He'd been broke, and Gustav had felt sorry for him and given him a helping hand; only then had Lina learnt that they were cousins.

For some years Gustav had been wanting to open another shop, and now he was able to realize his dream. Victor had no business training, but he learnt quickly. He wasn't overly bright, however, and many years were destined to elapse before he tumbled to it that Egil was his son. That was when he had started to pile on the pressure. Made desperate by his threat to tell both Gustav and Egil the truth unless she persuaded her husband to make over Boutique II to him, Lina had put forward a suggestion of her own which a more intelligent man than Victor Friberg would have seen through in a moment. She proposed that the two of them should kill Gustav and later, after a decent interval, marry and run the two shops together. But first they had to devise a plan that would ensure that no breath of suspicion fell on them.

It had been about that time that their neighbour of long standing, Oskar Mathisen, an old fisherman, had decided to go in for beekeeping, and she had helped him to get started. Shortly afterwards she had spent a holiday touring Austria by coach, and had there bought synthetic isoamyl acetate.

"Doesn't it affect you at all?" Victor whispered, his mouth close to her ear. "I don't mind admitting that I'm beginning to get cold feet. But you . . ."

"Feeling grateful to Gustav all of a sudden, that it?" Lina mocked him.

"It's not that. I'm scared we might be found out. You realize that, surely?" he whispered hoarsely.

Of course she realized it. "I can take your word for it that Pauline's all right at your cabin, can't I?"

He nodded. "Yes. But are you quite sure you didn't leave any fingerprints behind anywhere? You're not exactly a professional."

"You know darned well I wore gloves. Anyway, would it really matter—they're *our* shops. But for God's sake stop whispering in my ear! Act naturally. If Gustav's watching he'll wonder what on earth we're up to. I'm just going into the boathouse to get some suntan lotion. Wait for me."

She returned after a few moments carrying a small bottle.

"Turn over and I'll do your back for you," she said.

She had barely begun to rub the lotion in before a wasp started to circle her hand. It was soon joined by another. Then another and another. But *were* they wasps?

"Lina!" Victor gasped, terror in his voice. "There've never been bees out here before. You know I'm allergic! I'd never have come if I'd known there were bees."

"They're our neighbour's, Victor. Fierce little devils! I chose them myself, specially for you. I'd never kill Gustav! He's always been wonderful to me. I wouldn't need to, anyway. He has cancer and hasn't long to live. He doesn't know—Stefan Malo's told him it's ulcers."

"Specially for me! What d'you mean, 'specially for me'?" he cried, lashing out frantically at the bees.

"You're the one who's going to die, Victor," Lina said. Her voice was surprisingly steady, but she knew the reaction was bound to set in later. "You. You're a pest, always have been. And another one's going to kill you. You're going to find out what it's like to be bitten by a black widow!"

Dramatically she waved a little gauze bag in front of him.

"Here, Victor, here's the black widow!"

Before he could scramble to his feet Lina grasped the back of his bathing trunks and slipped the bag inside. Frenzied from its close confinement, the spider bit immediately. Victor gave a shriek and started to run towards the sea. Suddenly he stumbled and fell, to lie writhing by the water's edge.

"Poor Victor," Lina said sadly, shaking her head as the local policeman bent over the body. "He was allergic. Very. One bee sting can be enough for someone like him, and he must have been stung lots of times."

Her thoughts went to the post mortem. There was bound to be one, she realized, but she was convinced that whoever performed it would never look beyond the numerous bee stings for the cause of Victor's death. The stings would still be in his body, if proof were needed.

The black widow, on the other hand, had no sting, and the two tiny dots left by the bite would be practically invisible to the naked eye. The bag and spider she had thrown into the sea before calling the police.

Monday afternoon Lina phoned Sergeant Fossdal while Dr Malo sat at her husband's bedside. The shock of Victor Friberg's sudden death had proved too much for Gustav Lund and he had had to take to his bed.

"I just thought I'd let you know that I've got Pauline back," she said. "Because of the heat I've been leaving my car with the windows open when I knew I'd be away for only a few minutes and when I got back this morning after a bit of shopping, someone had put Pauline in the car. It was such a relief! I could hardly believe my eyes! Anyway, now you can forget the burglaries."

"But what about the tarantula and the black widow?" the policeman asked.

"Sergeant, I've a confession to make," Lina answered in a confidential tone. "Actually, it was only Pauline that was stolen. I think the thieves tried Friberg's shop first, and when they didn't find what they were looking for there, they burgled ours. Victor flushed the tarantula down the toilet—because I asked him to. I knew the police would never go to much trouble over a parrot—couldn't expect them to, really—but I reasoned that they'd be far more likely to take the burglary seriously if there were a couple of poisonous spiders missing as well. But—well, all that's water under the bridge. Pauline's back, that's the main thing, and she's all right. I'm sorry I deceived you, but—well, I hope you'll forgive me. I'm not exactly on top of the world at the moment, Pauline or no Pauline. First there was poor Victor, all those bee stings, and now my husband's very ill . . ."

"But what about the black widow?"

"It went the same way as the tarantula," Lina answered unhesitatingly, "except that I did it myself."

"That's strange," said the policeman. "I think I'll nip over and have a word with you, Mrs Lund, if you don't mind. Perhaps you can help me. You see, the pathologist's report on Mr Friberg says that he died from a black widow bite! There'd been so much talk about poisonous spiders, that I felt I ought to warn him to keep a special lookout, just in case . . ."

FAIR AND SQUARE

Margaret Yorke

Mrs Ford stepped aboard the *S.S. Sphinx*, treading carefully along the ridged gangplank, her stick before her. It would be unfortunate if she were to stumble and injure herself before her holiday had properly begun.

Her holiday.

Mrs Ford had developed the custom of avoiding some bleak winter weeks by going abroad. While ostensibly seeking the sun, she sought to give her family some relief from having to be concerned for her. She tried hard not to be a burden to her middle-aged sons and daughters and their spouses.

She had been cruising before. She had also stayed in large impersonal hotels in the Algarve and Majorca, where it was possible to spend long winter weeks at low cost, enduring a sense of isolation among uncongenial fellow weather refugees. On her cruise, Mrs Ford knew she could expect near insolence from certain stewards because she was a woman travelling alone. With luck, this would be counterbalanced by extra thoughtfulness from others because of her age.

Her cabin steward would be an important person in her life, and she had learned to tip in advance as a guarantee of service and her morning tea on time. There would be patient tolerance from couples who were her children's contemporaries; they would wait while she negotiated stairways and would help her in and out of buses on sightseeing excursions ashore. Older passengers in pairs would be too near her in age and too fragile themselves to spare her time or energy, and the wives would see her as an alarming portent of their own future.

There would be plenty of older spinster ladies in cheerful groups or intimately paired. Eleanor Ford would not want to join any such coterie.

The best times would be if the sun shone while the ship was at sea. Then, in a sheltered corner, she would read or do her tapestry while others played bridge or bingo or went to keep-fit classes. She would have her hair done once a week or so, which would help to pass the time. She hoped she had brought enough minor medications to last the voyage. The ship's shop would certainly sell travel souvenirs and duty-free scents and watches but might be short on tissues, indigestion remedies, and such.

Each night Mrs Ford would wash her underthings and stockings and hang them near the air-conditioning to dry by morning. For bigger garments she would be obliged to use the laundry service. She would go on most of the shore excursions, though they tired her and she had been to all the ports before, because to stay on board would be to mean she had abandoned all initiative. She would send postcards to her smaller grandchildren and write letters to her sons and daughters.

She would long for home and her warm flat with all her possessions round her and her dull routine—yet this morning she had been pleased, leaving it in driving sleet, at the prospect of escaping to the sun. Most people would envy her, she told herself, wondering which of her fellow-passengers, who had looked so drab waiting at the airport, would, by the whim of the head steward, be her table companions throughout the cruise. She had requested the second sitting and been assured by the shipping office that this wish would be granted—otherwise what did you do in the evening after an early meal? As it was, Mrs Ford would be able to go to bed almost at once when dinner was over with a book from the ship's library, which was likely to be one of the best features of the vessel.

Her cabin was amidships, the steadiest place in bad weather, and not below the dance-floor, where she might hear the band, nor the swimming pool, where the water might splosh to and fro noisily if the ship rolled. She had been able to control these points when booking. What she could do nothing about was her neighbours. They might be rowdy, reeling in at all hours from the discotheque, or waking early and chattering audibly about their operations or their love lives—Mrs Ford had overheard some amazing stories on other voyages.

As she unpacked, she thought briefly about Roger, her husband, who had died six years ago. He had been gentle and kind, and she had been lucky in her long life with him. He had left her well provided for, so that even now, with inflation what it was, she could live in modest comfort and put aside enough funds for such an annual trip. She had so nearly not married Roger, for it was Michael whom she had really loved, so long ago. Setting Roger's photograph on her dressing-table, she tried to picture Michael, but it was difficult. She seldom thought of him after all this time.

That night, climbing into her high narrow bunk, she had a little weep. It was like the first night away at school, she thought, when you didn't yet know the other pupils or your way around. It would all be better in a day or two.

In the morning she had breakfast in her cabin. The ship had sailed at midnight, and beyond the window the sun shone on a gently rolling sea. Mrs Ford had taken a sleeping pill the night before, and so she felt rather heavy-headed, but her spirits lifted. She would find a place on deck in the sun.

On the way, she stopped at the library and selected several thrillers and a life of Lord Wavell, which should be interesting. She found a vacant chair on a wide part of the promenade deck and settled down, wrapped in her warm coat. After a while, in the sunlight, she slept.

The voice woke her.

"You're not playing properly," it charged. "Those aren't the right rules."

Mrs Ford's heart thumped and she sat upright in her chair, carried back by the sound to when she was twelve years old. She was playing hopscotch with Mary Hopkins, and Phyllis Burton had come to loom over them threateningly—large, confident, and two years older, disturbing their game.

"This is how *we* play," came the present-day response, in a male voice, from the deck quoit player now being challenged on the wide deck near Mrs Ford's chair.

"They're not the right rules," the voice that was so like Phyllis's insisted. "Look, this is how you should throw."

Long years ago Mrs Ford's tennis racket had been seized from her grasp and a scorching service delivered by Phyllis Burton. "You played a footfault," she had accused—and later, umpiring a junior match, she had given several footfaults against Eleanor Luton, as Mrs Ford was then, in a manner that seemed unjust at the time and did so still. All through Mrs Ford's schooldays,

Phyllis Burton's large presence had loomed and intervened, interfered and patronized, mocked and derided.

She was good at everything, but though she was older she was in the same form as Mrs Ford. She wasn't a dunce, however—it was Eleanor who was a swot, younger than everyone else in her form. In the library she was unmolested; her head in a book, she could escape the pressures of community life she found hard to endure. Eleanor was no joiner, and neither was she a leader—it was Phyllis who became, in time, head girl.

There came the sound of a quoit, thudding.

Mrs Ford opened her eyes and saw large buttocks before her, shrouded in navy linen, as their owner stooped to throw.

"We enjoy how we play," said a female voice, but uncertainly.

"Things should always be done the right way," said the owner of the navy-blue buttocks, straightening up.

In memory, young Eleanor in her new VAD uniform stooped over a hospital bed to pull at a wrinkled sheet and make her patient feel easier. Phyllis, with two years' experience, told her to strip the bed and make it up over again, although this meant moving the wounded man and causing him pain.

"But the patient—"

"He'll be much more comfortable in the end, it's for his own good," Phyllis had said. And stood there while it was done, not helping, although two could make a bed much more easily than one.

Phyllis had contrived that Eleanor was kept busy with bedpans and scrubbing floors after that, until more junior nurses arrived and she had to be permitted to undertake other tasks.

Michael had been a patient in the hospital. He'd had a flesh wound in the thigh and was young and shocked by what he had seen and suffered in the trenches. He and Eleanor had gone for walks together as he grew stronger. When he cast away his crutches, he took her arm for support—and still held it when he could walk alone. They strolled in the nearby woods, and had tea in the local town. Phyllis saw them once and told Eleanor so, and soon after that Eleanor was switched to night duty so that she scarcely saw Michael again before he went back to the front. She didn't receive a single letter from him, and after months of waiting, although she never saw his name on the casualty lists, she decided he had been killed.

Later she met Roger, who was large and kind and protected her from the harshest aspects of life for so many years, leaving her all the more ill-prepared to battle alone, as now she must.

"Games are no fun unless you play fair and square," said the sturdy woman with Phyllis's voice.

Mrs Ford looked away from her and saw a thin girl in white pants and a red sweater and a young man in an arran pullover and clean new jeans—the deck quoit players. The older woman was leaving, walking away, but the damage was done.

"Come on, Iris, your turn," said the man.

"No, I don't want to play any more," the girl said.

That had happened long ago too. Eleanor had not wanted to play games after Phyllis Burton's derisive interventions.

There was some murmuring between the two. The man put his arm round Iris's shoulders but she flung it off and, head down, mooched off along the deck, disappearing eventually round the corner. The man watched her go, then moved to the rail and leaned over it, gazing at the water.

Mrs Ford was trembling. The woman was so like Phyllis, whom she hadn't heard of since "their" war, so long ago. Strange that someone else should waken her memory. Phyllis, if she were still alive, must be well over eighty now—eighty-four, in fact—and this woman was what? Getting on for sixty? It was hard to tell these days.

Mrs Ford found it difficult to settle back down after that, and spent a restless day.

Proper table allocations, not prepared the night before when seating had been informal as passengers arrived, had now been made, and Mrs Ford was pleasantly surprised to find that she was at the doctor's table, with two couples past retirement age and a younger pair. The doctor was also young, reminding Mrs Ford of her eldest grandson, who was thirty-five. She didn't know that her elder son, that grandson's father, now chairman of a group of companies, had personally visited the shipping office to request special attention for his mother, particularly a congenial place for meals. He and his wife had been on a cruise the year before—their first—and had seen for themselves what Mrs Ford's fate could be. Her children all loved their timid mother and respected her desire to maintain her independence—and, far from relaxing about her when she went away, they worried. On a ship, however, there was constant attention at hand, a doctor immediately available, and swift communication in an emergency.

Mrs Ford felt happy sitting next to the doctor, waiting for her soup. She would eat three courses merely, waiting while others ate their way through the menu like schoolboys on a binge. The doctor told her he was having a year at sea before moving, in a few months' time, into general practice. It was a chance to see the world, he said.

He was a tall blond young man with an easy manner and he liked old ladies, who were often valiant, building walls of reserve around themselves as a defence against pity. Mrs Ford, he saw, was one like that. There were others who thought great age allowed them licence to be rude, and took it, and the doctor liked them too for he admired their spirit. He ordered wine for the whole table and Mrs Ford saw the other three men nod in agreement; they would all take their turn to buy it and so must she. This had happened to her before and it was always difficult to insist, as she must if she intended to accept their hospitality. She liked a glass of wine.

Phyllis Burton, if she were a widow, would have no difficulty in dealing with such a problem. She would, early on, establish ascendancy over the whole table.

After all these years, here was Phyllis Burton in her mind, and just because of the dogmatic woman on the deck this morning.

Conversation flowed. The doctor asked about Mrs Ford's family and listened with apparent interest to her account of her grandchildren's prowess in various activities. It was acceptable to brag of their accomplishments, but not of one's children's successes, Mrs Ford had learned. Everyone disclosed where they lived and if they had cruised before—or, failing that, what other countries they had visited. Both retired couples had been to the Far East, the younger pair to Florida. The doctor revealed that he was unmarried, but his face briefly clouded—then he went on to describe the ship making black smoke off Mykonos (such a white island!) due to some engine maintenance requirement. He laughed. It had looked bad from the boats taking the passengers ashore.

Mrs Ford had enjoyed her meal. The passenger list was in her cabin when she returned after dinner but she didn't look at it. She read about Lord Wavell, falling asleep over him and waking later with her spectacles still on. Then, with the light out and herself neatly tucked under the bedclothes, she dreamed about Michael. They were walking in the woods near the hospital, holding hands, and he kissed her sweetly, as he had so long ago, her first kiss from an adult male, right-seeming, making it easy when afterwards Roger came along.

She woke in the morning a little disturbed by the dream, but rested.

The next night the captain held his welcoming party, and at it Mrs Ford, hovering on the animated fringe of guests, saw the doctor talking to a pretty girl in a flame-coloured dress. She saw them together again in Athens, setting off to climb the Acropolis.

Mrs Ford decided not to attempt the ascent—she had been up there with Roger on a night of the full moon and preferred to hold that memory rather than one of a heated scramble that would exhaust her. She waited in a tourist pavilion by the bus park, drinking coffee, till the groups from the ship returned. This time the doctor was alone. With her far-sighted eyes, Mrs Ford peered about for the girl but did not see her.

Then she heard the voice again.

"What a clumsy girl you are. I don't know why you can't look where you're going," it said, in Phyllis's tones. "Look at your trousers—they're ruined. Scrambling about like a child up there!"

"I'm sorry, Mummy." Mrs Ford heard the tight high-pitched reply of someone in a state of tension. "I slipped. It will wash out."

Mrs Ford, on her way to coach number four, glanced round. The tourists wouldn't pause for coffee—meals were paid for on the tour and they were returning to the ship for lunch before taking other excursions before the *Sphinx* sailed that night. Behind her she saw a tall, well built woman with carefully coiffed iron-grey hair in a tweed skirt, sensible shoes, and an expensive pigskin jacket. Beside her was the girl Mrs Ford had witnessed talking to the doctor, her blonde hair caught back in a slide at the nape of her neck. On her pale trousers there was a long, dirty smear.

It was to the mother, however, that Mrs Ford's eyes were drawn. Just so might Phyllis Burton have looked in middle age.

That evening Mrs Ford consulted the passenger list with a pencil, reading it with care to winnow out the mothers and daughters travelling together. The father might be present too, unobserved so far by Mrs Ford. She marked several family groups with a question mark. There were no Burtons. Of course not. But the resemblance was so uncanny, she would have to find out who the woman was.

In the end it was easy.

The next day the sun shone brightly and the sea was calm. Mrs Ford decided to climb higher in the ship than she had been hitherto and explore the sports deck in search of a quiet corner where she could sit in the sun. Stick hooked over her arm, a hand on the rail, she slowly ascended the companionway and walked along the deck to a spot where it widened out and some chairs were placed. In one sat the blonde girl. Beside her was an empty chair.

"Is this anyone's place?" Mrs Ford inquired, and the girl, who had been gazing out to sea, turned with a slight start. A smile of great sweetness spread over her face and, confused, Mrs Ford was again in a wood, long ago, with Michael.

"No—oh, please, let me help you," the girl said, and, springing up, she put a hand under Mrs Ford's elbow to help her into the low chair. "They're difficult, aren't they? These chairs, I mean. Such a long way down."

"Yes," agreed Mrs Ford, gasping slightly. "But getting up is harder."

"I know. We found it with my grandfather," the girl said. "But now he's got his own chair for the garden—it's higher, and he can manage."

"Your grandfather?" Mrs Ford wanted the girl to talk while she caught her breath.

"He's lived with us since my grandmother died—before I was born," said the girl. "He's still quite spry, but a bit forgetful. He's a lamb."

"And are you like him?" She was, Mrs Ford knew.

The girl laughed.

"Forgetful, you mean?" she said. "Maybe I am—Mummy always says I'm so clumsy and careless. But then, she's so terribly well organized herself. Granny was the same, Grandpa says. She always knew what to do and made instant decisions."

Roger had always known what to do and made quick, if not instant, decisions, Mrs Ford reflected. "I dither a bit myself," she declared. "I miss my husband a great deal. He cared for me so."

"That must have been wonderful," said the girl, seeming quite unembarrassed by this confidence.

They sat there in the sunshine, gently chatting. The girl's mother was having her hair done, she said. They were cruising together—her mother had had severe bronchitis during the winter and it had seemed a good idea to seek the sun. Her father couldn't get away and so she had come instead. What girl would refuse a chance like this? Her mother had a great desire to see the Pyramids and that would be the high point of the trip for them.

"But you've travelled before?" Mrs Ford asked. Her elder grandchildren, this child's generation, were always whizzing about the globe.

Mummy hadn't liked her going off just with friends, the girl said, but she *had* been to France to learn the language. There had been family holidays in Corsica, which she loved. They rented a villa. She had two brothers, both older than herself.

"What are their names?" asked Mrs Ford, still feeling her way. She didn't know the girl's yet.

"Michael's the eldest—he's called after my grandfather," said the girl. "The other one's William, after Daddy."

Mrs Ford's gently beating old heart began to thump unevenly. Should she say she had known a Michael, long ago? But the girl was going on, needing no prompting.

"Aren't names funny?" she said. "I'm glad I wasn't called after Mummy—her name's Phyllis, after her mother. It would be confusing to have two Phyllis Carters, wouldn't it?"

"I suppose it would," Mrs Ford agreed, and now bells seemed to be ringing in her head, for her Michael's surname had been Carter.

"I'm called after someone else Grandfather knew," said the girl. "It's quite romantic, really. There was this nurse he met in the war—the first war, you remember."

"Yes, my dear, I do," said Mrs Ford.

"She was very young and shy and kept being ticked off by this older, bossier nurse, Grandfather said. When he went back to France he wrote her lots of letters, but she never answered. Wasn't that sad? I'm named after her. Her name was Eleanor."

"Oh," said Mrs Ford faintly, and her head spun. Letters?

"She must have married someone else or something," said the girl. "Or even died. All the letters were sent back to Grandfather.

Mummy found them when she helped him clear up after Granny died, in her desk, locked up. She burned them without telling Grandfather. It would only have upset him."

"Yes, I suppose it would," said Mrs Ford. There was just one fact that must be confirmed. "Your grandmother?" she asked.

"Grandfather married another nurse," said the girl. "Mummy's exactly like her, he says."

Mrs Ford took it in. All those years ago Phyllis Burton had intercepted letters meant for her. Why? Because she wanted Michael for herself, or because she sought, as always, to despoil?

"And have you uncles and aunts?" she asked at last.

"No, there was only Mummy," the girl replied.

So Phyllis had managed just one child, and had died before this grandchild had been born, while Mrs Ford, with two sons and two daughters, had survived into great age. And Michael had never forgotten, for this girl bore her name.

She could cope with no more today.

"What a nice little chat we've had," she said. "We'll be meeting again." She began to struggle up from her chair and the girl rose again to help her.

In the days that followed they talked more. Seeing them together, the mother would walk past, but if Eleanor was talking to any man among the passengers, or a ship's officer, the mother would break in upon them at once.

In Mrs Ford's mind the generations grew confused and there were moments when she imagined it was this confident, domineering woman who had been so perfidious all those years ago, stealing letters meant for another, not this woman's long-dead mother. At night Mrs Ford shed tears for the young girl that had been herself, waiting for letters that never came and in the end giving up.

But she'd had a long, full, and happy life afterwards. And Michael hadn't persevered—hadn't tried to find her after the war. Perhaps Phyllis had already made sure of him; she'd borne him just one child.

On deck, Mrs Ford heard Eleanor being admonished.

"A ship's doctor won't do," came that dominant tone. "I've plans for you, and they don't include this sort of thing at all. It stops the instant you leave the ship, do you hear?"

Eleanor told Mrs Ford about it later.

"He's a widower. His wife died in a car crash when she was pregnant," she said. "But it isn't just that. Mummy wants me to marry an earl, if she can find one, or at least some sort of tycoon, like Daddy."

"It's early days. You don't really know each other," said Mrs Ford.

"I know, but he's only doing a short spell in the ship, then he's going into general practice. We could get better acquainted then, couldn't we?"

"Yes," agreed Mrs Ford.

"And as for earls and tycoons—" Eleanor put scorn in her voice.

She'd learned typing and done a Cordon Bleu cooking course, Eleanor said. She'd wanted to be a nurse, but Mummy hadn't approved. The girl seemed docile and subdued—too much so, Mrs Ford thought.

Michael Carter, she remembered, had seemed to have plenty of money, though neither had thought about things like that, when during that long-ago war they took their quiet walks and had tea in a café. Phyllis Burton might have destroyed the innocent budding romance simply because that was her way, but she wouldn't have married Michael unless he had been what was called, in those days, "a catch." She'd have made sure of the same for her daughter—and the daughter was repeating the pattern now.

"You're of age," Mrs Ford said. "Make your own decisions."

Later the mother spoke to her. It was eerie, hearing that voice from the past urging her, since she had become friendly with Eleanor, to warn her against the doctor.

"But why?" Mrs Ford asked. "He seems such a nice young man."

"Think of her future," the girl's mother said. "She can do better than that."

"He'd look after her," Mrs Ford said, and she knew that he would. The girl was timid and lacking in confidence; the doctor, experienced and quite a lot older, would make her feel safe, as she had felt with Roger. "It depends on what you think is important," she said, rather bravely for her, and Eleanor's mother soon left, quite annoyed.

Mrs Ford smiled to herself and stitched on at her *gros point*. She'd help the young pair if she could. Nowadays, as she knew from her own family, people tried things out before making a proper commitment, and though such a system had, in her view, disadvantages, there were also points in its favour.

Mrs Ford did not go to Cairo. The drive was a long one from Alexandria, and she'd been before—stayed with Roger at Mena House, in fact, years ago. She spent the day quietly in Alexandria. The doctor, she knew, had gone on the trip in case a passenger fell ill, as might easily happen. That evening he said that someone had fainted, but nothing more serious had occurred.

The next day was spent at sea, giving people a chance to recover from the most tiring expedition of the voyage. Among those sleeping on chairs on deck, Mrs Ford saw Eleanor's mother. Her mouth was a little agape and her spectacles were still on her nose. In her hand she held an open book. Perhaps she was not as robust as she seemed, Mrs Ford mused—her own mother, after all, the Phyllis of Mrs Ford's youth, had not survived late middle age.

On the upper deck, Eleanor and the doctor were playing deck tennis. Mrs Ford, seeing them, smiled to herself as she walked away. Youth was resilient.

Several days later the *Sphinx* anchored off Nauplia. The weather was fine, though a haze hung over the distant mountains and there was snow on the highest peak, rare for this area. Mrs Ford stood in line to disembark by the ship's launches with the other passengers going ashore. Stalwart ship's officers would easily help her aboard and she quite enjoyed feeling a firm grasp on her arm as she stepped over the gunwale into the boat.

A row of coaches waited on the quay. Mrs Ford allowed herself to be directed into one. She would enjoy today, for while Mycenae, their first stop, was a dramatic, brooding place, holding an atmosphere redolent of tragedy, Epidaurus, in its perfect setting, was a total contrast. They drove past groves of orange trees laden with fruit. The almond trees were in bloom and the grass, which later in the year would be bleached by the heat of the sun, was a brilliant green.

The haze had lifted when the coach stopped at Epidaurus. Mrs Ford debated whether to go straight to the stadium, which so few tours allowed time to visit and where it would be peaceful and cool, but in the end, walking among the pines and inhaling their scent, she decided to visit it again.

She walked past the group from her coach as, like docile children, they clustered around their guide and, sauntering on, using her stick, she turned up the track to the left of the theatre where the ascent was easier than up the steep steps.

At the top she turned to the right and entered the vast semi-circle of stone. She moved inwards a little and sat down, gazing about her, sighing with pleasure. Below stood her group; she had plenty of time to rest and enjoy her surroundings.

The sun was quite strong now and she sat thinking of very little except her present contentment. A guide below began the acoustic demonstration, scrabbling his feet in the dust, jingling keys, lighting a match. Mrs Ford had seen it all before. Then her eye caught a flash of bright blue lower down—young Eleanor's sweater. She was almost at the bottom of the auditorium and with her was a tall young man easily discerned by Mrs Ford's far-sighted eyes to be the ship's doctor. They were absorbed as much with each other as with the scenery, Mrs Ford thought as she watched them together.

Then a voice behind her called loudly.

"Eleanor!" she heard. "Eleanor! Come here at once!"

Mrs Ford reacted instinctively to the sound of her name and she turned. Her pulse was beating fast and she felt her nerves tighten with fear. Since her youth no one had talked to her in such a tone.

Down the steep steps of the aisle between the seats, Phyllis's daughter, whose name was also Phyllis, came boldly towards her, striding with purpose, Phyllis the malevolent, Phyllis the destroyer. Mrs Ford's grip on her stick, which was resting across her knees, tightened as the lumbering figure in its sensible skirt and expensive jacket approached. Her pace did not slacken as she drew near, Mrs Ford knew with a part of her mind that it was not she but her young namesake below who was the target of the imperious summons.

She acted spontaneously. She slid her walking stick out across the aisle, handle foremost, as Phyllis drew level, and by chance, not deliberate design, the hooked end caught round the woman's leg. Mrs Ford tightened her grasp with both hands and hung on, but the stick was pulled from her grip as the hurrying woman stumbled and fell.

She didn't fall far—she was too bulky and the stairway too narrow—but she came to rest some little way below Mrs Ford and lay quite still. No one noticed at first, for there were shouts and cries filling the air from tourists testing the amplification of the theatre and attention was focused below.

Mrs Ford's pulse had begun to steady by the time people began to gather around the body. Her stick lay at the side of the aisle. She retrieved it quite easily. She returned to her coach by the same way she had come, away from all the commotion, and was driven back to Nauplia where the ship waited at anchor.

There was talk in the coach.

"Some woman tripped and fell."

"It's dangerous. You'd think there'd be a rope."

"People should look where they're going."

"She must have been wearing unsuitable shoes."

The doctor was not at the table for dinner that night, and over the loudspeaker the captain announced that though sailing had been delayed this would not interfere with the rest of the timetable—the next port would be reached as planned.

Mrs Ford's table companions related various versions of what had happened ashore to cause the delay. The woman, Eleanor's mother, had stumbled in the theatre at Epidaurus and in falling had hit her head against a projecting stone, dying at once. Someone else thought she'd had a stroke or a heart attack and that this had caused her to fall, for she was a big woman and florid of face. The Greeks had taken over, since the accident had happened ashore, and the formalities were therefore their concern.

"Terrible for the daughter," someone remarked. "Such a shock."

"The father's flying out," someone else said.

Mrs Ford ate her sole meunière. She had only wanted to stop Phyllis from interfering. Hadn't she?

Her son, meeting her at the airport some days later, found his mother looking well and rested. He knew about the accident—it had been reported in the newspapers.

"What a terrible thing to happen," he said. "It must have been most distressing. Poor woman."

"Well, she saw the Pyramids," Mrs Ford replied.

What a heartless response, thought her son in surprise, and looked at his gentle mother, astonished.